TO *Love* the BROODING BARON

OTHER BOOKS BY JENTRY FLINT

Games in a Ballroom

TO *Love* *the* BROODING BARON

PROPER ROMANCE

JENTRY FLINT

SHADOW
MOUNTAIN
PUBLISHING

To my dad.

*His career in law enforcement and humanitarian
services hasn't left him without his own internal scars.
Never stop fighting and know that I love you.*

Library of Congress Cataloging-in-Publication Data
Names: Flint, Jentry, author.
Title: To love the brooding baron / Jentry Flint.
Description: [Salt Lake City] : Shadow Mountain Publishing, [2024] | Series: Proper romance | Summary: "Opposites attract and sparks fly when the vivacious Arabella falls for Henry Northcott, a baron who lives under the shadow of a scandalous family secret."—Provided by publisher.
Identifiers: LCCN 2023053149 (print) | LCCN 2023053150 (ebook) | ISBN 9781639932399 (trade paperback) | ISBN 9781649332554 (ebook)
Subjects: LCSH: Courtship—Fiction. | Nineteenth century, setting. | London (England), setting. | BISAC: FICTION / Romance / Historical / Regency | FICTION / Romance / Clean & Wholesome | LCGFT: Romance fiction. | Historical fiction. | Novels.
Classification: LCC PS3606.L569 T6 2024 (print) | LCC PS3606.L569 (ebook) | DDC 813/.6—dc23/eng/20231127
LC record available at https://lccn.loc.gov/2023053149
LC ebook record available at https://lccn.loc.gov/2023053150

Printed in the United States of America
Publishers Printing

10   9   8   7   6   5   4   3   2   1

ONE

Standing in his family's gallery, Henry Thomas Northcott, the perpetually accursed thirteenth Baron Northcott, stared at one of the paintings. Only it was not the current portrait on the wall he was seeing, it was the portrait of his family that had hung there before and had long since been taken down. How easily the past could be removed and rendered forgotten.

If only that could be said for the gossips of the *ton*.

"There you are, Henry," his aunt said, stepping purposefully toward him. The dark maroon color of her gown combined with the evening light filtering through the windows turned her graying auburn hair a shade of plum. "Why did you not come to the parlor? I was waiting to have tea with you."

There was neither anger nor worry in her tone. His aunt always held herself with the utmost comportment and control. Traits he himself tried to reflect.

"My apologies, Aunt," he said, turning away from the portrait. "I intended to be but a moment."

He shouldn't have come into this room.

"Is everything all right?" she asked, her brows drawing together as she stopped before him. "Did something happen in the House of Lords?" She reached up and adjusted the ermine collar of his red ceremonial robe.

"Nothing that was not expected," he replied, ignoring the sudden urge to rid himself of the anvil-like weight upon his shoulders. The barony mantle had never felt like it belonged to him, no matter how many times he donned the robes.

The Prince Regent had come to Westminster with all the pomp and circumstance he was known for. His extravagant crimson-and-gold carriage had been escorted by an entire host of cavalry, and he was welcomed with a cannon salute. Prorogation was then performed, closing out that session of Parliament and sending most of the aristocracy and gentry to their country estates.

It had been what Henry had overheard as he walked out of Westminster that led him to the gallery.

"That's him . . . the Brooding Baron."

"The heir whose predecessor was murdered?"

"The very one."

"I heard the previous baron was killed by his brother's widow."

"I heard the same, and that she was spared the noose in order to avoid a public trial and then sent to Bedlam."

"It's no wonder the baron broods, to have such a mother."

Henry had swiftly passed by the two new lords, not wanting to hear any more of the gossip. The many rumors about his family's past haunted him everywhere he went.

His aunt's eyes drifted to the portrait behind him. Her countenance faltered as her eyes lit with emotion, but there was no warmth to them. There was pain, there was heartache, and then there was anger. She stepped around him, moving closer to the painting. "His hair had just begun to silver at the sides and temples," she said in a distant tone, as if she were back in the library the day the portrait was commissioned.

Henry nodded, remembering all too well. He'd been a boy of fifteen, standing with his aunt and Uncle Thomas, the twelfth Baron Northcott. Henry's mother, four months widowed, had stood in the library doorway, her eyes like daggers pricking his soul. It had felt like a betrayal, standing for a portrait without his mother and sister, but he was the heir now that his father was dead, and his aunt had been insistent.

"Should we retire to the parlor?" Henry asked, wanting to move the conversation away from the past.

His aunt hesitated, her eyes still on the portrait until she delicately cleared her throat and stepped away. "Of course."

Henry held out his arm, and she placed her hand upon it.

She remained silent as they made their way to the parlor. Guilt consumed him for ending her moment to remember her husband, but it would've been wrong to let her believe he'd been there to do the same. Especially when he'd been recollecting the last portrait of his family, the one that held the visage of the person who'd killed her husband—his mother.

Entering the parlor, his aunt released his arm and went to the bellpull, summoning a footman.

"Have his lordship's valet come to collect his robes and have a tea service brought up," she said.

The footman bowed and quickly departed to see to his tasks.

Henry's aunt moved to the sofa and took a seat, leaving him to wonder if she intended for him to join her or wait for his valet.

"You had two letters come," his aunt said, retrieving them from the side table next to her.

Henry took them from her, noticing both wax seals had been broken. It wasn't uncommon for his aunt to read his missives. When he'd suddenly inherited the title of baron at fifteen, she'd been all he had to guide him, and he didn't have the heart to tell his aunt that her assistance was no longer necessary. Not after all she'd been through and all she had done for him.

"Your friend, Mr. Latham, writes that he must once *again* delay his return from Bath for another month," his aunt said.

Henry opened the letter, briefly scanning its contents. He had sent an express message to Emerson, warning him that Mr. Wilde—Emerson's brute of a father-in-law—had departed London after recovering from an injury sustained during a confrontation with Emerson as he, Henry, and their friend Bradbury helped to spirit away Emerson's new bride and mother-in-law to Bath. It appeared Mr. Wilde had indeed tracked them to Bath, and while there had been no encounters so far, Emerson, not trusting his father-in-law, decided to delay his return by another month to make certain his mother-in-law would be safe in her new living arrangement with Emerson's aunts.

Which meant Henry had another month of watching over Emerson's mother.

And his sister, Arabella.

He shook his head, not allowing himself to be distracted by thoughts of the dark-haired vixen who'd barely managed to keep herself and her curious mind out of trouble throughout the remainder of the Season.

Forcing himself to focus on the last half of the letter, Henry froze on one word that stood out from the rest.

Billiards.

Emerson was asking him to see to the delivery of a new billiards table that would be delivered in the coming week.

Why did it have to be billiards?

Swallowing down the lump forming in his throat, he glanced at his aunt. She was watching him as if she expected him to react.

He pushed back the awful memories. He wasn't his father. A billiards table had no hold over him.

Refolding the letter, he was forced to wait to open the second by the arrival of his valet, followed by a maid with a tea service. His valet saw to the removal of his ceremonial robe and helped him with his black jacket while his aunt saw to pouring them both a cup of tea.

Alone with his aunt once again, Henry sat in one of the cushioned armchairs adjacent to the sofa. His aunt watched him carefully out of the corner of her eye as she took a delicate sip.

He unfolded the second letter, which was from his solicitor. He was hoping to arrange a time to discuss the pressing details of Henry's sister's hospital transfer. Unease pooled in his stomach, and a sharp chill scraped across his spine.

"Do you still believe this to be wise?" his aunt asked before he could finish reading the missive.

Collecting his cup, he took a drink as if the tea could warm him. "It's necessary if I am to see her properly cared for."

Something he'd—to his growing regret—neglected to do until this last year.

"If the *ton* should somehow hear of it, or see you even entering where your sister will be held, it would undo all we have overcome these past ten years," his aunt said, a deep frown marring her lips.

His aunt spoke as if the *ton* had forgotten the harrowing series of events surrounding his family that were more fit for gothic novels than history. Today proved otherwise.

Every horrific thing the gossips ever said about his family was true. But what they didn't know—and what his aunt could never discover—was that, just like his mother and sister, he, the Brooding Baron, was mad.

TWO

Arabella Latham stood by the sitting room window, watching as the one—and only—gentleman to propose to her that Season turned a disappointed but amicable smile at her before dashing out into the rain to climb into his carriage. He was a good and amiable man, and she'd told him as much in her gentle refusal, but he didn't stir in her the feelings she knew she was searching for.

She'd gone her entire first Season searching for a spark. For a fire that would consume her and tell her beyond any doubt that she'd found love.

"Mr. Fulton did not stay long," her mother said, sweeping into the room as if she'd not been listening by the door the entire time.

She wore a simple gray dress. Her mother always wore gray. The sudden and unexpected death of Arabella's father almost two years ago had been hard for her mother to bear, but secretly Arabella had hoped by now to see her in a shade of purple. Her father had always loved her mother in softer colors. He used to say it brought out the rosy hues in her cheeks, and then her mother would always blush.

Theirs had been a love match, born from a spark, that had warmed their lives and brightened the lives of their children. To feel such true and abiding love was a blessing Arabella did not take for granted. She knew such love wasn't a standard of the *ton*. Marriages were meant for making alliances and elevating one's family's status or wealth.

Her father on his deathbed had been adamant that she and Emerson marry for love, wanting to know before he took his last breath that his children would find happiness. Emerson had kept his promise when he fought for and married Olivia, and Arabella fully intended to keep her promise to her father as well.

"He made an offer I felt I needed to refuse," Arabella said, turning away from the window to face her mother, uncertain how she would react to the news.

"I see," she said with a nod before moving to the sofa, where she retrieved that morning's paper, and, beneath it, her bowl of marzipan. She'd quickly hidden it beneath the paper when Mr. Fulton had been announced.

"That is all you have to say?" Arabella asked, stunned.

Mr. Fulton had courted her the entire last month of the Season, and she'd thought her mother liked the gentleman.

Her mother stared at her over her paper with a single raised brow as if the answer were obvious. "You said you did not feel anything. I know better than anyone that you do not do anything that you do not feel." She lifted the corner of her mouth to remove any sting her words might carry.

Arabella returned the smile as she moved to sit on the sofa set opposite her mother. She was notorious in her family for getting a feeling about something and immediately acting upon it without fully thinking it through.

"It does mean, however," her mother continued, picking up a cream-colored piece of marzipan from the bowl in her lap, "that you shall be unable to avoid Lady Bixbee's machinations."

Arabella's back stiffened. She'd forgotten about that. "I thought the nephew or grandson or whoever she wished to introduce me to was 'detained on a matter of importance'?"

"Grandson," her mother clarified before taking a bite of her marzipan. "She wrote this morning to say he was detained no longer."

A flicker of panic shot through Arabella's chest. The indomitable matron had spent the entire Season expressing her desire to introduce Arabella to a member of her family, which was both terrifying and flattering. If Arabella could feel a spark with Lady Bixbee's chosen gentleman, all would be well, but if she didn't . . .

An angry and disappointed Lady Bixbee wasn't an adversary she wanted to face.

"I see," Arabella replied, the room falling into a heavy silence.

After an awkward moment, as Arabella's nerves continued to thin and fray, she suddenly shot up from her seat. "I think I will go to the study and get a book."

"Of course, dear," her mother said, unsurprised, her attention remaining fixed on her paper.

Telling her mother she would return shortly, Arabella made her way to the study. She paused just inside the doorway, the familiar scent of old books, wood polish, and the undefinable something that was distinctly her father filled her senses. Even after Emerson had taken over the use of the study, a part of her father remained, and she prayed it never left.

Her father could often be found in his study. As a child, she would join him, reading on the sofa in front of a large window. He would eventually abandon his work and sit next to her, and they'd discuss recent events reported in the newspapers or share their favorite passages from the novels they had read.

A tightness formed in her throat and chest that felt as real as the day she watched him draw his last breath.

It was because of him that she'd discovered her love of Shakespeare.

At a time when her governess could no longer take her asking why about anything and everything, her father had given to her *The Comedy of Errors*.

"Tell me what you discover," her father had said, handing her one of Shakespeare's shortest comedies about two sets of twins who'd accidentally been separated at birth and then years later were reunited after a series of mistaken identities and unfortunate events. From it, she'd learned the importance of family and, more importantly, of her father's love for her despite what her governess called "her vexing and undesirable spirit."

Which play would he suggest for me now?

Arabella wished she knew.

Swallowing back the melancholy that threatened to overpower her, she followed her feet to the bookshelves. She could continue her search for love next Season; she would just have to find a way to distract herself until then.

She skimmed her fingertips along the familiar rows of books, easing into the comforting motion. She knew without having to look the moment she touched the volumes of Shakespeare's works. The leather covers were all dented or scratched, and the gold lettering had faded in places. But instead of stopping to select a book, she continued across the rows of bookshelves until she reached the blue-patterned wallpaper. A few steps more, and she came to the fireplace mantel, above which hung a portrait of her young father and mother.

"What will I do if I cannot find my spark?" she asked the portrait, wondering, for the first time, if perhaps she'd read too much *Hamlet*, considering how easy she found it talking to a ghost.

No answer came, of course, so she turned to collect one of her books. She stopped mid-turn, her eyes catching on a very familiar shade of green.

Hanging over the chair behind her brother's desk was an evening jacket that was unmistakably her father's.

How had it come to be there? Had Emerson or her mother arranged to have it brought down? Was that why her father's scent never seemed to fully leave the room?

Unable to ignore the pull toward something that was once her father's, she moved toward the chair, craving that connection. It was just as foolish as believing she could talk with a ghost, but she still gently stroked her fingertips across the material, her memory flooding with images of her father before his illness suddenly took him.

Lifting the jacket from the chair, she swung it over her shoulders, her eyes closing as her senses anticipated the feel of her father's warmth.

But it wasn't there. The jacket was cold, vacant, and the garment hung so limp and loose over her, she couldn't even feel the cuff of the jacket's sleeve with her fingertips.

"If you are trying to pass as your brother, you make for a poor look-alike."

Arabella's head jerked up to see Mr. Bradbury with his hands upon his hips, standing in the doorframe to the study. He wore his all too familiar teasing smile as he assessed her up and down.

"But perhaps if you did something with your hair and dress, you might be able to pass as a younger cousin in desperate need of a tailor."

A smile tugged at her lips. Mr. Bradbury was one of her brother's oldest and closest friends, and he could never resist an opportunity to have a little fun—especially at someone else's expense. "I do not know whether I should take that as an insult or a compliment, sir."

"Sir? Why, *Miss* Latham, you wound me." He playfully grabbed his chest. "Have I been so negligent these past four months in my shared duties to watch after you and your mother that you have completely forgotten who I am?"

"I doubt anyone would be able to forget you, *Mr. Bradbury*." She shook her head and laughed.

"Should I take that as an insult or a compliment?" He winked.

She didn't know who was more ridiculous, her in the oversized evening jacket or Mr. Bradbury with his teasing. "To what do my mother and I owe this great honor, Mr. Bradbury? As you said, it has been some time since we last saw you."

He flinched. "Ah, yes, I suppose I do owe your mother a visit."

Arabella nodded, knowing her mother looked upon Mr. Bradbury as one of her own. He had, after all, been friends with the family since he and Emerson were at Eton.

"I shall go and see her the moment my business here is done," Mr. Bradbury replied, reaching into his jacket and removing a small stack of banknotes. "I bring your brother's earnings from our last wager."

"What was the wager?" she asked, eager as always to discover what Emerson and his friends were up to inside their gentlemen's club.

"A gentleman never reveals such secrets." He grinned. "Especially when you are the one asking."

She gave an exasperated huff and folded her arms. Only instead of looking annoyed, she imagined she looked rather ridiculous with the excess sleeves of her father's jacket flopping about her.

Mr. Bradbury made a strangled sound in his throat that sounded an awful lot like repressed laughter and quickly turned away.

Squaring her shoulders, Arabella waited for him to look at her again. "If you have nothing further, Mr. Bradbury, you may leave my brother's earnings on the desk. Heaven only knows what secret wagers await you next."

"I am afraid that is not possible," he replied without moving from the doorframe.

"Whyever not?"

"I make it a priority never to enter a room where only a young lady is present. Deuced impossible to be accused of compromising a woman if I was never in the room."

Arabella looked heavenward. "How could I forget your fear of matrimony?"

"It's not fear," he said with all seriousness. "It's common sense. Not every man wants to be shackled into something so binding only death can free you."

"That was not the case for Henry VIII." Arabella couldn't help but argue, though she knew it would be futile. Mr. Bradbury would never change his mind about marriage.

"Weren't some of his wives beheaded while the rest conveniently died?"

"Not quite. He had to rid himself of the Catholic Church and then form the Church of England to divorce his first wife."

Arabella always wondered how Shakespeare would have written his play had he included the monarch's six wives and not just the first two. Although, it was said that the fourth marriage was annulled on the grounds that the marriage was never consummated. So should it only be considered five wives?

"That would still make it 'til death did they part,'" Mr. Bradbury argued. "For heaven's sake, the man ended the reign of an entire church."

She shrugged, if only to frustrate him as he'd frustrated her. "If you will not bring the winnings in, shall I collect them from you?"

The tension in Mr. Bradbury's shoulders eased, and a familiar teasing glint entered his eyes. "And risk you pulling me into the room so that you may compromise me? I think not."

Her shoulders quaked before a snorted giggle burst from her lips. Mr. Bradbury's laughter joined hers.

"You sound ridiculous," she said.

He puffed out his chest. "So Northcott likes to inform me."

Lord Northcott was the third friend in her brother's infamous Brooks's Brotherhood—at least that was what she'd once overheard Mr. Bradbury call the trio.

"But I think it is because he is in denial about how much he cares for me," Mr. Bradbury continued. "One day I am determined to crack a smile on the Brooding Baron's face."

All sense of laughter fell from her lips, replaced by the confusing stir of emotions she had about the baron. She'd first been introduced to him when he and Mr. Bradbury had accompanied Emerson to their home in Berkshire after her father had first taken ill. She'd thought the baron reserved and perhaps too serious, but upon further acquaintance, she'd begun to see glimpses of a different side of him.

As her father's health continued to decline, whatever time she didn't spent by his side was spent in the library.

Lord Northcott had often come to the library too. He never spoke to her but simply read in a chair not overly close to her sofa but in her line of sight, as if he knew she was trying to hold on to a piece of her father, who was slipping away, and offering her comfort in his steady and constant breaths.

It wasn't until she saw him again, after the mourning period had ended and she'd arrived in London for her first Season, that she learned the *ton* had a much different opinion of him. They called him the Brooding Baron, whispering dark tales about his family and portraying him in a beastly light.

She often wanted to ask him about the stories, but it never felt right to do so when he'd shown her such kindness. A part of her doubted he would answer if she did. He rarely said more than a few words to anyone. She could never truly get a sense of who he was because he always remained so stoic. Perhaps that was what unsettled her most.

He was such a dark and handsome towering wall of man surrounded by mystery.

"Is it true, what the *ton* says about his family?" she found herself asking before thinking the better of it.

For a moment, Mr. Bradbury's gaze darkened as though thinking of something unpleasant. "That is something you shall have to ask him if you wish to know. Your brother and I still have not discovered the full extent of the answer."

"What *have* you discovered?" she asked, wanting even a small piece of information to try to understand the mysterious baron.

Mr. Bradbury shook his head. "I have as much desire to talk to you about that subject as I did about Brooks's."

"You only make me more determined to discover both answers with your continued refusals," she replied.

"Believe whatever you wish, Miss Latham. But I am afraid that even if you used a disguise"—he gestured to the evening jacket she still wore—"you will never discover the secrets inside Brooks. You are a woman, and women have certain"—he waved a hand uncomfortably up and down her form, no longer able to directly meet her eye—"attributes that cannot go unnoticed by any warm-blooded man. I'd wager you would be outed before you even crossed the threshold."

"I see," Arabella said, smiling. She suddenly knew how she could distract herself until the next Season.

Mr. Bradbury made a valid argument. Even with a disguise, she would most likely never make it through the front door, but what he didn't understand was that she'd read Shakespeare's *Twelfth Night* many times. And therefore, she understood what was necessary to pull off the cleverest disguise.

She would take him up on his unintended wager and prove once again that, regardless of the situation, Shakespeare was always the answer.

THREE

Henry judged it best to visit his solicitor while his aunt was at her charity committee meeting with Lady Bixbee. He and his aunt had been at odds over the care of his younger sister for years. Though they both wished for discretion in the matter, his aunt wanted no contact with Sarah while Henry could no longer hold himself apart from his sister's treatment.

Wanting to know what to expect should your secret be found out? the voice inside his head whispered.

Henry pressed his back hard against his chair and crossed his arms over his chest, giving no visible reaction to the subject being discussed inside and outside his head.

"Your sister's transfer from Guy's Hospital to the new Bedlam on Lambeth has been secured for the first of next month," Mr. Tompkin read from one of his many papers before pausing to look at Henry.

Henry responded with a nod, though every muscle in his gut tightened. He didn't know what the right path was when it came to caring for Sarah. What did a man do when his mother had been an institutionalized murderer, his sister declared of a similar mind, and the victims of his mother's transgression were his now-widowed aunt and murdered uncle?

Not to mention the fact that you yourself are mad, the voice taunted.

Henry's jaw clenched.

For the past ten years, he'd been suffering alone and in silence, choosing to focus all his efforts on the care of his aunt and seeing that his uncle was remembered for the good he'd done and not his horrific demise.

But after the war with Napoleon ended, too many soldiers came home needing the specialized care found at what was then an old and crumbling Bedlam, forcing Parliament to begin its work with lunacy reform and construct a new Bedlam, and his family's past was ripe for the gossips once again.

As Mr. Tompkin outlined the discreet manner in which Sarah would be transported, Henry's memory went back to the first—and only—time he'd set foot inside the old Bedlam to visit his sister.

The 140-year-old building had shown its age with its coal dust-darkened stones and discolored patchwork along the roof. A haunting statue of two men sat above the front door. The man who lay across the left side appeared languid and calm, while the man on the right appeared to be raving and held down by chains. Perhaps the sculptor had thought it poetic for those crossing the threshold, but as someone who had a family member inside, Henry could barely stomach the sight of it.

Once he was inside, the warped floorboards bent unevenly beneath his boots; Parliament had learned the structure had been built on the marshlike Moorfields without a proper foundation. Visible cracks stretched along the corridor walls, the jagged lines often leading to flaking plaster, which created a buckling at the base of the wall. But what had ultimately turned his stomach wasn't the continuous signs of physical dilapidation nor the over-powering stench of urine. It was what he saw inside the common room. A single row of chairs ran down the center of the otherwise empty room. The chairs were spaced evenly apart, and each one held a patient strapped down by the wrists. The patients wore gray nightgowns; many had long hair that had become a tangled, matted mess. Several of them distractedly hummed, mumbled, or rocked, while others sat lifeless, staring blankly into nothing.

It was then that Henry fully understood why the new Court of Governors had ordered as many of the old Bedlam's patients removed to other hospitals until Parliament could collect the funds to purchase new land and construct a new Bedlam hospital. No ounce of humanity resided inside that place that was supposed to care for the afflicted. And his sister, sitting eerily still near the center of the room, had been one of the unlucky souls who remained, unable to be placed in one of London's other hospitals.

Henry hadn't been able to rest since that visit. The memories of the old Bedlam, and the thought that his sister would have remained there had he not gone to see her, haunted him whenever he closed his eyes.

Securing Sarah's transfer from the old Bedlam to Guy's Hospital had cost him his family's long-time solicitor, who'd worked for both his grandfather and his uncle. Henry had been forced to let the ancient man go when he refused to "dabble anymore with the devil." If only the old man had known that the moment Henry had taken up the barony, he'd been dabbling with a devil all along.

Henry's new solicitor cleared his throat, raising his brow slightly.

Henry shook off his dark musings and nodded, signaling for Mr. Tompkin to continue.

"I received a letter this morning from Dr. Stafford," he began in a cautious tone, sliding a piece of paper toward Henry. "He asks once more to meet with you."

The knot in Henry's gut grew tentacles.

Dr. Stafford was one of the newly appointed doctors trusted to oversee the treatment of the patients at the new Bedlam. He'd spent the entire Season requesting to meet with Henry, perhaps believing he'd found himself an ally in Parliament after discovering the sister of a baron was one of his patients. Henry had hoped the doctor would give up his pursuit the moment Parliament had ended.

He'd been mistaken.

What Dr. Stafford refused to understand was that, despite Henry's firm stance on the need for reform, he had purposefully taken a lesser role in that legislation. With the rumors still circulating about his family, his aunt thought it best for him to focus his efforts on the Corn Laws to avoid drawing any more unwanted attention. Little good it'd done in the end. The gossip remained, and his party had failed to stop the new Corn Laws.

A war-taxed England, in order to make its people more dependent upon its own economy and not on cheaper imports, was about to face a severe rise in the price of grain. The new law put the power in the hands of the landowners and not the people who needed help putting food on their tables.

"No," Henry said, not bothering to read the letter.

Mr. Tompkin, who'd proven to be a quick study, asked no further questions. "I've one last item of business." Pulling open one of his desk drawers, he retrieved a stack of papers darkened by age. "I finished reviewing what was given to me from your previous solicitor, and I've found a stipulation in your uncle's will that does not appear to be in effect."

Dread filled Henry as he stared down at the papers. His old solicitor must have stowed the old will away after realizing Henry had no intention of enforcing one particular item.

"According to the will, there's a separate household and income set aside for your aunt upon your uncle's death."

"I am aware," Henry replied, hoping his clear disinterest would dissuade Mr. Tompkin from asking the next obvious question.

Mr. Tompkin stared at him, confused. "I beg your pardon, my lord, but if you knew, then why does your aunt remain inside your home?"

Henry moved his hands to grip the armrests. "My aunt has expressed that she would be more at ease living in the home she once shared with my uncle."

Henry could still hear his aunt's anguished cries the day their old solicitor read aloud his uncle's will. His aunt hadn't been ready for the change then, nor was she ready now. She was aware of the income and the home, and when she was ready, she would come to him. He dared not risk upsetting her by pressing the point.

"I see." His solicitor nodded, though Henry doubted he did.

"Then might I recommend either reducing the staff or letting it out to try to balance some of the costs for keeping it in constant readiness?"

"Leave it be," Henry replied. It was ridiculous to pay for more than a skeleton staff in an unoccupied home, but after the return of Napoleon and the second war that ensued, coin and decent-paying jobs were scarce. If he could help some of those poor souls struggling, he would. The Northcott holdings had more than enough money.

"As you wish," Mr. Tompkin said, the hesitancy in his tone making his disagreement clear. "I believe that concludes our business then."

Henry nodded, ready for a reprieve.

Placing his hat atop his head, Henry readied himself for the ever-present summer rain. His carriage waited for him on the near-abandoned street, though a few people trapped by the rain stood underneath the shops' doorways.

His coachman opened the carriage door, and, before ducking his head to step in, Henry gave an address that fell easily from his lips. He knew he should return home. He'd already visited the Latham home twice that week. But the pull for a moment of distraction with Arabella was enough to make him ignore his better judgment.

Are you sure about that? The voice whispered. *She is rather beautiful and spirited.*

Henry's senses came alive at the thought of her. The smell of primroses filled his nose, and the most melodious laughter echoed in his ears. Arabella was everything he wasn't and everything he could never have.

He didn't trust himself when he felt so unrestrained. Control was needed to keep his and his family's secrets from hurting anyone else. Which was why he had a plan. He would die childless, thus, leaving no one to inherit, and the title would revert to the crown. His aunt, whose entire purpose was upholding her husband's title, would remain ignorant of his plan. A Northcott had been in possession of the barony since before the Magna Carta was signed. But Henry's blood was tainted, and for that reason, the curse and his family's secret would die with him.

His carriage slowed to a stop, dipping to one side before he heard his coachman's boots splash in a puddle. Henry had a matter of seconds to change his mind and ask to be taken home, but he didn't. His weakness for a pair of large, sparkling eyes and teasing lips had got the better of him.

Henry stepped from the carriage, walked quickly through the pouring rain to the front door, and knocked.

The shock on the butler's face reaffirmed Henry's suspicions. He shouldn't have come. This visit was going to draw attention.

The old man quickly recovered and stepped aside, taking Henry's rain-splattered hat and gloves. "Something amiss, my lord?" he asked.

"Nothing amiss, Smith," Henry replied. "Just a visit."

"Good. Good," Smith said before directing Henry down the familiar corridor. The Lathams, and even their servants, stood on little ceremony with him, as if he were one of the family. He was trying to get used to such treatment; his aunt ran their home very differently.

"Lord Northcott to see you, ma'am," the butler announced as they stepped into the parlor.

A low-lit fire crackled in the hearth, warming the small, intimate room. Mrs. Latham stood, her smile surprised but inviting. Her husband's death had taken a toll on her appearance, but he was relieved to see the dark circles under her eyes were beginning to fade with time. Fate had delivered her a painful blow, and yet she still cared for her children as any rational-thinking mother would. How different she was from his own mother after his father's sudden death.

"Lord Northcott, this is a most welcome surprise," Mrs. Latham said, holding out her hands to him as she always did.

Feeling awkward, as he always did, Henry approached and touched her upturned hands with his fingertips. "Pardon the intrusion," he said, pulling back his hands and looking about the room.

Where was Arabella?

"No intrusion at all. You know you are always welcome." She gestured for him to take a seat on the sofa opposite her. "This week has actually been quite full of surprises."

The hairs on Henry's neck stood on end. Surprises and Arabella weren't often a good combination.

"Do not trouble yourself," Mrs. Latham said, amused.

Had he given a visible reaction?

She instructed Smith to have tea sent up before turning her attention back to Henry. "For once, I believe her ambitions are of a more moderate nature."

This time Henry allowed himself a raised brow. Arabella was capable of moderation, but the definition of it wasn't something she and her mother often agreed upon. Arabella's curiosity, he'd quickly learned, was boundless, and if not properly channeled could become a headache for everyone around her.

"As you know," Mrs. Latham continued, "Lady Bixbee and your aunt have been involving Arabella and me in their charity work for the Foundling Hospital."

Henry nodded.

"Well, for the past two days, Arabella has been focused on tailoring some of my late husband's clothing to fit some of the orphaned older boys."

"I am glad to hear it," he said, relieved that Arabella's latest fascination appeared to be harmless and yet disheartened that he might not see her during his visit.

"So was I. It has done wonders for her restlessness. Allow me to have her come down and you can see for yourself." She rose to ring the bellpull, and Henry's heart traitorously quickened.

When the parlor door opened, his heart jumped to his throat only to plummet to his stomach when a maid walked in with a tea service. As Mrs. Latham rose and prepared them both a cup, Henry couldn't help but keep glancing at the door. He took his cup from Mrs. Latham, and, like a fool, swallowed a distracted sip.

The scorching liquid burned his tongue and throat, but he held the pain in.

A few moments later, Arabella burst into the room in a mesmerizing rush of soft blue skirts that pressed perfectly to her willowy frame. "My apologies. I am afraid I found myself quite literally stitched to a pair of men's breeches."

Henry sputtered and choked on another poorly timed sip of tea as his traitorous mind flashed with an image of Arabella in a formfitting pair of breeches.

Arabella and her mother watched him with concern as he set the cup on the table next to him and rose to his feet to greet *Miss Latham* properly.

Call her what you like, but we both know you are halfway in love with her, the voice whispered.

Clenching his jaw, he stiffened his spine before offering a formal bow. "Miss Latham."

The voice laughed.

Arabella smiled and offered him a polite curtsy. "Lord North-cott."

"I was just telling Lord Northcott about what you have been doing for his aunt's charity," Mrs. Latham said.

Arabella hesitated, her eyes darting from her mother's sofa to the open seat next to him, as if uncertain where to sit. "Yes, I am hoping to have the clothes finished in the next few days."

Henry nodded. A part of him wanted her to choose the seat next to him, as she had done often during his last few visits. He wanted her to playfully tease him for being so quiet and tempt him into playing her little Shakespeare game.

He'd first become aware of her game when he'd arrived with Emerson and Bradbury at her family home in Berkshire. She'd been the one to greet them with a soft smile at the door and the words, *"Prepare for mirth, for mirth becomes a feast."*

Henry had been taken off guard, not understanding why

she would choose to say something so spirited when her brother had been called home because of their father's poor health. But then Emerson had responded with "*Perciles, Prince of Tyre*" before wrapping his sister in a long, tight embrace. Henry had recognized the title of Shakespeare's play and put together that it must've been some sort of game the siblings played.

And then there was the single tear that had rolled down Arabella's cheek.

She was attempting to put on a brave face for her brother, and Henry had become entranced.

He had read more Shakespeare those few days of his visit than he had over the entire course of his life. He wanted to know such spirit, such connection. Things his family never had.

"Have a seat, dear," Mrs. Latham said, pulling Henry from his memories and rising from her seat. "I shall pour you a cup of tea while you entertain our guest."

The decision seemingly made for her, Arabella sat on the sofa next to him.

"Three visits in a week?" Arabella asked him, her tone playful though her eyes studied him. "Is something amiss?"

"No," Henry replied, careful to keep his tone indifferent. "I was nearby on business—"

Liar, the voice whispered.

"—and thought it best to look in." He swallowed, a lump forming in his throat the longer she stared at him. Did she see through his lie? "Given all the rain," he blurted out and resisted the urge to groan at his foolishness.

Her eyes lit with mischief, and his heart thudded hard inside his chest. "Oh, *the rain, it raineth every day*," she said as if it wasn't concerning that England was experiencing an unseasonably heavy amount of rain.

He purposefully held back his answer—it could be either *King Lear* or *Twelfth Night*; she was most likely trying to make the game easier for him to tease him into playing it with her.

Her mother approached, stopping any further play. She handed Arabella her tea, then returned to her seat opposite them.

"I think Lord Northcott suspects I am being a burden on you, mama," Arabella said, her teacup halfway to her tantalizing, rose-colored lips. Her eyes flashed at him over the rim. "Because of all the rain."

Henry was a dead man. The way she continued to look at him, teasing him by using his own words, while she took a tiny sip from her cup nearly stopped his heart. Heaven help him for once; he couldn't look away from this woman.

"Not entirely," Mrs. Latham said, snapping Henry's attention.

Arabella gasped much like a performer in a play. "Mama? Have I not been a paragon of a daughter with *a heart of gold* these past few days?"

Henry V, he thought.

She watched him out of the corner of her eye, as if waiting to see if he would play.

He said nothing, resisting the urge to smile.

She was a paragon. No one could tempt him to want to smile more than she did—which was saying something because he was friends with Emerson and Bradbury, whose idea of fun was sneaking a pig dressed in a waistcoat into White's gentlemen's club.

Henry and Arabella continued to watch each other discreetly, neither speaking, while Mrs. Latham took up the topic of the rain.

Arabella innocently sipped at her tea, while Henry nodded to Mrs. Latham when it was appropriate to do so.

The situation grew more unnerving when Arabella leveled her attention at him directly, something that was completely against social standards. She truly was the most tempting and infuriating mixture of determination and spirit.

A small smile slipped past his hold as he wondered how long she would hold his gaze.

"I knew it!" she cried out in triumph, startling him and Mrs.

Latham. She practically jumped out of her seat before settling back on the cushion and playfully slapping him on the arm.

Unwanted heat rose up Henry's neck.

"I knew you had to be playing inside your head. Go on, say it, name the play," she demanded with one of her breathtaking smiles.

Henry cleared his throat, suddenly finding it difficult to meet her eyes. He subtly looked between Arabella and Mrs. Latham, embarrassed to have had a reaction to such a simple touch.

He was simply not used to that sort of outward affection, that was all.

Keep telling yourself that, the voice whispered.

It wasn't because he enjoyed such contact. His family had simply never been that way with one another. And besides, a woman with Arabella's spirit would never truly look twice at a man like him.

Not that he wanted *any* woman to look twice at him.

He was meant to be alone.

FOUR

Shakespeare had been unerring when he'd written "all the world's a stage," and Arabella deserved applause. It had only taken her a few days to carefully construct a script that would—with an added bit of luck—see her walk through the front doors of Brooks's gentlemen's club.

Act one: under the guise of making clothing for the boys at the Foundling Hospital, Arabella—along with the desperately needed needlework skills of her lady's maid—would fit herself with an evening jacket, waistcoat, shirtsleeves, drawers, and breeches.

Act two: hair. This task took several attempts to perfect. Luckily for her, the dandy Beau Brummel had made the Brutus style popular with its longer and somewhat untamed curls at the top of the head. Using Emerson's pomade, and with some minimal—but unavoidable—cutting, her lady's maid was able to mold and arrange Arabella's curly hair to her head for a more tousled look.

Act three: under the cover of darkness—and with the help of her lady's maid's older brother, who also happened to be her family's groomsman—she practiced how to sound and behave like a man.

Act four: the day of her performance. Which she carefully selected for the day her mother would be visiting an ailing friend. Arabella stopped at the Foundling Hospital to deliver most but not all of the altered clothing to the boys, then dashed back to her carriage to perform the final act.

Act five: enter Brooks's gentlemen's club and locate the infamous betting book.

"I don't know why I always let ye talk me into things like this," Hattie, Arabella's lady's maid, groaned as she helped Arabella slip her white shirtsleeves over her bonnet and head. The bonnet was left on to keep any hairs from being disturbed while she dressed inside the moving carriage.

Arabella eyed Hattie skeptically as she fastened the two buttons at her neck, making the stiff collar reach up past her jaw. "You love our little adventures as much as I do."

Hattie scowled as she handed Arabella her dark-blue breeches with more force than was necessary. "Yes, but this time I'm not goin' with ye."

"And I have told you why," Arabella said, shaking out the stiff material before attempting to thread her leg through the hole. "This is nothing like the times we snuck out to watch the East Asian firework show at Vauxhall or to the Argyll Rooms to hear the Philharmonic Society of London perform. This is a private *gentlemen's* club. It will be hard enough to talk my way inside. To try to get us both in?" She shook her head. "It would overcomplicate things."

"I don't like it," Hattie huffed. "What if somethin' happens and I'm not there to help ye?"

"Nothing will happen," Arabella said, reaching out to squeeze Hattie's hand. Her excitement for what secrets she would learn inside those walls far exceeded any nerves she had about the possibility of being caught. "I very much suspect I shall find an empty club. The *ton* has left London for the summer, and I specifically chose an early hour for today's adventure. The odds of me being recognized is very small."

"I still don't like it," Hattie grumbled, shaking out the waistcoat.

Arabella looked to the heavens for patience—something she had most assuredly not been born with—and shoved her other leg into her breeches as the carriage bounced and swayed. "This is not about me running into trouble. This is about you missing out on a chance for gossip."

Hattie had a natural talent for making friends anywhere she went and was therefore privy to all sorts of information. If she hadn't turned out to be the most loyal lady's maid, Arabella would've recommended her to work for the Bow Street Runners.

A smile tugged at Hattie's lips. "It's a *private* club. Can ye imagine the secrets happenin' inside?"

Arabella shook her head and laughed. She stood to pull her breeches the rest of the way up and secure the buttons at the waist. "If I promise to keep an ear out for the most juicy piece of gossip, will you stop grumbling and help me finish dressing? We must be nearing St. James's Street by now."

Before Hattie could respond, the carriage bounced violently, knocking Arabella backward with a yelp, landing her in Hattie's lap.

"*For goodness sake*," Hattie giggled as she pushed Arabella onto the bench beside her.

"*Henry VIII*." Arabella laughed as she righted herself. For the first time since she'd thought of her plan, she was grateful she didn't have to contend with skirts.

Wearing breeches had been a strange thing to get used to. It was a bit like wearing a corset, only they ran all the way down her legs, molding to her shape and hiding very little. If it weren't for the added bulk from her brother's old, leather, knee-high top boots, she would've feared her delicate ankles would give away the ruse.

She wanted nothing to ruin this opportunity. She *needed* this. She needed to try to fill that part of her soul that had felt empty since her father's death.

"Waistcoat?" she asked, holding out her hand.

Hattie handed her the light-blue garment, which had darker, horizontal stripes to give the illusion of a broader chest and shoulders. In addition to binding her chest, they'd sewn extra pleats into the sides of the shirt to hide what Mr. Bradbury had described as her "attributes" that would certainly give her away.

Slipping into the waistcoat, she began to fasten the row of

ivory buttons. There was nothing of splendor or pomp about her appearance. She intended to stay below anyone's notice by looking the part of a humble, country-bred gentleman.

For the next several minutes, Arabella and Hattie worked together in silence, tying her cravat and slipping her into her dark blue jacket. They'd just managed to put on her boots when the carriage rolled to a stop. There was some noise coming from the street outside, but nothing compared to how loud London could be during the Season.

The carriage swayed, indicating Hattie's brother had jumped down from his perch.

Arabella released a shaky breath and ran her hands down the length of her thighs, her nerves prickling with anticipation.

This is it.

Getting up from her seat, she moved toward the door.

"Miss?" Hattie called out, stopping her progress.

She turned around. "Yes?"

Hattie's eyes shot to the top of her head. "Yer hat."

"My hat?" Arabella knew she hadn't forgotten her hat; she could feel it atop her head.

Hattie's eyes widened as if to emphasize her point, and she nodded toward Arabella's head once again.

Exasperated, Arabella reached up and her fingers grazed the familiarity of her bonnet—

Devil take it! She'd almost forgotten to switch out her bonnet.

Tugging hard on one end, she untied the ribbon beneath her chin and then pulled out the long pins that'd been added to secure the bonnet while she changed.

Hattie took the pins and the bonnet with one hand while handing her the dark-blue topper hat with the other. She gave her a smug grin. "What was that about how ye wouldn' need me if ye ran into any trouble?"

"I have not yet left the carriage," Arabella argued. "It does not count."

Hattie snorted.

Arabella let out a breath and shook her head. Perhaps she was more nervous than she originally thought. Taking another calming breath, she donned her correct hat and turned back toward the carriage door.

"Be careful, miss," Hattie called out in a more serious tone.

"I will," Arabella replied, her hand shaking as she reached for the door handle. "No matter what happens, remember our plan."

"Of course. Jim and I'll be here waitin' when ye come out—with no one the wiser."

Arabella sent up a quick prayer for that to be true as Jim opened the door.

Stepping onto the pavement, Arabella exchanged a nod with Jim. He would drive around the row of buildings in a circle, constantly passing by until she made her exit.

Hattie and Jim each possessed a letter, signed by Arabella, to be used should the worst happen during one of her adventures and she were caught. The letters acquitted them of any guilt, stating she would've gone through with the plan with or without their help, and as faithful servants, they remained by her side, seeing that she was as safe as the situation allowed.

Approaching the Portland stone structure, Arabella did her best to avoid eye contact with anyone she passed. The two-story building, with its long rows of arched windows evenly spaced across its front, blended well with the other buildings along the popular street. It was what was inside the club that made it stand out from the others.

Her steps quickened, matching her rapidly beating heart. She could barely hold back her excitement, which was, no doubt, taking away the impression she wanted to give of casual indifference. She was supposed to be playing the part of a gentleman, not a child rushing to eat an entire cake. She needed to pace herself or find herself sickened with regrets.

Using the gold door knocker, she tapped twice against the black surface.

The door opened, revealing the world's tallest butler standing between her and her goal. The man was a veritable giant, his square stature blocking even a glimpse inside the door.

Goliath cleared his throat. "May I help you, sir?"

Sir. That was promising.

Retrieving the letter she'd forged with her brother's signature, she took a shaky breath. "My name is Sebastian Latham," Arabella began, tucking her chin closer to her chest hoping it would give her voice a deeper tone. She extended the letter to the butler.

She'd chosen the name from her inspiration, *Twelfth Night*, in which the main character, Viola, had disguised herself as a man and used the name of her twin brother, Sebastian.

"I am here on the voucher of my cousin, Mr. Emerson Latham," she continued, grateful her hand and her voice remained steady, though a nervous sweat had broken out on the back of her neck and under her arms.

Goliath studied her for several long minutes.

Finally taking the letter, he opened it. "Mr. Emerson Latham is not in town?" Goliath asked, his thick, black-and-gray brows lifting as he stared at her from over the top of the forged letter.

"He is not," she replied, swallowing back the lump in her throat. Her nerves hummed with anticipation and the fear of disappointment, making her heart race.

Would he let her in?

"I am afraid you will have to come back when the other Mr. Latham—"

Goliath's words were cut short by a familiar and very slurred voice.

"Latham? Latham, you say?"

Goliath turned in the doorway, revealing Lord Digby, the *ton's* infamous drunkard. Rounder in the middle, the white-haired man teetered to the right and then the left, his next words somehow sounding even more inebriated.

"Why, Latham never"—he hiccupped—"never s'ought—"

Lord Digby scowled and wiggled his jowls, as if the gesture would remove the numbing from his tongue and lips. "What are you doing here?" he managed to finish.

There was a good chance the blurry-eyed lord had mistaken her for her brother; they did, after all, stand at almost a similar height and had the same nose and color of eyes.

Before the butler could question Lord Digby's conclusion, Arabella followed that undeniable feeling in her gut, urging her to seize the opportunity that presented itself.

"Lord Digby," she called out with a tone of complete familiarity and offered a friendly bow, proud of herself for not automatically curtsying. "A pleasure to see you, my lord."

With any luck, she could get the drunkard to help her through the door. She just had to find a way to trick him into offering her an invitation. Goliath wouldn't dare argue with a member who had the added benefit of being a lord.

Lord Digby took a few tipsy steps toward the door, his feet stumbling on everything and nothing.

She moved closer to the threshold, but Goliath didn't budge.

"Perhaps you would permit me to be of some assistance, my lord?" Arabella called out around Goliath's shoulder.

Lord Digby had either grown weary in his struggle or the entrance hall had a serious slant, but he was most assuredly leaning closer to one of the side walls.

"Assistance?" He hiccupped mid-scoff. "My boy, when I need assistance holding down my drink, you can put me in my grave."

Arabella twisted her lips in annoyance. The man wasn't proving to be useful.

Lord Digby's struggle intensified when his left foot connected with his right, launching his upper half sideways while his bumbling feet attempted to catch up. "Confound it, Latham," he shouted, his arms flailing in an effort to steady himself. "What is taking you so long? Get in here." He was half bent over and falling fast.

Caught by surprise, it took Arabella a moment to react.

Goliath moved out of her way, and with horses stampeding in her stomach, she ran toward the fumbling lord.

Grabbing one of his arms, she attempted to stand him upright while Goliath grabbed the lord's other arm.

"Took you long 'nough," Lord Digby grumbled, his weight proving to be far more substantial than she'd anticipated.

"My apologies, Lord Digby," Arabella said, "but in my defense, you had just said—"

"Hang what I said, man, and help me to the coffee room."

"Of course, my lord," she replied, unable to hold back the smile that curved her lips.

Her nervous sweats were gone, replaced by lightning bolts of excitement that coursed through her and brought every sensation inside her to life.

She'd found a way inside.

FIVE

"Is it not early in the day to be reading?" Bradbury moaned, dropping languidly into the empty chair directly across from Henry inside the coffee room at their club.

"Is there a time of day you *do* read?" Henry asked with an indifferent tone he struggled to maintain as he snapped the book closed, his thumb remaining inside the pages. He stared at his friend over the top of his book, his heart racing, and silently upbraided himself for allowing Bradbury to sneak up on him.

"Not if I can help it." Bradbury smiled, his eyes briefly scanning the room, which held only a few members. "But if the task cannot be avoided, then the subject matter had better be entertaining." Leaning forward, Bradbury squinted at the cover of Henry's book. "Agriculture?" He lurched back in disgust. "For pity's sake, man. You truly cannot think of anything better to do with the bounty that surrounds you?" He held his arms out to the room.

"I cannot," Henry replied. The leather-bound book began to bow beneath the press of his fingers. His thumb brushed the edge of the lunacy pamphlet pinned inside the pages.

Henry had always come to Brooks's seeking solitude. It was the one place he could go where his aunt couldn't follow. But this time he'd taken his search for solitude even further by choosing the coffee room over the cardroom in the hopes of avoiding Bradbury. To be found reading a pamphlet about lunacy was an invitation for questions he didn't want to answer.

Afraid to speak the truth? The voice inside his head whispered.

Henry's hand gripped harder on the book. As if that could somehow contain everything.

"Honestly, Beasty, when am I going to convince you to have

a little fun? You are far too serious. When was the last time you took a chance on anything?"

The answer was never. And for good reason. His father's poor example had rid him of any desire to gamble. "I took a chance on befriending you," he replied, knowing he needed to say something to satisfy Bradbury.

Bradbury snorted. "We both know that was Emerson."

He was right. Emerson had been the first to befriend Henry, and that was only because Bradbury had wagered with him to sit at Henry's table one afternoon. Emerson had struck up a mostly one-sided conversation that had left Henry both bewildered and intrigued. But even more surprising, after that initial encounter, Emerson sat with Henry again, and just like that, he became part of the Brooks's Brotherhood.

Bradbury cleared his throat.

Henry found his friend watching him with a questioning look.

"If you enjoy taking risks so much," Henry began, wanting to redirect Bradbury's attention, "I wonder why you are here and not in the cardroom."

Bradbury let out a frustrated breath. "That beef-witted Mr. Deighton ruined a perfectly good game of cards by wagering the hand of his well-dowered sister." He shuddered. "I had to leave fifteen guineas on the table just to get out of there before it was too late."

Henry resisted the urge to shake his head. "Did it not occur to you that Lord Deighton wanted you to withdraw from the game?"

Bradbury's brow furrowed as he slipped into a contemplative silence. Once realization dawned, he shot upward in his seat. "That conniving, odious bounder! I ought to march right back up there and fleece him of his inheritance."

"By the sounds of it, he would have to pay you with the hand of his well-dowered sister."

Bradbury turned his scowl on Henry. "For once in your life, can you stop thinking with your head and more about a man's pride?"

"*He that is proud eats up himself.*" The words slipped off Henry's tongue before he could stop them.

"Was that Shakespeare?" Bradbury asked, tilting his head.

Henry didn't answer. To do so felt tantamount to admitting he'd read all of Shakespeare's plays because of Arabella.

A commotion at the doorway on the far side of the room saved Henry from further questions. Everyone else in the room turned their heads toward the noise, but Henry did not. It was easy enough to recognize the owner of the overly loud voice, his slurred words, and the heavy, uneven footsteps.

Lord Digby had managed to find his way to the coffee room.

"This is interesting," Bradbury said, turning more fully in his chair to face the doorway, leaving Henry with nothing but a view of the back of his head. "Who is that with Lord Digby?"

Not caring which poor soul Lord Digby had latched himself onto to get him to the room, Henry took the opportunity to secure his book inside his jacket pocket. It slid in easily, which was why he'd chosen that book in the first place.

"Step lively, Latham," Lord Digby called out just before an audible crash of furniture filled the room.

Latham? Emerson wasn't due home for several more weeks.

"Did he say Latham?" Bradbury vacated his chair, and Henry stood in time to see his friend reach Lord Digby's side.

"Steady on," Bradbury said, swooping in and taking hold of the drunkard's free arm as the butler stepped aside to stop another table from toppling.

Looking to Lord Digby's other arm, Henry's heart stopped.

No. Henry shook his head and closed his eyes before he dared look again.

It cannot be.

How could it be?

The person standing next to Lord Digby in a dark blue jacket and—he swallowed—breeches was Arabella. He knew it without a doubt. Though her curves were disguised beneath carefully tailored wool and linen, he'd been discreetly gazing upon her for long enough to know those unique, fawn-colored eyes and full red lips. They'd tempted him many times.

"And you are?" Bradbury's voice cut through the room, snapping Henry to the present.

Panic constricted his lungs, and Henry wondered how obvious his panic would be if he plowed through the tables and chairs separating him from the disaster playing out before him. He had to get Arabella out of the club before anyone else recognized her.

"Sebastian Latham," Arabella said in a ridiculously deep tone. She gave Bradbury a quick nod as they continued their struggle to steady Lord Digby. "I am—I am a cousin of Emerson Latham."

Bradbury smiled, but his expression was nothing in comparison to the gleam of satisfaction in Arabella's eyes as she appeared to fool him.

Shaking himself from his initial shock, Henry moved toward Arabella with a determined but unsuspecting pace.

Was this some sort of joke to her? A game?

Sebastian? This was no Shakespearean comedy to be performed for her entertainment. One wrong move and she risked utter ruination for herself and her family.

His temper rose with every step, forcing him to clench his fist to regain some control. He knew better than anyone how quickly one mistake could become fodder for the gossips.

"Aiden Bradbury," his friend replied, pulling on Lord Digby's arm and leading them away from Henry and toward the wingback chair specifically placed in the corner of the room where Lord Digby liked to sleep off his drink. "I am sure your cousin has mentioned me. I am, after all, his closest friend."

Arabella grunted out an acknowledgment, straining under Lord Digby's weight as one of his legs dragged behind him.

Henry vowed then and there to have Bradbury checked for the need of spectacles and an ear trumpet. Could he truly not detect the ridiculously forced tone?

Bradbury looked up, his eyes quickly finding Henry. "Beasty?" His forehead creased with confusion. "Is everything all right?"

Henry gave no reply, his eyes locking on Arabella as her head jerked quickly in his direction and then back to Lord Digby. Only a few tables and chairs separated them, and Henry had no intention of slowing his pace until he reached her and removed her from the building.

"Did you not hear me, old man?" Bradbury called out while still pulling Lord Digby along.

"I am only one year older than you are," Henry replied, the urge to make that perfectly clear suddenly very important to him.

Worried she will think you a dull, old man, compared to the intrepid Mr. Bradbury? The voice taunted.

Shoving back the voice, Henry kept his focus on Arabella, who, with the significant aid of Bradbury, was almost to the wing-back chair. When she finally looked up at him again, he shot her a sharp look of warning, telling her he wasn't fooled by her disguise.

Her eyes widened and darted away just as her foot caught on one of the chairs, sending her sprawling to the ground with Lord Digby tumbling after her, leaving Bradbury helpless to stop them.

Henry spanned the remaining distance in a matter of seconds, his hands going to Lord Digby. He grabbed hold of the lord's jacket and yanked him off Arabella, pulling him up in almost an arc, and then down hard onto the cushion of the wingback chair.

Lord Digby grunted from the force of the impact, but Henry didn't care. He had already moved to Arabella, who clutched at her chest, struggling to regain her breath.

Henry knelt beside her, using his larger frame to shield her from the few patrons occupying the room. He reached out, his only thought to assess her for injuries, but she pushed his hand away with a grunt.

"I can manage," she said in a strained but deep tone, keeping her eyes averted from him as she quickly worked to straighten her appearance. Her hands were shaking.

Henry's anger returned full force. She'd nearly injured herself with this foolishness.

"Devil take it, Northcott," Lord Digby spewed and sputtered

from behind him. "With a grip like that, you should have been a pugilist, not a lord. You could have killed me."

All the air in the room vanished, and the hairs on the back of Henry's neck stood on end.

He could feel every eye in the room turn upon him. No doubt everyone, including Arabella, remembered who had murdered his uncle.

A hand pressed upon his shoulder, and he twisted his body around to look behind him.

Bradbury stared down at him with an uneasy smile that Henry suspected he used for the benefit of watching eyes. "You help our new friend. I will see to Lord Digby."

Henry nodded, finding it hard to do much of anything else. In the eyes of many members of the *ton*, he was just as guilty for his uncle's death simply because he shared the same blood as his mother.

Bradbury offered him a solemn nod in return and turned his attention to Lord Digby. "How about some coffee, my lord?" he said loud enough to draw the attention of everyone in the room. "We would hate for you to take another stumble. How fortunate you were to have Lord Northcott assist you the rest of the way to your seat."

The air slowly returned to the room, followed by the soft hum of chatter.

Henry pushed out a breath and looked down at Arabella.

A book lay open across her stomach. Dread iced his veins as he recognized both the cover and the folded piece of paper she held in her hand.

Color drained from Arabella's skin as her eyes focused on the cover of the pamphlet.

Bile rose in his throat, and his hand pointlessly clutched where the book should've been inside his jacket.

The situation had gone from bad to worse.

SIX

Arabella's heart pounded hard inside her chest, matching her rapid breaths. The sound filled her ears, blocking out everything else in the room. In a matter of seconds, she had gone from being crushed beneath Lord Digby to being hit in the stomach by a book that had fallen out of Lord Northcott's jacket.

A crisp, folded piece of paper had slipped free from somewhere inside the book's pages, landing flat on the floor. She reached over to pick it up and froze the moment she turned it over. The cover showed the most frightening image of a person thrashing about, tied down with heavy chains, and the title on the pamphlet read:

Lunacy: mastering the animality after the loss of humanity.

The words were chilling, and her stomach twisted into a sickening knot.

She'd heard the gossip during the Season about Lord Northcott's mother being a patient at the old Bedlam. But that story was contradicted by another claiming she was buried somewhere in an unmarked grave.

Before Arabella could puzzle anything out, she was unceremoniously lifted off the floor. She landed on unsteady feet and was practically dragged out of the room by the large and domineering figure that was Lord Northcott.

"Let me go," she demanded in a panicked whisper.

He didn't even look at her as they exited the coffee room.

Lord Northcott pulled them through the corridor and into a nearby room. It was much smaller, with only one tall window at the back, which didn't fill the space with much light.

Keeping his grip on her arm, Lord Northcott turned Arabella around so his back was to the closed door.

"What are you doing?" He growled the words like he wanted to shout.

She'd never seen such a reaction from him. He was always so controlled, but standing here, looming over her with his fists clenched, he appeared the beast the *ton* accused him of being.

Unfortunately for him, she'd just spent the past year with an overprotective brother, so she wouldn't be so easily intimidated.

"I owe you no explanation," she replied, lifting her chin and taking a step toward him.

His eyes shot to the space she'd closed between them, and his back stiffened.

She squared her shoulders, prepared to argue further, but then he did the strangest thing.

He took a step back.

"You need to leave," he said after a moment, his voice emotionless as he met her gaze.

"Not until I find the betting book," she replied. "I came here for a reason, and I intend to see it through."

"No."

She felt her temper flare. "You cannot physically stop me. It would only draw more attention, which is something neither of us wants." She placed her hands on her hips, and the sound of crinkling paper filled the tense room.

Lord Northcott's eyes locked on her hand.

She'd forgotten she still held his pamphlet. She couldn't read his exact reaction but, given his rigid stance, she knew it meant something to him—which meant she could bargain with it.

With slow movements, she held the pamphlet between them. "If you take me to the betting book, I will return your pamphlet and leave willingly."

He said nothing, though she had the distinct impression his mind was weighing out all the consequences behind his dark and penetrating gaze.

Unbidden her body shivered. Not from fear, but from heat. Never before had a man stared at her in such a way.

"All right," he said, his voice gruff. "The betting book for the pamphlet, and then I am taking you home."

"To my carriage," she countered. "It will be on the street waiting for me, along with my change of clothes. I understand you will have to tell my mother, but I do not want her to have to bear the shame of seeing me like this when you do."

Lord Northcott nodded.

She tucked the pamphlet inside her jacket pocket, his eyes carefully watching her movements.

"Do not leave my side," he said, an odd strain to his tone as if he feared more for her safety and less about what was in her possession.

"I will not," she replied softly, feeling unbalanced by the different reactions he was causing in her.

The sudden urge to take his hand to reassure him overtook her, but he turned away just as her hand lifted, and he moved with stiff steps toward the door. Had she imagined something more happening between them?

They walked to the entrance hall in silence. Goliath stood at his post near the front door, his eyes following her as if he still had his suspicions. Her nerves prickled, making her eager to be away.

But instead, Lord Northcott approached him and engaged him in a brief conversation. Panic gripped her as Goliath abruptly left his post, leaving her to fear Lord Northcott had gone back on their arrangement.

"What did you—" she began, but Lord Northcott cut her off.

"I called for my carriage to be made ready for when we are finished," he said, his expression guarded as if he expected her to think the worst of him.

And she had.

He walked away, and she felt as if someone had punched her in the stomach. He didn't have to reassure her. He could've let her suffer in her panic, but he hadn't.

Could a man the *ton* painted to be dark and brooding truly be so selfless? And if he wasn't who the *ton* continuously made him out to be, then why didn't he do anything to prove them otherwise?

She puzzled over the enigma that was the man before her as she followed him up a set of stairs. With her every step, she began to feel the weight of his every step, pulling her closer to him. The pressure of his large hand as it slid and then gripped its way up the wood banister left a warm, lingering caress that continually stroked the palm of her hand, igniting every nerve throughout her arm. His breaths, which were heavy and controlled, drove her to match his every inhale and exhale as if they were somehow becoming one.

She didn't know how to explain what was happening between them, but she knew she'd never felt this way before. Never looked upon a man this way before.

"The book is in the cardroom," Lord Northcott said, startling her into realizing they'd reached the landing. His eyes narrowed. "Are you all right?"

"I—I do not—" She blinked, their connection broken. "I—"

Her words were cut short by the arrival of Mr. Bradbury, who had come up the steps behind them. "There you are. I was beginning to think you'd left." He stopped next to Arabella, a grin on his face. "Are we going to the cardroom?"

Arabella shot a glance at Lord Northcott, who held his usual stoic expression.

"We were," he replied.

"Splendid," Mr. Bradbury said, rubbing his hands together before leading the charge into the cardroom.

She waited for Lord Northcott to say something—this hadn't been a factor in their plan—but he said nothing. His expression was like stone, unmovable, and his eyes stared right through her as he motioned for her to precede him. The moment her back was to him, she could *feel* his eyes upon her.

Walking into the cardroom, Arabella took in every sight she

could. She would never have this opportunity again, and it was much simpler to focus on her surroundings than on the way Lord Northcott was making her feel.

There were three large, half-circular gaming tables running along one side of the room with a row of smaller, more private, square tables running along the opposite wall.

Only one of the larger tables was in use, while the rest of the room sat empty. Two of the four gentlemen at the table looked toward them but quickly averted their eyes the moment they landed on Mr. Bradbury.

"I would suggest a game of cards," Mr. Bradbury began, glaring at the backs of their heads, "but trust me when I say you would not like what is being wagered in that game."

Not wanting to stray from her promise to Lord Northcott, who remained directly behind her, she took Mr. Bradbury at his word, though she was curious to know what else besides money might be wagered at a gentlemen's card game.

"My cousin talked of a betting book," Arabella said, taking the opportunity to direct Mr. Bradbury to what she wanted.

A fire lit in Mr. Bradbury's eyes. "The next best thing."

He led them to a sideboard centered along the back wall. A very large, very ornate book lay open on top of its polished surface, a black feathered quill resting next to it, along with a crystal inkwell.

"This is our infamous betting book," Mr. Bradbury said, motioning for her to come closer.

Arabella's heart raced, and her hands shook as she stepped forward. Despite all that had happened, she'd done it. She was about to see the secrets that had been denied to her. Until now.

Placing her fingers on the tabletop to steady herself, she leaned over the pages, her eyes hungry for every word.

Mr. Bradbury stepped up beside her. "Let me show you one of our most recent wagers."

Arabella resisted the urge to laugh. Mr. Bradbury was making winning his wager far too easy. She would have to find the perfect opportunity to tell him. How fun that would be!

"Ah, here it is," Mr. Bradbury said, holding a finger at the top of a page.

Biting her lip to hold back her grin, she leaned forward to read the ledger:

1815. March 12th.

Mr. Bradbury and Mr. Latham bet Lord Digby and Lord Masdon twenty pounds to twenty-five pounds. A pig wearing Beau Brummel's waistcoat shall be released inside the morning room of White's gentlemen's club without the participants ever being caught.

There were a few more wagers listed below it, all adding up to quite a hefty sum should her brother and Mr. Bradbury win. Then, on the last line, she read:

Won by Mr. Bradbury and Mr. Latham. Paid.

"My congratulations." She smiled at Mr. Bradbury while secretly congratulating herself. She'd heard speculation about this very rumor during the Season, but Emerson had always denied it. Now she knew for certain.

Mr. Bradbury puffed up his chest and grinned. "I had to climb out a first-story window with a makeshift rope while your cousin jumped onto the roof of his carriage to avoid capture."

"It sounds as if your bounteous winnings were well-earned. Are there any involving Lord Northcott?" she asked, curious to discover more about the stoic baron who had chosen to remain a few steps behind them.

Mr. Bradbury laughed and turned wry eyes on Lord Northcott. "Beasty refuses to take part in any fun."

Arabella looked at Lord Northcott, wanting to know what that exactly meant, but he remained silent, his expression unreadable.

"Do not look for answers from him, Mr. Latham," Mr. Bradbury said, patting her across the back and startling her into remembering she was *Mr.* Latham. "I have been asking that same question for years." He scoffed. "Do not let his dour mood spoil this moment. Let me show you some of my other favorites."

Arabella nodded, trying and failing to feel that strange connection with Lord Northcott once again. It was like he had built up his walls within himself and completely cut her off.

Mr. Bradbury flipped through several pages before he stopped and directed her to a certain spot on the page.

1814. October 22nd.

Doctor Fleetwood bets Lord Digby ten guineas to thirty guineas. Lord Digby will be dead by the end of the year if he does not reduce his consumption of spirits.

Won by Lord Digby. Paid.

Arabella blinked in shock. Had they truly wagered about a man's death?

"Can this be true?" she asked Mr. Bradbury.

Mr. Bradbury nodded. "Lord Digby has been fleecing Doctor Fleetwood of his guineas for years. The man is like a fish happily swimming in his drink, much to the good doctor's chagrin."

Arabella laughed and shook her head as she turned back to the book. What other ridiculous things did gentlemen feel the need to gamble over?

She stopped turning the pages when a familiar name jumped out at her.

1815. June 18th.

Mr. Deighton bets Mr. Bradbury twenty guineas to fifteen guineas. Mr. Bradbury will be unable to walk down the streets of Pall Mall during daylight hours without being recognized by any passersby.

Won by Mr. Bradbury.

"This bet was completed, correct?" she asked, noticing something missing.

Bradbury leaned forward, looking at where she pointed. A

grin spread across his face. "Yes, it was. Deighton thought he had me on that one, but I claimed my victory thanks to the protective covering of Beasty's"—he pointed a thumb to Lord Northcott—"great-great-something-or-other's armored helmet."

Arabella gaped at Mr. Bradbury's brilliance. "A very clever solution, indeed."

Mr. Bradbury smirked. "Clever does not even begin to describe my many traits."

Arabella resisted another urge to laugh at her brother's boisterous friend. "Would you say noticing finer details is one of those many traits?"

Lord Northcott moved directly behind her, his unease palpable to her. Did he fear she would out her disguise to make her point?

"I suppose," Mr. Bradbury said, his eyes darting toward Lord Northcott, a befuddled wrinkle forming between his fiery brows.

She was about to shock them both.

"Then tell me, Mr. Bradbury, has Mr. Deighton indeed paid you for this wager, or am I reading this incorrectly?" She slid her finger down to the empty spot on the ledger where it should have been marked as paid.

Bradbury's eyes jerked to the page, then opened wide. "What in the blazes!" Pivoting on his heel, he stormed toward the one large gaming table currently in use. "Deighton, you brummagem, you still owe me twenty guineas—with interest—and do not even think that I will accept the hand of your sister."

Arabella stifled a laugh.

"We should leave," Lord Northcott said, leaning so close to her ear his breath sent shivers up and down her spine.

"Of course," she said, suddenly breathless and trying to remember how to move her legs.

He was right; if she wanted to leave unnoticed, now was her chance. Every eye in the room was focused on the heated argument between Mr. Bradbury and Mr. Deighton.

"Miss Latham?" Lord Northcott whispered, her name on

his lips so soft it felt more like a caress along her cheek. Had he moved even closer?

She swallowed, daring a look over her shoulder, the sudden scent of sandalwood and leather weakening her sensibilities.

"Yes?" she breathed.

His eyes dipped to her lips, but just as quickly, he looked away and took a large step back.

The connection severed, he held out his hand. "My pamphlet?"

His sudden indifference sliced through her, and she didn't know what to think of that.

SEVEN

The tension in Henry's shoulders didn't ease until his carriage turned onto Kensington Street. Rapping his fist on the carriage ceiling, he signaled for his coachman to pull over.

Leaning forward, he watched out the window as Arabella's carriage came to a stop in front of her home. A few moments later, she alighted from the conveyance, properly dressed in pelisse, day dress, and bonnet—much to the relief of his mind and body.

Every moment he'd spent inside Brooks's with her dressed in those clothes that—

Letting out a frustrated groan, Henry scrubbed a hand across his face.

He would *not* think of how their encounter today confirmed that she was the most exquisite creature he'd ever beheld. He felt like a rake for staring at her form as often as he had. He should be focusing on how angry he was with her.

Are you angry or afraid? the voice inside his head taunted.

Henry swallowed, watching her as she paused at her front steps. She looked up and down the street—looking for him, no doubt.

The truth was, he was afraid.

Afraid of feeling so out of control merely by being in her presence. Which was why he wouldn't be accompanying her inside. With both their reputations still intact, he would distance himself from her. For both their sakes.

He waited until Arabella walked inside before instructing his coachman to take him home. As soon as he could put quill to paper, he would ask Bradbury to take over the weekly visits to the Lathams until Emerson returned.

As soon as his carriage came to a stop, Henry jumped out

onto pavement, only to be met by a sudden downpour. He muttered an oath. How fitting that the day's looming clouds would choose that exact moment to open. He would add that to the growing list of reasons why he knew he was cursed.

His aunt's butler, Samson, was waiting for him at the front door. His eyes briefly traveled over Henry's wet clothing and the growing puddle on the floor.

In his youth, Henry thought of the man as a gargoyle, and looking at him now, unchanged by time, he almost believed it to be true.

Handing over his rain-soaked hat and gloves, Henry growled as he struggled to free his arm from his jacket.

"Allow me, my lord," Samson said, intervening.

"Thank you," Henry replied, grabbing his book from the inside pocket and tucking it securely under his arm.

"Would you care for some tea?" Samson asked, folding the damp jacket over his forearm.

"No, thank you, Samson. I would like to be left alo—"

"Henry. What on earth happened?" His aunt's concerned tone echoed inside the entrance hall.

"I was caught in the rain, Aunt," Henry said, moving his book behind his back. The last thing he wanted was for his aunt to discover the pamphlet.

She studied him with penetrating gray eyes. "Samson, have the floor mopped, then send a footman to fetch Lord Northcott a new jacket. We shall be in the music room."

If it had been anyone else, Henry would have made an excuse, but he could never do that to his aunt. He would hold the book in the hand of the arm she didn't take and pray it remained unnoticed until Samson returned with a new jacket.

Entering the music room, Henry escorted his aunt to the elegant, cherrywood pianoforte, a wedding present to her from his uncle, where she took a seat on the cushioned bench.

His aunt cherished music, and she had tutored Henry to sing when all they had was each other. He only wished he could enjoy

singing as much as she loved to play. His aunt was bred for attention, while he preferred the shadows.

"Nothing warms the soul like song," she said, shuffling
through the music carefully stacked atop the pianoforte.

"I'm actually quite warm, Aunt," Henry said.

"Nonsense," she said. "And besides, we need to practice."

"Practice?" Dread filled him for what was sure to follow.

"Yes," she said, lifting a stern brow. "For a small charity event
held by Lady Bixbee."

"The Season is over," Henry argued.

"Yes," she said slowly, making him feel like a recalcitrant
child. "Though most of the gentry have gone to the country, the
Foundling Hospital remains. *And* it is in need of our help."

A wave of guilt washed over him. His aunt had never had
children, so her charities of choice always involved youth. And he
had an obligation to attend with her.

Devil take it, he truly was cursed.

"Of course, Aunt," he replied.

She offered him a soft smile. "Now, put down your book—"
Before Henry could react, she grabbed it from his hand.

Inwardly he cursed as he struggled to keep an outward appearance of calm.

"What have you been reading?" his aunt asked, turning it
over in her hands and scanning the cover.

Henry held his breath and prayed.

"Agriculture?" She looked at him, puzzled. "Is there a problem with one of our estates?" She opened the book and began
flipping through the pages.

He should've known better than to waste his time praying.

She stopped on the page where the pamphlet lay hidden, and
his stomach dropped.

"What's this?" she asked, pulling out the folded paper.

Henry said nothing.

A shadow fell across his aunt's countenance as she studied

the pamphlet, ushering in a cold he hadn't felt since the night his mother killed his uncle.

"Why do you have this?" she asked through a clenched jaw.

Henry again remained silent, knowing nothing he said would make her understand. He didn't fully understand why he'd kept the pamphlet that day in Westminster when a man had been handing them out.

A tense silence filled the room. His aunt's eyes darkened until her irises were indistinguishable from the pupils. "What is it you hoped to find, Henry?" she snapped with both rage and disgust.

Again, he said nothing. Whatever he'd hoped to find inside that pamphlet was gone now.

Her nostrils flared, and she rose from her seat. "I do not like these sudden changes in you." She said each word carefully, as if she wanted to make certain he heard and understood every single one. "First, you replace your *uncle's* solicitor with a man whom we do not even know can be trusted to hide *your* family's secret. And now this."

When Henry still remained silent, she shoved past him and moved directly to the low-lit fire and threw the pamphlet into the flames. "I want no more of this. Whatever you are looking for, you will never find it. *Your* family is tainted. Your father. Your mother. Your sister." His aunt visibly shook as she spat out each name, sending sharp barbs into his chest.

The final death knell would be if she ever thought the same about him.

She stormed away from the fire, her eyes flashing their own flames. "Only you and I are left to see that the Northcott family name is remembered for the reputable family it once was. Not the fodder for the gossip mills that your parents have made of it."

Henry nodded, the stabbing pain in his chest becoming more painful with every word. He—his family—had done this, and it was up to him to redeem them.

Starting with distancing himself from Arabella. She made him want more from his life, and that he couldn't have.

EIGHT

It was late in the evening, and all Arabella could do was pace. A low fire flickered in the hearth in her room, warding off the dampness after yet another day of rain. The flames cast a faint, ghostly shadow that followed her across the light-blue patterned wallpaper, while her night rail, loosely tied about her waist, wrapped around her ankles with every abrupt turn.

"Yer goin' to wear a hole in that floor, pacin' it like ye are," Hattie said, eyeing Arabella as she dropped a pile of dirty linens by the door.

"I cannot help it," Arabella replied, continuing to pace as her nerves twisted into a knot in the pit of her stomach.

She'd waited all day for the knock on the door that would be Lord Northcott coming to tell her mother what she'd done. But it never came.

He never came.

She didn't understand it.

"Why does he stay away?" Arabella asked, abruptly stopping mid-turn, one hand on her hip.

Hattie looked at her as if she'd grown a third arm. "And yer upset about this, why? If he doesn't come, *we* don't have to face the consequences of our actions."

"I know that," Arabella said, throwing her hands up in exasperation. "But I cannot help feeling that if he does not come, it is only because—" She paused, letting out a flustered breath. It was never easy to admit one's insecurities out loud. "Because he no longer wants anything to do with me."

Hattie tilted her head. "Do ye want him to want somethin' to do with ye?"

Arabella had been just as surprised as Hattie when she first had the thought. But there it was, unbidden, and so in earnest she couldn't deny it no matter how confused she felt. She'd never thought about Lord Northcott in that way throughout the Season, yet something had changed inside Brooks's.

"I do not know," she replied, frustrated with herself.

Walking to her bed, she flung herself—a little too dramatically—backward onto the coverlet. She couldn't seem to let the matter go. He was a dark enigma with a gentle appeal that tugged at her emotions. She couldn't help but want to know more about him.

"He is nothing like me," Arabella said more as an argument to herself. Her thoughts and feelings battled one another.

Hattie scoffed. "That's for certain."

Arabella shot her a glare.

"What?" Hattie balked. "Ye said it first."

Arabella sat up. "That does not mean I need you to agree with me."

Hattie sat down next to her with a look of concern. "What is this really all about, miss?"

Arabella let out a breath. She hadn't told Hattie *everything* that had happened inside the gentleman's club. Lord Northcott's secret wasn't hers to tell, but if she was going to understand these new feelings she was having, she needed advice.

"There was a pamphlet," she blurted out.

"Where?" Hattie asked, confused.

"Inside Brooks's. It fell out of Lord Northcott's pocket. It had been tucked inside a book. And I told him I would return it—the pamphlet; I did not keep the book—to him, and that I would leave willingly if he took me to see the betting book." Her words were coming out fast, but she couldn't seem to slow them down or make them make much sense. "It had the most frightening title—*Lunacy: mastering the animality after the loss of humanity.*"

Hattie's eyes bulged.

"I am sorry I did not tell you about it, but he—Lord North-cott—was very uneasy about me having it, and then I did the horrible thing of using it against him." She cringed; it hadn't been her finest moment. "I did give it back, but I also cannot stop thinking about that pamphlet and why he had it and why he was hiding it." She gulped in her next few breaths, feeling suddenly lightheaded.

Hattie blinked for a moment before meeting Arabella's gaze. "I'm goin' to forgive ye for not tellin' me, because I might know somethin' that I didn't tell ye—only because I didn't feel it was my place to talk about a close friend of the family."

It was Arabella's turn to gape.

Lord, how this world is given to lying.

"What do you know?" Arabella asked.

Hattie clasped her hands in her lap and took a deep breath. "I heard from one of the maids in Lady Bixbee's home that her aunt once worked in the Northcott home, and she says there was a sister."

"*Was* a sister?" Arabella repeated, her mind furiously coming up with its own explanations.

Hattie nodded slowly. "As in, she was in the home but was admitted to Bedlam . . . like the mother."

A sudden chill swept through the room, sending shivers up Arabella's spine. She turned to see which of her windows had been left opened but found all were closed.

A knock firm and clear sounded at her door, causing both girls to jump.

"Arabella?" her mother's voice called out.

Her already pounding heart continued to pound for an entirely new reason. Had Lord Northcott finally told her mother what she'd done?

Forcing an outward appearance of calm that she did not feel, Arabella stood and smoothed down the front of her night rail. "Co-come in."

Her mother opened the door and stepped inside the room.

Her brown hair, which matched the color of Arabella's, hung over one shoulder of her dark-blue night rail in a finely woven plait. "I thought I heard talking." She looked between Arabella and Hattie, who stood beside her.

"Pardon me, mistress. I'm late getting these linens down to the washroom." Hattie curtsied and shot a quick look of apology to Arabella before gathering up the linens at the door and leaving. The lucky coward was getting out before the situation turned bad.

"Did we wake you?" Arabella asked with a forced smile.

Nothing will come of nothing. She repeated the words of King Lear, praying them to be true.

"No, I was still awake. This was just delivered." She held up a letter, the wax seal unbroken. "Apparently, it could not wait until morning."

Arabella was going to be sick. Needing to move, needing to do something to contain the riotous nerves fighting inside her, she returned to her bed. Snatching up one of the pillows, she hopped onto the cream coverlet, pressed her elbows onto the pillow, and clasped her hands in her lap as if everything was perfectly fine.

"Oh? Who is it from?" she asked with far too much nonchalance in her tone. She might as well hold up a bell that clanged out "guil-ty, guil-ty" every time it rang.

Her mother gave her a curious look before joining her on the opposite corner of the bed. "Are you all right?"

"Yes," she said far too quickly. "It was just a strange day," she blurted out again, wanting to cover her face with the pillow. Where was the control she'd had when she was inside Brooks's? If she had acted like this, she never would have made it through the front door.

"At the Foundling Hospital?" her mother asked, one delicate brow raised.

"Yes," she replied. What else could she say?

"How so?"

Wonderful. Now she would either have to risk making up a

lie to add to the growing list of her transgressions or simply ask for her sentencing once the letter was opened.

"It was—that is to say—it *felt* strange, I guess. Parting with father's clothing." There. It was not a lie, nor was it admitting the full truth. Arabella had felt strange handing over the items. She knew her father would never wear them again, but it felt so final. Almost like the day he had been buried. Life was moving on, and once again she had to leave another part of him behind.

Tears glassed over her mother's eyes, and she forced a smile Arabella knew was for her benefit. "That's understandable," she said in a soft tone.

Abandoning the pillow in her lap, Arabella moved to her mother's side and wrapped her arms around her shoulders. "Forgive me, I was not thinking. I should not have brought it up."

Her mother sniffled and wiped a stray tear from her cheek. "No, no, I am the one who should be sorry." She patted Arabella's clasped hands at her shoulder. "I want you to feel free to talk of him. It is good for me, even though I might not be strong enough yet to do so." She tilted her head, resting her temple against Arabella's forehead. "He would have been proud of what you did today."

Arabella's stomach clenched. She very much doubted that.

"Who is the letter from?" she asked, letting go of her mother and taking a seat beside her. It was time to face the consequences of her actions.

Her mother lifted the letter from her lap and opened it with painful slowness.

Arabella held her breath.

"It is from Lady Bixbee," she said, shooting Arabella a teasing glance.

"What?" Arabella exclaimed, lunging for the letter to see for herself. Relief flooded over her, followed swiftly by another rush of nerves.

Her mother scanned the letter's contents. "She writes to inform us that her grandson will be at the charity musicale, and she wishes for you to play your harp, not the pianoforte as you had previously committed."

Arabella scoffed in disbelief. "She wishes?"

"Very well, she says you *will* play your harp so that you may stand out from all the other ladies performing."

Arabella shook her head and laughed. That sounded much more like Lady Bixbee. "And she had to inform us of this now? The charity musicale is not for two days."

"She wants to know what song you will play so her grandson might not 'look a fool' and learn ahead of time when to turn the pages." They both giggled. That was just like the heavy-handed Lady Bixbee.

Her mother stood from the bed. "Try to get some sleep." She leaned forward and kissed Arabella on the forehead. "Tomorrow is a new day."

Arabella's smile faded as she nodded, not at all certain what the next few days would bring.

NINE

A charity musicale? Henry inwardly scoffed. That was the intent of the evening, yet so far, there hadn't been a single musical note uttered, strummed, or stroked. Instead, he, his aunt, and twenty or so members of the *ton* stood hostage inside Lady Bixbee's ridiculously pink parlor.

The walls were a solid deep pink. The columns framing every window and doorframe were a lighter pink. The pillows were all varying patterns and shades of pink. The drapes were a darker pink, and the sofas were—a yellowish-green.

It was all utterly absurd, as was the way Lady Bixbee managed to continuously block the face of the gentleman currently making Arabella laugh on the opposite side of the room. Why did the cumbersome matron feel the need to wear an entire peacock atop her head?

So much for distancing yourself from the lady. You cannot even keep your eyes off her, the voice inside his head taunted.

Heaven forgive him. It was impossible to keep his eyes from her.

Arabella looked resplendent in cerulean blue. Yellow-gold roses were stitched around the gown's high waistline and cascaded toward the hem. The color matched her fawn-colored eyes, enchantingly contrasting the darkness of her beautifully arranged curls.

She smiled—the one that formed adorable creases at the corners of her eyes and made her shoulders rise toward her flushing cheeks. Henry loved that smile. It was truly genuine, and one she only used when she was enjoying herself, yet secretly self-conscious about something someone had said. And her smile was directed toward the gentleman Henry could see now that Lady Bixbee had moved.

"Henry?" His aunt gently tugged on his arm with her gloved hand. "What do you think?"

He looked down at her, and she glanced carefully toward Arabella, whose entire party consisted of her mother, Lady Bixbee, and *that* gentleman. Her brow rose subtly.

Henry cleared his throat, reminding himself that tonight was about fixing the damage the pamphlet had done to their relationship. "Forgive me," he said to his aunt, and his aunt's friend, Mrs. Fowlhurst.

"Do not tease him, Dowager Baroness Northcott," Mrs. Fowlhurst said with a simpering laugh that put Henry on edge. "I believe we both observed how his lordship was admiring . . ." Her words drifted off while her eyes playfully bobbed in Arabella's direction.

His aunt's fingers tensed around his arm, drawing Henry's attention. "I am certain my nephew is only curious about who the gentleman is across from Lady Bixbee. I, for one, have never seen him before," his aunt said.

"That is Lady Bixbee's grandson," Mrs. Fowlhurst replied with a pretentious smile. "Apparently, he is making quite a name for himself after studying underneath Dr. Robert Darling Willis, one of the king's personal physicians." She whispered the last part as if the king's relapse into madness was some greatly kept secret.

A prickling trepidation crept up Henry's spine.

"His name is Dr. Brandon Stafford," Mrs. Fowlhurst said, and Henry's back went rigid. Hearing the name of the doctor who had been relentless in his desire for a meeting with him was like having a bucket of ice water poured over his head.

"He is the son of Lady Bixbee's third son," Mrs. Fowlhurst continued. "Certainly you have heard of him during one of your sessions at Parliament, Lord Northcott?"

"I have heard the name," Henry said with the controlled,

indifferent tone that had earned him the name of the Brooding
Baron.

Mrs. Fowlhurst, visibly shaken by his demeanor, quickly
looked away and engaged his aunt in conversation.

Out of the corner of his eye, Henry caught Arabella watching
him. He looked to her, unable to resist. Despite the distance between them and the other people in the room, it suddenly felt as
if he and Arabella were alone.

Something constantly pulled him to her, and his fingers
twitched, wishing to reach out and touch her.

A hesitant smile tugged at her lips, as if she were unsure of its
reception. It was so unlike her, and he hated it because he knew
he was the reason.

He was not good for her.

Closing his eyes, he turned away.

"Henry?" his aunt spoke.

He opened his eyes to find his aunt and Mrs. Fowlhurst both
watching him worriedly.

"Is it your head?" his aunt asked.

He had suffered from headaches shortly after his mother's
committal to Bedlam, but they had eventually gone away—and
been replaced by the voice inside his head.

"It's nothing, Aunt," he replied, angry with himself for being so
open with his emotions. "The color of the room is—overpowering."

His aunt and Mrs. Fowlhurst shared a knowing look.

"Yes, according to Lady Bixbee, it's supposed to reflect her
favorite flower," his aunt said, as if it weren't a compliment.

"A rose," Mrs. Fowlhurst added, which was news to Henry.
He could have guessed at least a dozen flowers with similar color-
ing. "Ever since Sir Joseph Banks named that flower after Queen
Charlotte—the Bird of Paradise"—she said the words with much
exaggeration—"Lady Bixbee has been relentless in getting a flower
named after her in the Royal Gardens."

As if the matron had known they were whispering about her,
she announced it was time for the musical portion of the evening.

Henry was relieved, ready for the evening to progress, but then suppressed a frown when he saw Dr. Stafford escort Arabella and her mother into the music room. Would he be forced to watch them together for the entire evening?

Escorting his aunt and Mrs. Fowlhurst, he followed the other guests into the music room, which, to his relief, was a much more soothing shade of green. Henry resisted the urge to groan at the sight of the rosewood chairs—all with pink rose-patterned cushions—that faced an ornately carved harp and an elegant pianoforte that supported a large bouquet of pink roses.

His aunt directed him past several preferable rows of chairs toward the back and settled on the third row from the front, which only left a single row of occupied chairs between himself and Arabella, who sat next to Dr. Stafford and Lady Bixbee on the front row.

The heavens were continuing to conspire against him.

Dr. Stafford leaned close to Arabella, her head dipping toward him, as the doctor whispered into her ear. A smile played about Arabella's lips before she whispered something back to him.

Henry wanted to lunge over the rows of chairs and force them apart.

It was tantamount to torture. Was she playing her Shakespeare game with him?

Dr. Stafford let out a chuckle, and Henry's jaw clenched.

The musical performances began, each one as painstakingly long as the next. Henry tugged at his cravat, the temperature rising with every passing minute. There were far too many bodies in the room, judging by how close Dr. Stafford sat next Arabella. Henry had half a mind to open a blasted window. For pity's sake, it was nearing the end of July; open windows should be a common occurrence.

A crack of lightning flashed, and thunder crashed outside the window, cruelly reminding Henry why his wish couldn't be granted. The sound momentarily obscured whatever song was being pounded out on the pianoforte. Did the lady have hams for fists? And why was it always raining!

His chest began to tighten, a familiar feeling, but not one he'd felt since his boyhood when his mother and father were having one of their many rows. He sat straighter in his seat, trying to focus on drawing individual breaths through his nose and exhaling subtly through his mouth.

His concentration lasted until ham-for-fists took her curtsy and Arabella stood.

A whiff of primroses reached his senses, launching his heart into a pounding rhythm.

Heaven—for once—help him, everything about her was bewitching.

Dr. Stafford stood, placing a hand at her back as he helped her onto the raised stage.

Henry should've known better than to pray.

Arabella sat at the harp, not the pianoforte, which had been the only instrument played so far that evening. He shouldn't be surprised to see Arabella standing out from the rest. He'd heard her play the harp many times before, but that didn't stop his nerves from humming in anticipation.

That was, until Dr. Stafford moved to the right of Arabella, helping lay out her music on the stand. Their hands accidentally brushed, and they shared a blushing smile.

Henry bit back a groan. He couldn't take much more of this.

Tilting the harp back to rest in the delicate nook between her neck and shoulder, Arabella raised her hands and gently placed her fingers on the strings. What should've been a small, insignificant moment was the most graceful act Henry had ever beheld.

Her first gentle plucks echoed in the hushed room, and Henry could feel his lungs release a natural breath.

His enjoyment of the music, however, did not last long.

Dr. Stafford reached across Arabella and turned one of the pages. He hovered over her so closely, he was practically blocking all light from the tall, gold candelabra behind them. Arabella's eyes had to be straining just to read the notes. Henry should say something. Did the man not know it was raining outside? There was practically no natural light filling the room. Henry was going to say someth—

"Henry?" His aunt's concerned whisper penetrated his frayed senses. But it was her hand resting on his knee that brought him back to his surroundings.

He was halfway out of his seat and about to draw unwanted attention.

"What is the matter with you?" She looked up at him, her brow sharply raised.

His stomach clenched. If only she truly knew.

"Nothing, Aunt. I will return shortly." Unable to stay a moment longer, Henry abandoned his seat and made his way out into the corridor. He needed a moment to clear his head and regain control of his senses.

Or as much control as you can, the voice whispered.

Closing the music room door behind him, he ignored the butler's inquiry and turned left, knowing there was an alcove farther down the corridor.

Once assured of his privacy, he took a seat on the cushioned bench and dropped his head into his hands. What he wouldn't give to see this evening come to an end.

His traitorous ears caught the faint strumming of the harp just as the song came to a flourishing conclusion. There was applause, and, after a moment, the pianoforte began to play once again.

It was safe to return; he would no longer have to watch Arabella and Dr. Stafford at center stage, and yet Henry didn't move. He *needed* to move. His and his aunt's performance would be coming up next.

"Lord Northcott?"

His head still in his hands, Henry slowly opened his eyes, spotting a pair of cream-colored slippers and the hem of a cerulean blue dress.

Unable to stop himself, he let out a groan before looking up to meet Arabella's gaze.

She stood just inside the alcove, her eyes carefully watching him. "Are you all right?"

"No," he replied.

Her eyes widened as if surprised by his honesty. Good. He was tired of being the only one thrown by something that evening.

"Is there anything I could do?" she asked after a moment.

"Unfortunately, no," he replied, looking to the floor and dragging his fingers through his hair. He immediately regretted the motion. Using the palm of his hand, he attempted to smooth his tousled hair back down.

"It looks"—Arabella paused—"handsome." She said the last word with such heart-pounding nervousness that his eyes shot to meet hers. Color tinged her cheeks as she stared down at him.

Henry swallowed. He was in a world of trouble. He needed to return to the music room before he did something foolish like ask her to hide away with him for the rest of the evening. He stood abruptly, gripping the lapels of his black evening jacket to keep his hands from reaching for her.

"Would you like me to escort you back to your mother, Miss Latham?"

The corners of her lips dipped downward. "No, thank you." She hesitated, her eyes finally glancing away. "I—I shall return on my own." One of her hands reached across her stomach and gripped her upper arm. She looked wounded, and again, he hated himself for any pain he caused her. But nothing could happen between them.

Needing to end this encounter, he offered her a brief bow and moved to step around her.

"Lord Northcott?" she spoke, the uncertainty in her tone halting his steps.

They stood shoulder to shoulder at the edge of the alcove. He looked at her out of the corner of his eye while she tipped her chin over her shoulder to look up at him. He breathed in the slightest hint of primroses, and he reprimanded himself for wanting to lean closer and press his nose to the delicate curve of her neck.

"Yes?" he asked, his voice rough.

She took a deep breath. "After what I did"—she swallowed—"that day at Brooks's. Do you no longer want anything to do with me?"

He held back a mirthless laugh.

No longer want anything to do with her? If only she knew how badly he wanted her.

The right thing to do, for everyone's sake, would be to end this now and say yes.

But you are going to be selfish, the voice whispered.

But he was going to be selfish.

"No," he replied, his gut twisting as his pulse rampaged.

Slowly she turned to face him. "Thank you," she said, her heart completely in her eyes. "When you did not come, I—I feared I had lost your good opinion of me."

"*There is nothing either good or bad, but thinking makes it so.*" The Shakespeare line rolled off his tongue without thought, and the way her expression brightened nearly stopped his heart.

"*Hamlet,*" she replied, her eyes softening. "It was wrong of me to use the pamphlet against you like I did. I hope you will forgive me."

Henry nodded, his shoulders growing tense. The pamphlet was the last thing he wanted to discuss, but he appreciated her humility in admitting she'd done wrong. Not many in this world would be willing to do that, which only proved her goodness.

"Why were you even at Brooks's?" he asked, needing to know.

A corner of her lip ticked up. "Mr. Bradbury unwittingly challenged me to a wager when he said I would never get inside Brooks's and discover his and my brother's secrets."

Henry shook his head and rubbed the back of his neck, bemused. Left to their own devices, Bradbury and Arabella made a dangerous pairing.

"Lord Northcott," Arabella spoke, her tone earnest. She

somehow seemed closer. "I know none of this is my business, and my mother would probably advise me to leave it alone, but I wanted to say that if you ever need to talk to someone about—" She hesitated as if choosing her words carefully. "About life or— or your family—you can always talk with me." She gently reached out and placed a hand on his sleeve. "It must be hard to be so nearly alone."

The feel of her slim fingers on his arm nearly brought him to his knees. Her genuine care washed over him like a danger- ous siren's call. He couldn't pull away from her even if he had wanted to. She had obviously heard the many rumors about his family and somehow put those together with the pamphlet, but he couldn't think poorly of her. He doubted he could ever think that way about her, no matter what outrageous thing she did. Her heart was good—unrestrained—but always good.

He only wished he could think the same way about himself.

"Thank you," he said, his voice heavy, knowing she would always be the light and he would always be the shadow.

They fell into an awkward silence. He, unwilling to pull away; she, waiting for him to say more.

"I should go," Arabella said after a time, slipping her hand from his arm. Immediately he felt the loss of her soothing touch. "My mother, no doubt, is starting to wonder what I am doing." She smiled his favorite smile at him before curtsying and walking back toward the music room.

TEN

Arabella walked into the breakfast room, her spirit lighter than it had been in days.

Her conversation the evening before with Lord Northcott had left her feeling better about their growing friendship. He hadn't opened up to her as she'd hoped, but he was a private man. Perhaps he needed time.

"Good morning," Arabella singsonged to her mother as she went to the sideboard and collected a plate.

"Good morning," her mother replied, setting down the letter she'd been reading. "You seem quite cheerful." Her mother watched her with a suspicious smile.

"I am." Arabella shot her a sly smile of her own. "The sun has finally returned." She nodded toward the window in the corner of the room where the sunlight warmed the glass.

Her mother shook her head in amusement while lifting her teacup to her lips. "Indeed." She took a sip, still watching Arabella over the rim.

Picking up a pastry with her fingers, Arabella took a bite right there at the sideboard.

Her mother gave her that chiding stare that only a mother could, though it was dulled by the smile she couldn't seem to hide.

Arabella dropped the pastry onto her plate, her eyes darting toward the butler. "Good morning, Smith. You must tell Cook the pastries are exceptional this morning. I simply could not wait to take a bite."

Smith was struggling to hide a smile of his own. "Of course, Miss Arabella."

He'd been with the family long enough that she doubted

anything she did could truly shock him—well, perhaps her going inside Brooks's. But she hoped no one would ever learn of that.

She took a second pastry—blueberry this time—and took her usual seat next to her mother at the small, round family table. Almost at once, she noticed the addition of a fifth chair. Her heart warmed even as tears pricked at her eyes. After the earth-shattering blow of losing her father and then her brother's recent marriage, their family had lost and then grown by one. It was both heart-breaking and comforting to see the chair still set at the table for her father even with the added seat for Olivia.

"Have you heard from Emerson?" Arabella asked, hoping for some good news after his last letter had informed them that he and Olivia would be staying longer in Bath.

Her mother set down her fork and picked up the letter from the table. "Just this morning, as a matter of fact." Faint worry lines appeared along her forehead. Not enough to make Arabella fear the worst had happened but enough to prompt her to inquire further.

"And?"

"Olivia's father remains in Bath."

A pit formed in Arabella's stomach. Her brother hadn't walked away unscathed from his last encounter with Olivia's father. And that had been before he'd eloped with the man's daughter and hid away his wife with Emerson and Arabella's aunts in Bath. Arabella feared what the monster of a man might do for revenge.

Reaching for her mother's hand, Arabella squeezed it. "Emerson was able to best him before. He will do so again. They will be safe."

"I am sure you are right." Her mother forced a smile and squeezed her hand in return. "Olivia sent you something inside your brother's letter." She picked up a smaller, folded piece of paper and handed it to Arabella.

She snatched the note out of her mother's hand, eager to hear from her closest friend, now sister by marriage. She opened the torn piece of paper that she suspected had been used out of necessity and haste.

Arabella,

Forgive me for taking so long to write since your last letter, and for doing so now in such haste. I had hoped we would have returned to London by now.

Arabella laughed at how right her assumption had been and continued reading.

Your brother has been the most controlling—

Arabella huffed in total agreement.

—the most handsome—

Oh, for goodness sake. Not this again.

—and loving of husbands, and I thank the heavens every day for my friendship with you, because without it, I would never have found such happiness.

She smiled, despite the fact that Olivia was gushing about her brother. Olivia deserved to have such love and contentment.

Now, if you would be so kind as to hide all your brother's cravats before we return home, I would greatly appreciate it.
You will DO NOTHING with my cravats, Arabella!

Her brother's handwriting joined the note, followed by another line from Olivia.

Your brother is being unfair and reading over shoulders. I shall close with this, and I know you shall understand its meaning: He that is thy friend indeed, He will help thee in thy need.

Your loving sister,

Olivia Latham

Arabella laughed at her friend's clever use of Shakespeare.

"Do I dare ask what was in the note?" her mother asked with an amused smile.

"Rapture." Arabella beamed, extending the note to her mother.

Her mother read the note, her smile wrinkling the corners of her eyes. "I believe you are right."

Arabella took a large bite of her pastry. It was going to be a splendid day; she could feel it.

"We received an interesting invitation to dinner for tomorrow evening," her mother said, picking up another letter.

"Oh? Who is it from?" she asked before taking a sip of her tea.

"The Dowager Baroness Northcott."

Arabella's eyes widened as big as the saucer that clattered beneath her teacup. They'd never received a dinner invitation—or any sort of invitation—from the Dowager Baroness Northcott before, and to receive one now seemed . . .

Had Lord Northcott asked his aunt to extend an invitation to them? A hopeful warmth swirled inside her chest.

"May we go?" Arabella asked.

"If you would like."

Biting into her second blueberry pastry, Arabella leaned back in her seat and smiled in contentment.

A knock sounded at their front door, and Smith excused himself to answer it.

"It's a bit early for callers," her mother said, removing her serviette from her lap and wiping her lips.

Arabella's heart beat faster in nervous anticipation. Could it be Lord Northcott making another impromptu visit?

A ruckus soon ensued out in the corridor, and Arabella could hear muffled voices and the distinct tapping of a cane. When the main instigator had drawn close enough, there was no mistaking her voice.

Lady Bixbee.

"A calling card?" The old matron scoffed. "I can assure you, sir, that the sound of my voice is calling card enough for your mistress to know it is I."

Arabella and her mother exchanged a silent giggle at Lady Bixbee's incomparable spirit and abandoned their plates to save Smith from the domineering matron.

Stepping out into the corridor behind her mother, Arabella stopped short as her eyes landed on Dr. Stafford, who stood beside his grandmother, looking uncomfortable.

His gaze found hers. He offered an apologetic shrug just as Lady Bixbee pushed past Smith and greeted her mother.

Arabella offered him a sympathetic smile. It couldn't be easy having such a grandmother.

ELEVEN

"I feel I should apologize once again," Dr. Stafford said, glancing from where they walked along the back terrace toward the parlor room window behind which Lady Bixbee stood, watching them with the most satisfied grin. "When I told my grandmother I intended to call on you tomorrow because of a previous engagement with a colleague today, I should have foreseen she would press-gang me into her carriage today despite the early hour."

"Truly, think nothing of it," Arabella replied as they descended the terrace steps. Last night's rain had made them slick, forcing her to grip tighter to the young doctor's arm while her other hand lifted her soft pink skirts.

He immediately slowed his steps and moved with such gentle care, she couldn't help but smile. She was no delicate flower, which made her think he was this attentive with everyone.

It was a quality any woman would appreciate in a husband. But, despite his good-natured spirit and handsome aquiline nose and soft, light-brown hair that complemented his darker eyes, Dr. Stafford, so far, lacked the one feature she wanted most in a husband.

A spark.

"If there is one thing I have come to know about your grandmother," Arabella said, as they reached the last step, "it is that she should never be underestimated."

"As the Royal Gardens is currently discovering," Dr. Stafford chuckled, and Arabella couldn't help but do the same.

They'd spent most of the musicale coming up with names the Royal Gardens could bestow upon Lady Bixbee's rose. Arabella liked "The Rose of Bixbee" best, and its petals would, of course, contain several shades of pink.

As they stepped into the garden, Dr. Stafford guided them along the circular, gravel path lined with green hedges and color-ful flowers. Many puddles dotted the walkway, making it neces-sary for them to separate to avoid them. In some instances, they shared one side of the path.

When they reached the purple plum tree at the center, Arabella was pleased that the stone bench beneath its branches appeared free of any water. They took a seat in direct view of the parlor room window, though Lady Bixbee was absent from her post. Arabella was certain the old matron would be back.

"I must confess," Dr. Stafford began after a short period of companionable silence, "I am not certain how to go about a sit-uation such as this. I know my grandmother's expectations . . ."

"Perhaps it would be best to set our own expectations," Arabella replied, grateful and yet nervous that he'd brought up the subject of courtship. Despite the level of enjoyment she'd shared with him at the musicale, she couldn't ignore the fact that she felt no spark between them. "We could start by simply getting to know one another."

She was trying to have patience and believe that one day her spark would happen.

Dr. Stafford nodded. "I cannot argue with that plan. And thank you, for speaking your mind. I know it could not be easy with my grandmother pushing our every encounter."

Arabella smiled, relieved that he didn't appear to be in as much of a hurry as his grandmother was. "You might come to regret that statement. I have been told by my brother that I give my opinions rather freely."

He chuckled. "I shall take that under advisement."

"And what is something I should be forewarned about con-cerning you?" Arabella asked.

"According to my grandmother, I work too much. Which was

something she also accused my father of doing. He was a doctor as well."

Arabella playfully gasped while putting a hand to her lips. "But a gentleman does not work."

"This one does," Dr. Stafford replied, his tone half teasing, half defensive.

"I think it admirable," she replied.

A memory of her father entered her mind. He'd returned home late one evening, disheveled and covered in dirt. He'd been out all day helping one of their tenant farmers who'd recently been ill and needed to bring in a harvest before it was too late. When she'd asked her father why he had gone, he responded: "A good man works hard to take care of his family, but a better man also works just as hard to care for those around him."

Her father was the best of men, and she'd be lucky to find her spark with a man as good and hardworking as he was.

"What is it about your work that requires so much of your time?" she asked, wanting to know if Dr. Stafford was a similar kind of man.

"Much." He let out a heavy breath. "The majority of my time is divided between treating patients and helping our government with the lunacy reform and the construction of the new Bedlam."

The word "Bedlam" immediately pulled Arabella's attention, turning her mind to Lord Northcott. Perhaps Dr. Stafford might be able to help her in her efforts to help him. "May I ask you your opinion about something?" she asked before her mind could warn her against it.

"Is that not what we have been doing?" he asked, his lips quirked.

"Yes, but this question is more—" She paused, trying to think of how to explain it without giving either herself or Lord Northcott's secret away. "It's about something I recently saw."

His brow lifted. "You have my attention."

She took a deep breath. "A lunacy pamphlet recently came

into my possession"—more like *fell*—"and I was somewhat taken aback by what I read."

Dr. Stafford's eyes narrowed, and he looked tense. He'd thanked her earlier for speaking her mind, but perhaps he didn't think lunacy was an appropriate topic for a woman.

"What did it say?" he asked.

Surprised that he was willing to continue the conversation, and feeling nervous about what she was about to ask, Arabella fidgeted with her hands in her lap. "The title of the pamphlet specifically read *Mastering the animality after the loss of humanity.* Are patients with lunacy truly considered more animal than human?"

Her heart ached all over again for Lord Northcott. She couldn't imagine reading such a thing and having to think of a family member in such a way.

Dr. Stafford shook his head. "No, and that is a belief I have been trying hard to disprove." He turned slightly on the bench to face her. "There is much we are still learning about the mind, but I refuse to believe any of that tripe you might have found inside that pamphlet. And I hope you will advise the person you got it from to burn it."

Arabella nodded, a mixture of feelings coursing through her. On one hand she felt lightened—relieved to hear Dr. Stafford contradict the words written on the pamphlet. But on the other hand, should she even broach such a subject with Lord Northcott? During their last conversation, she'd offered the option for him to talk to her, and he'd not chosen to do so.

Would it not be good to tell him about Dr. Stafford's opinion? Or would bringing up the matter do more harm than good?

"What do you believe about the cases of insanity?" Arabella asked, wanting to educate herself further.

"I will admit that I used to believe most of the things similar to those published inside that pamphlet. It was what we were taught at the Royal College of Physicians, and I had not yet spent much time around institutionalized patients. But as I studied directly under Dr. Robert Darling Willis—whose father, if you did not know, cured the king after his first bout of madness—I began to see patients differently. Dr. Willis taught me to see beyond the symptoms to the man—a father, a brother, a husband—a person similar to myself, but who had experienced something so traumatic that his mind had retreated so far into shadow that not even his family knew how to reach him." There was a faint bleakness to his eyes, as if he gave a piece of himself to every life he saved, and Arabella found herself swallowing back a rising lump in her throat.

What pain he must've witnessed. What suffering those families must've endured while feeling so helpless. She knew how her heart had broken at the loss of her father. What would it be like to have the physical reminder of him be present but to be told that his mind was just as lost to her as if he were dead?

And Lord Northcott had experienced just that—once with his mother and supposedly again with a sister.

Tears slipped down her cheek, and she turned away to wipe them, not wanting Dr. Stafford to sense she had a personal connection to the subject. She wished she knew what she could do to better help Lord Northcott. It couldn't be easy to fight against a monster you couldn't even see.

She felt a hand press upon her shoulder and she turned back to Dr. Stafford.

His smile was gentle and soothing. "Your tears are a testament to your heart, Miss Latham. There are many who cannot even conjure up the smallest sympathy. That is why I, and a few of my colleagues, are working tirelessly to gain more support for our way of treatment."

"What is your way?" Arabella asked, her voice strained.

"We still follow some of the old practices. Blistering, bleeding, and restraints have still proven to show results in the most extreme cases. But what we add is *humanity*." He spoke the last word with such fervor, Arabella could feel it down to her soul. "Dr. Francis Willis's medical journals told of how he encouraged fresh air and exercise to help his patients. He even went so far as to have them be properly dressed, which I am sure was shocking to most people when they saw a man working out in the field in a dress coat and powdered wig." A corner of his mouth twitched upward, and Arabella found herself pressing her lips together to keep from giggling. It would, indeed, be a baffling sight.

"Those practices yielded the best results," Dr. Stafford continued. "Dr. Francis Willis's goal was to encourage his patients to come back to find connection, purpose—even meaning—in the lives they had once known. This is why my colleagues and I pushed so hard for outdoor airing grounds at the new Bedlam hospital. Being trapped in a dark hell, figuratively or imaginatively, is not good for anyone."

Arabella reached out and squeezed his hand, comforted that he would care so much. "Your devotion to your patients is commendable."

She anxiously waited for that spark to ignite. Surely this was the moment her heart would call out to another. But it never came, and she grew frustrated with herself.

Time . . . thou ceaseless lackey to eternity.

"Unfortunately, it is not enough," Dr. Stafford said, pulling his hand from beneath hers and rubbing his chin. "If we are going to make *real* change, we are going to need more than the Church changing its views and saying that madness is no longer a direct punishment from God. And more than Parliament passing its lunacy reform in the wake of the war with Napoleon. What we need is to have doctors—and even members of society—properly educated."

"Is such a thing possible?" Arabella asked, knowing the heartless way society fed upon the gossip about the insane.

"I hope so," Dr. Stafford said, though he sounded more frustrated than confident. "Though so far, it has been near impossible to find anyone who wants to discuss such matters with me, even if it involves members of their own family."

Again, Arabella's mind went to Lord Northcott, whose own family was well-known for their connection with insanity. Would he be willing to work with Dr. Stafford to bring about such important changes? She had a sinking feeling in her stomach that he wouldn't, especially after her own much simpler offer to help him had been refused.

"But I will always continue to hope," Dr. Stafford said with determination. "Why, just this morning I received an invitation to dinner from a family I have been trying to meet with for the past year."

"I wish you all the luck in the world," Arabella said, her heart praying for that family to be open and willing to listen.

"Thank you," he said with a warm smile.

He glanced upward, and Arabella followed his gaze. Her mother and Lady Bixbee were watching them from the parlor room window.

"It would appear our time is up," Dr. Stafford said. "Shall we return to hear what else my grandmother has planned for us?"

Arabella nodded and took his proffered hand, her mind trying to sift through all she'd learned, and what she should do with that information.

TWELVE

When Henry's aunt informed him that morning that they would be having a small dinner party, he didn't think anything of it. Dinner with Mr. Collingsworth, a thousand-year-old clergyman who'd been a close acquaintance of the family for many years, was a weekly occurrence. So long had the clergyman been with Henry's family, he often boasted that there weren't many Northcotts in history that he hadn't either buried or blessed.

Staring at the old man from Henry's position across the sitting room, no one would ever mistake the clergyman for having found the fountain of youth. He sat in his usual spot upon the sofa, closest to the fire, a blanket spread across his lap. His celestial-white hair had thinned in many places, while the wrinkles across his forehead sagged, one on top of the other, until they rested heavily atop his scraggly, white brow.

Henry's aunt sat next to the clergyman, their heads tipped together in conversation. She seemed . . . lighter than she had in the last four days. There was no smile upon her lips, but there was an ease about her. Whether it was because of the familiar comfort of visiting with a family friend or that his aunt had finally decided to move on from the incident with the pamphlet, Henry didn't know. But he was relieved to see things returning to normal.

Samson entered the room, and Henry moved to rise, though it was early to be going into dinner.

"Mr. Bradbury, my lady," their butler announced, halting Henry's movements.

Bradbury sauntered into the room with a swagger that came as natural to him as breathing. He shot Henry the largest, smuggest grin before greeting his aunt. "Dowager Baroness Northcott,

I cannot thank you enough for this much anticipated invitation," he said with a flourishing bow.

Henry stared, completely dumbfounded. His aunt never invited his friends to dinner. Any invitation was always for political gain.

Henry's aunt rose, and Henry collected himself enough to do the same. What the devil was happening?

"We are glad you could accept," his aunt replied.

Henry watched her, trying to understand the situation, but she portrayed nothing beyond being a proper host welcoming their guest.

Samson entered the room again. "Lady Bixbee, my lady."

Henry's head whipped toward the door.

The formidable matron marched into the room with a bigger grin than Bradbury's, who, at the moment, was making his way toward Henry.

"You never said my aunt invited you to dinner," Henry said the moment Bradbury reached him. They had seen one another at their club for the past two days, and he never said a word.

"And what would you have said if I had?" Bradbury asked with a smirk and a raised brow.

"I would have uninvited you," Henry said in a flat tone, because that was what Bradbury expected from him.

"Exactly." Bradbury chuckled.

The truth of it was, Henry would've liked inviting his friends, but the planning of dinner parties had always belonged to his aunt, and knowing what his parents had taken from her, Henry never had the heart to challenge it.

"Come on, Beasty," Bradbury said, playfully nudging Henry with his shoulder. "A man's got to eat. And with Emerson gone, I've had to eat too many meals at the club. It's getting awful expensive."

Henry scoffed. It was so like Bradbury to never pass on an opportunity for a free meal. But why would Lady Bixbee accept an invitation? And perhaps more importantly, why would his aunt extend her one? What was to be gained from this evening?

Samson entered the room, and Henry felt ill at ease.

"Mrs. Latham and Miss Latham, my lady," their butler announced.

Mrs. Latham wore her usual mourning gray while Arabella was devastatingly beautiful in a gown of the softest yellow.

Henry's heart stopped, and he stood there, gaping like a fool as pinpricks of heat scattered across his skin. He needed to stop staring at her.

"I take it you were not expecting them either?" Bradbury spoke, the teasing in his tone gone.

"No. I was not," Henry said, watching as his aunt politely greeted the ladies.

He noted the primroses in Arabella's dark brown tresses, and his chest naturally expanded, anticipating the floral scent he had grown to associate with her.

As Lady Bixbee monopolized the conversation among the ladies, Arabella glanced in his direction and whispered a greeting to him.

His heart rate quickened, and his palms began to sweat. There was nothing flirtatious about her, but her natural beauty and spirit would enchant even a saint.

Or a sinner, in your case, the voice inside his head taunted.

"I wonder whom else we should expect?" Bradbury asked, snapping Henry's attention away from Arabella.

"What are you talking about?"

Bradbury stared at him with confusion. "Are you feeling all right?"

"Would you just answer my question?" Henry snapped, his temper growing short. With all that was happening, he had no patience for Bradbury's games on top of his aunt's unexpected invitations and Arabella's frustratingly bewitching glances.

Bradbury narrowed his eyes. "Growl at me all you like, Beasty.

But if *I* am the one pointing out an observation to *you*, something is most assuredly amiss."

Henry glared at his friend.

"Fine," he said, pointing a finger at Henry. "But something is not right." He dropped his finger. "Look around us. There are four ladies, but only three gentlemen. We need one more to even out our numbers."

Henry inwardly cursed. That was more than obvious, but he was so thrown off, he'd not noticed. Who else could his aunt have invited? And why had she kept all of this from him?

Samson came into the room. "Dr. Stafford, my lady," he announced, and Henry's blood ran cold.

Dr. Stafford entered the room, his steps faltering the moment he noticed his grandmother. "My—my apologies for my late arrival, Dowager Baroness Northcott."

Henry's aunt greeted the doctor as if his connection to the issue of lunacy meant nothing to her, while a cold sweat broke out across the back of Henry's neck.

"Grandmother," Dr. Stafford said to Lady Bixbee, struggling to contain the shock upon his face. "I did not know you would be in attendance." He turned to Arabella and her mother. "Nor you, Miss Latham."

"It's a surprise to me as well," Arabella replied.

A nagging suspicion instantly formed in the back of Henry's mind. Was his aunt aiding Lady Bixbee in her machinations?

Lady Bixbee mockingly laughed. "And miss all your shocked faces? I think not."

Henry looked to his aunt, wanting to see her response. He found her watching him, and then she turned back toward the others. Was she hoping to see a certain reaction from him?

Samson entered the room, and Henry held back a groan. He couldn't take any more surprises.

"Dinner is served, my lady," the butler announced.

Mr. Collingsworth startled from his nap, confusion on his face as he took in the new arrivals. "What—what?"

"Dinner!" Bradbury yelled for the benefit of Mr. Collingsworth.

A smile spread across the old clergyman's lips as he attempted
and failed to scoot his way off the sofa.

"Thank you, Mr. Bradbury," Henry's aunt said after an awkward silence fell over the room, the only sound coming from Mr.
Collingsworth's struggles. "Henry?" his aunt said, signaling with
her eyes for him to help the clergyman.

Henry nodded and moved to assist, but Dr. Stafford proved
to be a few steps ahead of him.

"Allow me," the doctor said, offering his hands to the clergyman.

"And who might you be?" Mr. Collingsworth asked, squinting up at the gentleman.

"Dr. Brandon Stafford. Your servant, sir."

"A doctor?" Mr. Collingsworth looked to Henry's aunt. "You
invited a doctor?"

"And others," his aunt said with a strained smile as she waved
her hand about the room. "We shall make for a lively party this
evening."

Mr. Collingsworth took Dr. Stafford's hands and finally
made it to his feet. "Oh good. Good. I enjoy lively conversation. Heaven knows that boy"—he pointed a crooked finger at
Henry—"has not spoken more than a few words at a time since
his father's death."

Henry stiffened, not daring to look at his aunt, whose dislike
for his father ran almost as deeply as her hatred for his mother.
His eyes caught on Dr. Stafford, who studied him with a puzzling
look.

"Shall we, Mr. Collingsworth?" Henry's aunt said, rushing
over to the clergyman and slipping her arm through his, leading
the way into dinner.

Lady Bixbee approached Henry and offered him her hand.
"Come along, Lord Northcott. Let us leave the younger set to

their coquetry." She shot Dr. Stafford a glance over her shoulder and then bobbed her brow in the direction of Arabella.

Henry clenched his fists before offering his arm to Lady Bixbee. He was getting tired of being referred to as old. He was just as youthful as the other men in the room—Mr. Collingsworth excepted.

"Well, I certainly do not fit in with that grouping," Mrs. Latham said with a soft laugh.

"And I certainly have no want for coquetry," Mr. Bradbury said, offering Mrs. Latham his arm.

Which left Dr. Stafford to escort Arabella.

Henry suppressed a sigh. It was going to be a long evening.

THIRTEEN

Dinner, as Henry had predicted, was akin to torture. With each course that was brought out, the topic of conversation always circled back to marriage.

When Mrs. Latham brought up the long winter and recent heavy rainfall, Lady Bixbee brought up the fact that, if one had to deal with the elements, it would be more prudent to have a wedding in winter and enjoy the white backdrop of snow.

When Mr. Collingsworth complimented the excellent boiled potatoes, Henry's aunt was reminded of a most memorable wedding breakfast.

When Dr. Stafford brought up the war with Napoleon . . .

"If our predominant and ancient bloodlines do not continue," Lady Bixbee huffed, "then we might as well hand Britain over to the French." She stabbed her fork into a roasted artichoke. "A gentleman *should* marry."

"Says the woman who has been widowed for nigh on a century," Bradbury grumbled as he sliced through his roasted duck. He'd not been happy to have been placed next to Lady Bixbee.

The overly opinionated matron sat to the right of Henry's aunt, who was at the head of the table. Perfectly positioned to coordinate an attack on Arabella and Dr. Stafford, who sat next to each other across from Lady Bixbee.

Lady Bixbee glared down her nose at Bradbury. "Says the lady who has *actually* done her duty to marry *and* has successfully seen her five sons and fourteen of her grandchildren married."

Bradbury's nostrils flared as he looked across the table to Dr. Stafford. "Look out. It sounds like she's on the hunt for number fifteen."

Dr. Stafford gave a slow nod. He seemed unsurprised and un-concerned by the observation, which made Henry grip the handle of his fork until it nearly bent in the palm of his hand.

Curious how your aunt has never played matchmaker for you, the voice whispered.

Henry's shoulders tensed. What the voice said was true. His aunt had never spoken to him about marriage. She, of course, didn't know of his plans to remain unmarried. So why hadn't she pressured—or even asked him—when he would marry?

He looked to his aunt, who was watching him over the pyra-mid of oranges and lilies placed at the center of the table.

Did she feel the same way he did about not continuing his tainted family line? It would make sense, considering how impor-tant it was to her that society remember her husband. If Henry married and begat children, her husband would become a more distant memory.

Sounds rather manipulative, the voice whispered.

Henry set down his fork, his appetite diminished. His aunt had, no doubt, suspected his interest in Arabella after catching him watching her at the musicale. Which would explain her alli-ance with Lady Bixbee that evening.

"I hear congratulations are in order, Mrs. Latham," Henry's aunt said, catching the attention of the table. She set down her fork and dabbed her lips with the serviette she pulled from her lap. A signal for the butler to start clearing plates for the last course.

"What's this?" Lady Bixbee demanded with an excited smile, her eyes intent upon Mrs. Latham.

Mrs. Latham's eyes briefly shot to Henry, worry creasing her brow. Emerson and Olivia's elopement to Gretna Green had been kept a secret to protect them for as long as possible. Joshua Wilde wasn't a man who would easily accept defeat.

And your aunt is bringing up the subject in front of one of the biggest gossips of the ton, the voice whispered.

Henry bit the insides of his cheeks and shot his aunt a warn-ing glance. He regretted allowing her such freedom to read his correspondence. In doing so, he now hurt a family who'd always been good to him.

His aunt responded by tipping her chin, as if she believed she'd done nothing wrong.

"Well?" Lady Bixbee demanded. She wouldn't let such a juicy morsel remain out of her reach.

Mrs. Latham glanced around the table with an uneasy smile. "I am happy to say that I have recently gained a wonderful daughter-in-law."

"I knew it!" Lady Bixbee said. "It must be that Wilde girl. That son of yours was chasing her the entire Season."

"It is," Arabella spoke up. "And I am happy my brother and my best friend were able to make a love match." Her smile was proud, and she looked ready to take on anyone who would mock the notion.

They were saved both by Mr. Collingsworth, who sat next to Arabella and to Henry's right, as he offered praise for the sanctity of marriage and the preservation of England, and by the arrival of the dessert course, which was an orange cream, a jelly of two colors, and a dish of varying fruits.

"I am curious, Dr. Stafford," Henry's aunt said, starting up the conversation after everyone was served. "As a man of science, what do you think of love?"

Henry should've known better than to think the topic would be so easily forgotten.

Dr. Stafford paused, his spoon in his orange cream. "I am afraid I do not fully understand your question. Are you asking if I believe love exists?"

She nodded. "I believe love is a product of fiction, used to entice the younger generations into ill-suited marriages. When I married my husband, it was out of duty to my family, king, and country. I never found disappointment because I knew what was expected of me. The simple illusion of believing someone has found love has a way of disappointing all involved."

If Henry held any more doubts about why his aunt had orchestrated such an evening, they were dispelled.

"Love exists," Arabella argued, gaining the attention of the table. She held a spoon in her hand, and she looked as if she were ready to slay dragons with it.

"How so?" Lady Bixbee asked, looking far too entertained.

"Well, to quote one of the most renowned playwrights," Arabella began, watching Henry's aunt out of the corner of her eye, *"Love is not love which alters when it alteration finds, or bends with the remover to remove: O no! it is an ever-fixed mark that looks on tempests and is never shaken."*

A ghost of a smile hovered at the corners of Henry's lips. Heaven help him, she was a remarkable spirit. Shakespeare couldn't have described the way he felt for her any better than the words from *The Merchant of Venice*: "Thus hath the candle singed the moth."

"I must agree with you, Miss Latham," Dr. Stafford said, his voice cutting through Henry's musings. "Love, if true, can be a most powerful thing." They exchanged smiles, and Henry's gut clenched.

"Here! Here!" Lady Bixbee raised her glass. "And if I have any say on the matter, we shall all soon have another reason to congratulate Mrs. Latham."

Mrs. Latham smiled, her eyes darting toward her daughter while Lady Bixbee continued to voice her approval, but all Henry could focus on was Arabella. She'd moved her attention to her plate, her spoon dipping into the yellow-and-pink jelly but coming up empty. Was she uncomfortable with the attention? She was no shy flower. Could he hope that she didn't entirely welcome these assumptions?

Her eyes flicked up from her plate, crossing the long span of the table that separated them. He caught and held her gaze for several agonizing seconds. Neither looked away. His breathing grew uneven.

"Shall we leave the gentlemen to their port?" Henry's aunt

said, the sudden screeching of her chair sliding across the floor snapping his connection to Arabella.

She stood, her lips pressed into a firm line as she snatched her serviette from her lap and tossed it onto the table. She offered a polite smile to everyone but Henry.

Henry stood, along with Bradbury and Dr. Stafford, who helped Arabella pull back her chair. She smiled and thanked him, and Henry clenched his fists at his sides until his knuckles cracked. Arabella linked her arm with her mother's, and the ladies left the room.

The gentlemen retook their seats, and Samson was efficient with the port, pouring each man a small glass before taking his leave. Henry briefly thought to stir the slumbering Mr. Collingsworth before he found himself with a painful crick in his neck, but his mind decided on a more selfish decision.

"I need you to leave," he said to Bradbury.

"What? Why?" he asked, sitting up from the relaxed position in his chair.

"I need to speak with Dr. Stafford," Henry replied, deliberately not looking at the man.

Bradbury frowned. "And what shall I do? Go join the ladies?"

There was a taut silence between the two men.

"I'm not going in there by myself," Bradbury said, breaking first. "I'd be a rabbit thrown into a pit of wolves. I would be eaten alive." His tone rose in exasperation.

"Only if they catch you," Dr. Stafford said, joining their conversation.

They both turned to the doctor, who sat to Henry's left. He looked far too at ease for someone who was about to have a private conversation with the Brooding Baron.

"I might end up liking you," Bradbury said to Dr. Stafford with a wry grin. Rising from his chair, he picked up his untouched glass of port and tipped the drink to his lips. He shook his head with a hiss following the port's distinct bite at the end. "But if I could offer you a word of advice?"

"By all means," the doctor replied, taking a smaller, slower drink of his port.

"Do not let old Beasty"—Bradbury pointed a finger toward Henry with the same hand that held his glass—"intimidate you with his brooding. He is about as threatening as a mother goose. Get too near his nest too soon and he will come at you hissing and biting. But earn his trust, and he may just let you get close enough."

Dr. Stafford blinked, bafflement written clearly across his stunned expression.

All Henry could do was shake his head. A goose? The man called him Beasty a hundred times a day, and he chose now to compare him to an infernal waterfowl?

Bradbury turned to Henry. "I believe there is a card game at Lord Darby's residence. Please give my regrets to your aunt." He swallowed the last of his port and disappeared through the door.

Henry excused the remaining servants. What he intended to discuss would go no farther than the room.

"What are your intentions with Miss Latham?" he asked the moment the door was shut.

Dr. Stafford raised a brow. "Are you the lady's guardian?"

"I am looking out for her and her mother while her brother is away," Henry responded, folding his arms over his chest.

"Then you should know that Mrs. Latham has been most receptive of my visits to Miss Latham. I was there only yesterday, and Miss Latham also appeared happy to receive me."

Dread and jealousy swirled in Henry's gut. He wanted to order Dr. Stafford to never visit the Latham home again. But Arabella was not—could not—be his.

"If that is all, Lord Northcott, might I ask you a question?" Dr. Stafford asked.

Knowing he could no longer avoid this long-awaited conversation, Henry forced his shoulders to relax and nodded. He would let the doctor speak his mind and then end the matter once and for all.

"Mr. Collingsworth made an interesting remark before dinner."

It was Henry's turn to raise a brow at the topic of conversation.

"As I understood it," Dr. Stafford continued, "you spoke very
little in your youth?"

Henry stared at the doctor, baffled. He'd given the man the
opportunity to discuss what he'd been petitioning to speak to him
about for months, and that was the question he asked?

"My mother was prone to headaches and preferred silence,"
Henry responded, though it was half a lie. His mother *was* prone
to headaches, but only after one of her screaming matches with
his father. It was better for everyone in those instances if Henry
and his sister remained quiet in one of their rooms.

Dr. Stafford nodded. "Are you aware that one of your sister's
original diagnoses for her committal was mutism?"

"What are you after?" Henry demanded, his anger rising as he
suspected he was about to be blackmailed or called mad himself.

He would be right, the voice laughed.

Dr. Stafford held up his hands. "It is merely an observation.
If the doctor who admitted her did not know of your mother's
previous condition, or that you yourself were quiet because of it,
perhaps parts of your sister's diagnosis were—incorrect."

An inkling of hope entered Henry's thoughts. Could his sister
have been misdiagnosed? Could she have something less severe
that had gone overlooked? Perhaps something that didn't require
the constant care found at a hospital. Something that could be
cured.

Could he be cured?

"I understand your sister is scheduled to be moved from
Guy's Hospital to the new Bedlam Hospital in a fortnight," Dr.
Stafford continued carefully.

Henry nodded, still too unnerved to trust himself to make a
verbal reply.

"Have you been to visit her?" Dr. Stafford asked, watching him over the rim of his glass.

Henry immediately tensed as the sickening weight of guilt filled his stomach and rose into his throat like bile. He swallowed and shook his head. He didn't know if he could look upon his sister again. Not after he'd failed her as a brother for so long.

Dr. Stafford set his glass down and met his gaze head-on. "You should."

"Why?" The word escaped Henry's mouth before he could think better of it.

Dr. Stafford studied him for a moment before speaking. "I am afraid the answer would take more time than we have. If we stay here for much longer, my grandmother will remark on my absence, and I would prefer not to have our conversation interrupted."

He is luring you into another talk, the voice whispered.

Henry pressed his lips together and studied the doctor. Even if that were true, and Dr. Stafford had some ulterior motive to his game, could Henry afford not to play?

Especially when he and his sister might have a chance for a real future, to be a family again, and to one day have families of their own?

"Another time, then," Henry replied, finding it hard to ignore a new, flickering hope for the future. "I must see that Mr. Collingsworth gets to his carriage," he said, rising from his seat. "Then I will join you and the ladies."

Dr. Stafford stood. "I will wait to hear from you, then," he said, surprising Henry by leaving the choice to meet up to him.

Ignoring his duty for the first time he could remember, Henry instructed two of the footmen to assist Mr. Collingsworth to the carriage, while he retreated to his study. He needed a moment to himself before he faced his scheming aunt.

And a certain Shakespeare-quoting vixen, the voice laughed.

FOURTEEN

Given Lady Bixbee's talent for dominating the conversation at dinner, Arabella wasn't surprised to see her reign continue the moment they entered the parlor.

"What do you think of my choice of husband for your daughter, Mrs. Latham?" Lady Bixbee asked with a haughty chuckle as she settled her round bottom on the dark maroon sofa.

Arabella dropped inelegantly next to her mother on the adjacent sofa, growing rather tired of being the center of everyone's attention.

Her mother placed a hand atop her knee and gave her a look that communicated everything and yet said nothing.

While thou livest, keep a good tongue in thy head.

It wasn't her favorite Shakespeare line, but it would do. She would practice patience and not inform the old matron exactly what she thought of her heavy-handed machinations.

The evening had gone nothing like Arabella had hoped. Instead of having time with Lord Northcott, she'd been all but forced to give her vows to Dr. Stafford. It was, of course, not Dr. Stafford's fault. But against Lady Bixbee and, surprisingly, the Dowager Baroness Northcott, who hadn't paid her any interest until now, it had been impossible to subvert their attentions.

"Any mother would be happy to have such a son-in-law," her mother said rather diplomatically to Lady Bixbee and the Dowager Baroness Northcott, who sat next to each other. The matrons shared a pleased smile. "But I shall leave the final choice of husband to Arabella."

Lady Bixbee's smile dipped into a frown while Arabella felt

nothing but relief. Showing patience in this instance might have paid off.

"If I had done that," Lady Bixbee scoffed, "I would still be waiting on half my children and half of *their* children to marry. Take my advice—a firm, guiding hand is the better way. They will thank you for it in the end."

Arabella's mother nodded politely, but Lady Bixbee didn't look convinced.

"Tell them, Beatrice," she said to the Dowager Baroness Northcott.

"In some things, wisdom and experience are needed," the other woman added.

"*Doubt truth to be a liar, but never doubt I love,*" Arabella recited for the room.

The Dowager Baroness Northcott pinned her down with a hard stare. "What *fiction* are you prattling on about now?"

"*Hamlet,*" Arabella said proudly. "And it means when it comes to marriage, I would much rather follow the love that I know is in my heart than the words of others."

Lady Bixbee and the Dowager Baroness Northcott both balked at the statement, and Arabella opened her mouth to argue her point further when her mother stepped in.

"Arabella, would you be so kind as to fetch my shawl? With the late spring and this continued rain, I find myself growing chilled at the strangest times."

Arabella was more than happy to remove herself from the current situation. "Of course, Mother," she said, standing up with a smile.

She had nearly made it to the door when it opened, and Dr. Stafford walked in.

"Have you come to welcome me to the parlor?" he asked with a teasing smile.

"I have not," Arabella replied in a hushed tone.

"Is everything all right?" he asked, his smile fading to caution as he glanced toward the others.

"Where is my nephew?" the Dowager Baroness Northcott called out.

Arabella looked past Dr. Stafford. She could have sworn she saw a glimpse of a shadow move across the far wall of the corridor. A footman perhaps?

"He is seeing Mr. Collingsworth to a carriage, my lady," Dr. Stafford replied before raising a brow at Arabella. He could, no doubt, feel the tension in the room.

Arabella should warn him, but it would do no good. Nothing, it seemed, would stop his grandmother.

Dipping one of the quickest curtsies of her life, she offered "Good luck" and swept out of the door, cringing as she heard Dr. Stafford's stumbled words.

"Wait. What?"

The moment the door shut behind her, Arabella leaned her back against the wall. Closing her eyes, she let out a frustrated breath.

"Miss?" a man's voice spoke.

Arabella's eyes flew open, and she pressed her hand to her throat, her breaths coming out in rapid pants. Thank heavens she'd not screamed and summoned the occupants of the parlor.

"Forgive me," Arabella said to the footman standing a few feet away. She straightened from the wall and smoothed out her skirts. "I did not see you there."

"May I be of assistance?" he asked formally.

Arabella resisted the urge to look to the heavens. The footman was just as serious as the Dowager Baroness. "Would you be so kind as to bring me my mother's shawl?" she asked.

He nodded, stiffly bowed, and left her in the flickering candlelight.

Frustrated, and wanting a moment to herself, she moved aimlessly down the corridor, sliding her fingers along the dark blue—nearly black—wallpaper and trim.

Everything about the house felt somber. From the darker-colored furnishings, polished wood floors, amber-colored carpets, and gold sconces, everything seemed . . . haunted. Weighed down by time and memories.

A breeze suddenly whipped past her, making the candles flicker and nearly burn out. Her eyes darted toward the direction it came, looking for a source. All she saw was an empty corridor that grew darker the further it went. There was one sconce lit near the end, which was curious.

Why only light the farthest sconce and none of the others?

Arabella stepped from the light and into the shadows.

The carpet muffled her footsteps, the only sound her slow breaths as she waited to feel another breeze. With the little light, she was able to make out the darker shapes of a few paintings, but no open window. And no breeze.

Could she have imagined it?

Then she heard it: a soft creak followed by the quick rush of a breeze across her skin. The single lit sconce at the end of the corridor flickered, prompting Arabella to hasten her pace. She didn't know how much time she had before the footman returned.

Stopping before the lit sconce, she scanned her surroundings. Nothing stood out to her, and once again, the breeze seemed to have vanished.

"How odd," she said to herself, turning in a circle.

Nothing.

And then she heard the creak, followed by a stronger breeze.

A shiver ran up her spine, and her eyes locked on a dark void. A door had been left open, beckoning her to enter.

"*But soft, behold!*" She whispered the lines of *Hamlet*, her footsteps guiding her ever closer. "*Lo, where it comes again! I'll cross it though it blast me.*"

The breeze came again, but this time it pushed the door forward and then pulled it back again.

She lunged, grabbing the handle before the door could slam closed. "*Stay, illusion!*" she whispered, resting her head against the chilled wooden door and collecting her breath, her heart racing.

Was something guiding her here?

She waited another moment, listening, and heard nothing.

"If thou hast any sound, or use of voice," she continued to recite, straightening from the door, and taking a deep breath. *"Speak to me."*

She slipped soundlessly through the door and into the darkened room.

Her eyes struggled to adjust, squinting and blinking rapidly to try to make sense of anything. It was noticeably cooler in the room, and there was an earthy taste that settled on her tongue that predicted a coming rain.

Following silver rays of moonlight that cascaded partway across the room, her eyes rested upon two bay windows, their drapes pulled back. A breeze rippled, but her eyes were fixed on a pair of broad shoulders and the tall muscular form standing before the opened window.

Lord Northcott.

The atmosphere in the room became still and charged, as if lightning could strike at any moment.

He didn't turn, and she doubted he'd heard her come in. His large hands were crossed behind his back, his legs spread shoulder-width apart.

What was he doing in the dark?

For the briefest moment, she thought about leaving, but she'd been wanting to spend time with him, and this might be her only chance.

With slow, anxious steps, she moved toward him.

"Lord Northcott?" she said softly.

His head snapped around, though his stance remained the same. His shadowed eyes watched her, and she felt her breaths grow heavy the longer they stood in silence.

"Is everything all right?" she asked, swallowing.

A breeze rustled the dark strands of hair that hung over his forehead. Her fingers itched to run through his hair to recreate the handsome picture he'd made, all disheveled the night of the musicale.

Slowly he turned to face her. His entire body was in shadow, the moon at his back. "What are you doing here?" he finally asked, his voice deep and husky.

"I felt a breeze," she said, not certain if he would appreciate her suspicion that his house was haunted. "What are you doing in here?"

"I needed some air," he said. "To think."

"Would it help to talk?" she asked, hoping he wouldn't send her away.

They were pushing the bounds of propriety being alone together, but the door was open—much like it had been in the library while they were in the country during her father's illness, and no one had said anything then.

He remained silent, which only made her want to talk more just to fill the silence.

"I find talking about things with others—like my mother or Olivia—to be helpful."

She was met with more silence, but then he finally spoke. "How long have you been acquainted with Dr. Stafford?" he asked, surprising her.

"Not overly long. The musicale was our first introduction."

He nodded.

"Are you acquainted with him?" she asked, trying to continue the conversation.

"In a way." He paused, as if rethinking his statement. "Though tonight was our first introduction."

She waited to see if he would say more, but when didn't, she took a step closer. "And what is your impression of him? Is he as wonderful as Lady Bixbee claims?" She was trying to lighten the mood, hoping it would help him to open up more.

"Not for you," he said, his voice gruff.

The air caught in her chest. "I—I beg your pardon?" She wished he wasn't cast in shadow so she could read his expression.

He met her question with silence, and then he took a step toward her.

And then another.

And another, until she was forced to tip her head back to look at him.

Her nerves prickled with awareness.

His breathing changed, growing deep and then slowing, as if he were trying to regain some inward sense of control. A heat, like a blaze in the hearth in winter, built between them, and though she couldn't see his eyes clearly, she felt herself being drawn in.

She didn't move—she couldn't—but she felt it, the pull. She wanted to place her hand on his chest, feel the rapid beat of his heart to see if it would match her own.

Something was happening between them. Could this be her spark?

Slowly, hesitantly, he reached a hand up and grazed the tips of his fingers across her cheek. They caught a strand of her misbehaving hair that whipped about in the breeze. She sucked in a startled breath when his touch, so soft it might as well have been a caress, slid up and around the back of her ear.

"Lord Northcott?" Her voice trembled.

He swallowed. "Talking with you is dangerous."

"Why is that?" she asked, not daring to move lest he pull away.

"Because more and more I want to give in . . . to you," he replied, his fingers gently gliding from behind her ear and down her neck.

"You can trust me." Her voice was little more than a whisper.

Slowly he pulled his hand away, but she could still feel his gaze upon her. "Dr. Stafford is treating my sister. I *have* a sister. And he says I should go see her."

Her heart broke for him. The rumors Hattie had heard were true. "I think you should listen to him," Arabella replied softly, making sure to hold his gaze, though it was still cast in shadow.

"Why?"

"Because from what I have come to know of Dr. Stafford, he is a man who is fighting for *humanity*." She emphasized the word, hoping he would know it contradicted his awful pamphlet. "And if he believes you could have a connection with your sister again, then you should fight for it too."

Silence once again filled the dark room for one heartbeat and then two. She wished she knew what he was thinking.

"I should return you to your mother," he finally said, though he didn't move away.

"Before we return, will you promise me something?" she asked, not wanting to lose what they'd started.

He nodded.

"Will you call on me and my mother—soon?"

He was silent for a long moment, making her nervous. He'd kept away after the incident at Brooks's; she didn't want that to happen again.

"I will," he said, his voice gravelly and thick.

"Thank you," she replied, a sense of relief washing over her. "I'll go now, and you can follow in a few minutes to avoid suspicion."

He nodded, and she did the same, a smile cresting her lips. He was a man of few words, but the way he made her feel was overwhelming.

FIFTEEN

Entering through the tall, black iron gate, Henry stepped into the cobblestone courtyard of Guy's Hospital. A crawling sensation skittered up his spine, and his stomach twisted in a sickening knot. The part of himself that still believed he and his sister were incurable, like their mother, shouted for him to turn and run before they could lock him inside.

But he couldn't—not yet. Not if there was a chance.

The nearly one-hundred-year-old gray stone building stood proud despite its age. Originally founded by Thomas Guy, whose statue commanded the rectangular courtyard, the hospital was a place to treat the incurables discharged from other hospitals.

Arabella's words filled his head: *"Dr. Stafford is a man who is fighting for humanity."*

And Henry wanted that fighting chance. He wanted to feel free to do more than brush his fingers along Arabella's cheek and tuck an unruly strand of hair behind her ear. That touch had sent his nerves to humming, and it had taken everything he had not to lean forward and taste her lips. But if he was ever going to consider marriage, he needed to know he would not be a threat to her and that his blood would not be a threat to whatever children they would be blessed with.

Pushing forward, Henry kept his eyes on the three-story building and its three-arched doorway, avoiding eye contact with the few weary souls who passed by him.

Dr. Stafford had wanted him to come here. Wanted him to see something. Was it to recognize something in his sister's expression that would make him believe she was still there?

A flash of his sister as a young girl filled his vision. She had the biggest, round eyes that had always looked to him for comfort, for reassurance that despite the never-ending upheaval of their lives, he would be her constant.

And look how you abandoned her to the care of others, the voice whispered.

A stab of guilt pierced Henry's chest. He'd only been a boy of fifteen, he told himself. The title might've come to him, but he'd needed the guidance of his aunt.

And when you became a man? the voice asked, plunging the knife even further.

It was right. He could've come to see her, long before the reports of the old Bedlam had been presented at Parliament. Guilt, both hot and clammy, settled over his skin.

He deserved the discomfort this encounter would bring.

With a shaky breath, Henry entered the hospital.

The sound of his footsteps echoed in the room that stretched back like catacombs. Death, pain—he could smell it in the air, yet there was movement everywhere. People sat along a row of chairs lining the wall or were huddled in corners, coughing, wheezing, and moaning. It was a place of sickness, a place where none wanted to go unless there was no other choice. And for people like his sister, if she couldn't be cured, there was no other choice.

A choice that would be made for him if he couldn't find a way to help them both.

"May I help you, sir?" an older woman wearing a serviceable gray dress and a white apron asked from behind a tall wooden desk. She eyed him questioningly, which was understandable; he was the most well-kept person there. Members of the gentry didn't go to hospitals because they could afford to have a physician come to them.

A man bumped into him, coughing and hacking into an overly soiled, blood-splattered cloth.

On instinct, Henry reached for his own handkerchief to offer it to the man, but the nurse behind the desk shooed the coughing man away and stared at Henry with a raised brow.

"Sir?"

"The Baron Northcott," he said, keeping his tone detached and neutral, though a bead of nervous sweat trickled down the back of his neck.

Her eyes flashed with instant understanding. It had to be well-known amongst the staff that one of the patients meant for the new Bedlam was the sister to a baron. She quickly dipped into a curtsy. "Of course. If you will follow me, my lord."

Henry nodded, relieved he had to say no more, and waited for the nurse as she rounded the desk.

Two younger nurses descended a set of stairs that wrapped around the tall desk, their arms full of linens. They shot a questioning glance at the older nurse, who came to stand near Henry.

"Stay at the desk, Mary, Alice," she directed.

They nodded, eyeing Henry with a probing stare that made it hard to remain in place.

Careful, Beasty, the voice whispered. *You wouldn't want them to grow even more suspicious.*

Henry clenched his jaw. He really was beginning to hate that moniker.

"This way, my lord," the older nurse said.

Henry followed her to a door on the far side of the room. She reached for a ring of keys at her hip and slid one into the lock.

The door opened with an eerie creak, and she waved for Henry to enter. He tried to ignore the way his heart knocked an odd, panicked rhythm against his rib cage.

She closed the door behind her, and the click of the latch being locked into place echoed in his ears while the empty, white-washed corridor appeared to narrow and extend in his vision.

His chest grew tight, and he bit down on the side of his cheek, needing to maintain control. He wasn't a patient. He could leave when he was done.

"Your sister is this way," the nurse said, making her way down the corridor.

Every few steps, he passed an arched window, filling the

barren space with sunlight. He could feel the heat on his hands and face, which helped him to push down some of the panic.

At the door, the nurse reached for her keys again and unlocked it.

So many doors. So many locks.

He took a steadying breath and stepped into the next whitewashed corridor. This time there were only four windows, and the rest were doors.

A handful of nurses bustled about, their arms full of either linens or trays. Many also had keyrings about their hips.

The nurse closed and bolted the door behind them, the lock clanking into place.

Studying the doors more closely, Henry noticed each individual door had a small rectangular slot at about eye level.

"Your sister's room," the nurse said, stopping at the second door. She opened the slot and peered inside and then stepped back to allow Henry a glimpse.

His boots felt anchored to the floor, his chest tightening with every breath.

"My lord?" the nurse prompted.

"Is the doctor in?" Henry asked, needing a moment.

"I believe Dr. Gladstone can be made available."

"Dr. Gladstone?" Henry asked in confusion. "I was told Dr. Stafford was her physician."

"Dr. Stafford is *one* of her physicians," the nurse replied. "Dr. Gladstone is also one of the physicians who will be at the new Bedlam."

Henry nodded. The new Bedlam was due to open at the start of next month. His sister would be transferred there in little more than a week.

"Would you like to wait here while I go in search of him?" the nurse asked.

"That will not be necessary," Henry quickly replied. The last thing he wanted was to deal with another doctor. "If you will unlock the door, I shall look in upon my sister and wait to speak with Dr. Stafford another time."

The nurse hesitated, no doubt wondering why he asked for the doctor if he didn't want to speak to him. But then she moved to comply, unlocking the door and stepping aside.

"I will have to lock the door behind you. But simply knock three times, and I or one of the other nurses will let you out."

Henry nodded, though his nerves were screaming for him to run. It wasn't that he feared what his sister might do, but rather his own reactions. What could he say to a sister he'd not spoken to in ten years?

"Hello, I'm the brother who abandoned you" would be a good place to start. The voice laughed.

Henry swallowed the overpowering feeling of guilt and regret, forcing his legs to enter the room. Whether his sister was incurable or not, he owed her this much.

The door closed behind him, and his stomach twisted into a sickening knot as the nurse's keys scratched against the door, locking them in.

His sister sat on a chair next to a single bed. The walls around her were whitewashed, the linens on the bed were white, and she wore a simple dress of white, though the hem was yellowed. Her feet were bare, and her black hair had been plaited to the side.

She stared forward, not even acknowledging his presence.

A long silence stretched between them, tormenting him until he could take no more of it.

"One of us should say something to *break the ice.*"

He shook his head. Of all the things, it had to be Shakespeare.

His sister remained silent and unmoving.

He took a few hesitant steps toward her. "At least that is what my friend would say if she were here." His mouth continued to run away with itself. "My friend is never one for silence. Well, she is not exactly my friend. She—she is—"

He had the sudden urge to pace. So he did. "That is to say, she is unabashedly the most perplexing, frustrating, beautiful creature I have ever beheld. One moment she has me utterly transfixed, and the next, I want to pull my own hair out."

He stopped pacing, his back to Sarah, and pushed out a breath. "I'm rambling." He raked a hand through his hair. He couldn't remember the last time he'd talked so much.

Actually he could, back when he and Sarah were younger, and she would ask him to tell stories to distract her from their parents shouting. He wasn't a great storyteller, but he'd done it. For her.

"I should, in truth, be apologizing to you." He turned slowly to face his sister. "I have not been a good brother to you, and I have no excuse."

Still she didn't move.

Moving closer, he knelt on the floor before her, lowering himself enough to meet her eyes.

They were dark like his, though larger. He could see no recognition inside their depths.

"Can you hear me?" he whispered. "Sarah?"

Her eyes remained fixed forward.

Was she always like this?

His heart aching, but not wanting to give up hope, he slowly reached up and gently placed his hand on her knee. He *needed* to get through to her. Needed her to understand. *He* wanted to understand.

A knock sounded at the door.

Henry shot to his feet, his heart threatening to pound its way out of his chest. The sound of keys turning in the locks followed, and the door opened.

A thin gentleman stepped through the doorway, dressed in a very fine black, tailored jacket and a crimson waistcoat. The colors were a stark contrast compared to the whites and grays found throughout the rest of the hospital. A pair of gold spectacles sat proudly upon his nose, and he offered Henry a wide smile.

"Forgive the intrusion, my lord," the gentleman said, stepping up to Henry and giving him a bow meant for Queen Charlotte's court.

Oh, let the fop kiss your boots, the voice whispered. *It would be better to keep him simpering than have him realize what you are.*

Henry tensed and tried to focus on taking even breaths.

"When I discovered you were visiting," the gentleman continued, "I knew I needed to make myself available to you. Dr. Perceval Gladstone—your servant, sir." He bowed again.

Henry nodded. "Is my sister always like this?"

The doctor looked past Henry before replying. "I am afraid we had an incident this morning, and she had to be . . . subdued."

"Drugged?" Henry asked, sharp and direct because he could be nothing else. The entire visit had been for naught. He made no claim to understand the human mind, but he couldn't see the good in altering a person until they were a shell of themselves.

"It was for her and the other patients' safety," Dr. Gladstone replied with an air of self-importance.

"What was the incident?" Henry asked, doubt and fear creeping in. His mother in her madness had killed someone; if Sarah was the same . . .

"She viciously attacked one of our newest patients."

Henry's stomach dropped, his hope all but gone. Visions of the chaos and the screaming that occurred the night his mother stabbed his uncle threatened to overwhelm him.

Dr. Stafford had said Sarah might have received the wrong diagnosis because of a lack of information. Could his belief be wrong because of the same reason? Did he know of Henry's mother's violent past?

Henry realized he didn't know what his aunt and the old family solicitor had given as a reason for his mother's admittance to the old Bedlam.

Rumor and gossip had run rampant after that horrific night, but because his uncle was a member of the aristocracy, the matter was dealt with in private, saving the reputation of one of Britain's upper families.

All information needed to be laid bare if Henry was going to allow himself to hope.

Does that include informing the good doctor of what is going on inside your head? the voice whispered.

Henry's blood turned to ice, chilling him to the bone.

He could never tell anyone.

"Is there anything in particular I can do or answer for you, my lord?" Dr. Gladstone asked, pulling Henry from his thoughts. The doctor's chest was puffed out, enhancing his ridiculously overly knotted cravat.

"No," Henry said, not trusting the man. "Good day, doctor." He walked past the pompous dandy and out of the room.

The nurse who'd brought Henry stood outside the door, waiting for him. "Leaving, my lord?"

"Yes," he replied, not bothering to stop and wait for her. He was ready to be out of the infernal place.

"I will take his lordship from here," he heard another woman say from behind him.

Within moments, a nurse much older than the one before came up alongside him. She had a head of solid gray hair and deep wrinkles that ran from her cheeks to her neck. She matched his stride, not bothering to say anything while she collected her keys and unlocked the first door.

Inside the next corridor, the nurse turned hard on her heel and stared him down.

"Whatever that doctor said to you, your sister did not mindlessly attack anyone," she said, her hands firmly planted on her hips.

"You were there?" Henry asked, crossing his arms over his chest. After seeing his sister's current state, he was wary of trusting anyone inside the hospital without sufficient reason.

"No," she said in a tone that implied it did not even matter. "But I know my Sarah. She would not make a noise unless it was necessary."

My Sarah?

"Who are you?" Henry demanded.

"Nurse Maggie," the elderly woman replied.

"Well, then, Nurse Maggie, might I ask why you have gone

out of your way to tell me all this? And out of earshot from every-one else?"

She smiled, further confusing him. "You are starting to ask the right questions, my lord. And I am glad to see Dr. Stafford has finally convinced you to come."

"Where is Dr. Stafford?" Henry asked.

"He was called to—"

The sound of a key turning in the lock on the door behind them filled the corridor, and Dr. Gladstone stepped through.

"Nurse Maggie?" the doctor barked out. "Do not bother his lordship. I am certain he would like to be on his way."

"Of course, Doctor," she replied in a clipped tone. She re-trieved her keys and unlocked the last door for Henry.

"Thank you," Henry said to the nurse before looking to the pompous doctor.

"Good day to you, my lord," Dr. Gladstone called out, bow-ing his head as if he had just done Henry the greatest of favors. "Do not hesitate to reach out to me at any time."

Henry doubted he would ever be so desperate. He walked out of the hospital with more questions than answers, which made his promise to visit Arabella even more difficult to navigate. He wanted to pursue a future with her but still didn't know if he should.

SIXTEEN

Sitting up from her relaxed position across the sofa, Arabella clamped her book shut, pushed out a frustrated breath, and dropped the leather-bound volume to the floor. The loud, singular thud died a sudden and hollow death.

Shakespeare, it seemed, was mocking her.

Tomorrow, and tomorrow, and tomorrow, creeps in this petty pace from day to day.

Four days. It had been four days since the dinner at Lord Northcott's, and he'd yet to keep his promise to visit her. She knew she needed to have patience, but it was growing very difficult.

Her mother cleared her throat. She sat on the sofa opposite Arabella, reading the morning newspaper, a bowl of marzipan on her lap. Her paper was lowered, and she watched Arabella with a raised brow. "*King John?*"

"What?" Arabella asked, stunned.

"Your reeenactment." Her mother nodded to the book on the floor. "*King John. Life is as tedious as a twice-told tale, vexing the dull ear of a drowsy man.*"

A laugh exploded from Arabella's lips. Retrieving her book, she walked over to her mother and showed her the cover. "*Macbeth.*"

"At least I got the author correct." Her mother winked before reaching into her bowl of marzipan. Marzipan was to her mother as Shakespeare was to Arabella: a necessity to treat the soul.

The parlor door opened, and Arabella looked over her shoulder to find Smith entering. "Lord Northcott and Mr. Bradbury, ma'am."

Arabella spun on her heels, her dark green skirts whipping around her ankles.

He was here!

"Well, that certainly was interesting," her mother said, coming to stand beside her.

Heat flooded Arabella's cheeks, and it took a considerable effort to meet her mother's curious gaze. For once, she wasn't entirely certain what to say. She'd never felt such a pull, such a desire to be noticed by a man. It was all so overwhelming and confusing how it had come about. He'd spent an entire Season dancing with her, and she'd felt no such nerves then.

"Take a breath," her mother whispered, rubbing a hand up and down Arabella's back as the gentlemen entered the room.

Lord Northcott appeared first, closely followed by Mr. Bradbury, whose bright and boisterous grin quickly commanded the attention of the room.

"I hope you did not put away your marzipan on my account," Mr. Bradbury said, moving past Lord Northcott and squeezing her mother's outstretched hands.

Arabella gave a giggle-snort, and she quickly covered her mouth with her hand.

Her mother didn't so much as blink at Mr. Bradbury's accurate assumption.

"I am afraid I do not know what you are talking about," her mother replied.

Mr. Bradbury quirked his lips before stepping around her mother and dropping onto the sofa. His hand slid across the blue-and-cream-striped cushion until it disappeared beneath an awkwardly slanted, blue velvet pillow and retrieved her mother's hidden bowl.

He settled the bowl in his lap and waggled his brow before taking a triumphant bite. "As I said, no need to hide your treat because of me. We have known each other long enough."

Arabella's mother shook her head and shot him a look that

only a mother could. "One would think after all that time I would have instilled in you a few more manners."

Mr. Bradbury shot her a boyish grin. "My apologies." He sat up straighter in his seat. "May I *please* have some of your marzipan?"

A smile stole across her mother's lips. "You may, but I shall hold the bowl."

Amusement gave way to another giggle as Arabella turned toward Lord Northcott, excited and nervous to have some time with him.

She found him watching her, only this time it was with an urgency that nearly took her breath away. His dark, hooded eyes tracked her every step, taking in every detail of her appearance as she approached as if he *needed* to look upon her. It wasn't like him, showing such emotions.

Her entire body warmed, and her heart picked up its pace. "Did you also come for some of my mother's marzipan?" she asked, wanting to almost laugh at the way her voice and hands were shaking.

He shook his head. "I made a promise to you," he replied, his expression serious, yet there was a hint of a smile in his tone, causing shivers to run up her spine.

"I'm glad you kept it." Her smile grew, and her heart raced when his eyes dipped down to her lips.

He swallowed and quickly gripped his hands behind his back as he glanced over her shoulder.

Was he just as nervous about all this as she was?

Following his gaze, she wasn't surprised to find her mother discreetly watching them. Heat flashed up Arabella's neck and into her cheeks, and she was grateful when Mr. Bradbury pulled her mother into a conversation.

"Walk with me?" she asked Lord Northcott, thinking a man as guarded as he was might wish for some privacy.

For a moment, she thought he'd turn her down, but then he

glanced toward the gloomy, gray-filled window, its glass speckled with that day's rain. "And go where?" he asked.

She studied him. Was he teasing her?

A corner of his lips twitched upward.

He *was* teasing her. Her heart did an excited flip. Two could play at that game.

"*The world's mine oyster*," Arabella said, holding her arms outward. "Though in truth, I was thinking the card table." She nodded toward the back of the room.

He hesitated before nodding his approval and held out his arm to her. She tucked her fingers into the crook of his arm, and they walked in silence toward the card table conveniently situated behind the sofa. They'd walked together like this many times over the Season, but somehow this time felt different. She was much more aware of him, like how he was using the corded muscles in his forearm to pull her even closer to him.

"*The Merry Wives of Windsor*," he murmured, completely catching her by surprise.

He was playing her game. She squeezed her fingers around his arm and smiled up at him with a lightness that filled her heart and lungs.

This feeling, this spark, had to be what her father wanted her to find.

They sat across from the other at the card table.

"I know you do not gamble," she said, reaching for the stack of cards at the center of the table, "but I hope you will find the game I have in mind innocent enough."

"And what game is that?" he asked, watching her hands as she shuffled the deck.

"I'm certain it will become your favorite." She grinned as he warily met her gaze. "I think we should play battle, only the person who flips over the highest card also wins the chance to ask the other a question."

His eyes narrowed before looking away. She didn't know why

he was always so guarded, but she had hoped he'd begun to trust her.

"*Our doubts are traitors,*" she began, wishing to regain his attention. "*And make us lose the good we oft might win, by fearing to attempt.*"

For an endless moment, she held her breath.

"*Measure for Measure,*" he replied, meeting and holding her gaze. "I will play your games, but I cannot promise I will answer all your questions."

Her heart sank. She would have to do more to prove to him she was worthy of his trust.

Dividing the cards equally between them, she straightened her stack, which remained face down. "Ready?" she asked, finding Lord Northcott had done the same with his stack.

He nodded, and they both flipped over their top cards. Hers was a seven of clubs and his a ten of hearts.

Zounds! Of course, he would win first.

"What is your first question?" she asked, watching him collect his newly won cards.

He set them in an orderly pile next to his larger stack of cards. "Do you plan to have any more secret adventures before your brother returns?"

She blinked and opened her mouth, but no words came out, feeling almost called out by his choice of question. And then the corner of his lips twitched. Was he teasing her again?

The so-called Brooding Baron was proving to be far more charming than people believed.

Biting the insides of her cheeks to hide her amusement, she leaned over the table as if she were about to impart some great secret.

He leaned forward as well, his eyes darting toward her mother and Mr. Bradbury.

"The answer is—" She paused, wanting to draw him in even further before she teased him. Only it was she who was taken in when she caught the most alluring and distracting scent of leather and warm spice.

"Miss Latham?" His tone was soft, but it was enough to return her to her senses.

She shook her head, breaking the spell that had overtaken her.

"My apologies," she said. "And my answer is no. Though if I am ever given the chance to see inside Sadler's Wells Theatre, I can make no such promise."

Lord Northcott's soft smile vanished into a thin line.

The infamous theater sat just outside London and was only open during the summer months. It'd been a dream of hers since she was a girl of sixteen and her father first mentioned a stage made of water. She'd thus far been denied that dream because the crowds that frequented that theater were often unruly, requiring the theater to provide escorts for its higher-paying patrons.

"Do not worry yourself," she said, leaning back in her seat. "I am fairly certain my luck will change once Emerson and Olivia are home. My closest friend may prove to be the perfect chink to break through my brother's overprotective armor."

The corners of his mouth twitched upward, and he shook his head. "No doubt."

Her heart warmed at seeing another small crack in his armor.

"Shall we draw again?" she asked, unable to keep a smile from her lips.

He nodded, and they flipped over their top cards once again. The knave of clubs against the six of diamonds. She'd won!

Collecting her winnings, she looked to him only half apologetically. "Are you ready for my question?"

He nodded slowly, his entire body tense and rigid in his seat.

"What is something you enjoy?" she asked, struggling to stifle the smile at his apparent relief in her choice of question.

She was practicing patience in order to gain his trust. Eventually she would ask him if he'd visited his sister.

"Reading," he replied after a moment's thought.

"What do you read?" she asked, glad to hear they had that in

TO LOVE THE BROODING BARON

common. She could picture evenings by the fire where they'd read to one another . . . perhaps with his arms wrapped around her.

Her body overheated at the thought.

"That is two questions," he replied.

"I gave you a more detailed answer," she argued.

"You gave that willingly. I am only following your rules of the game."

She began to argue but was cut off by Mr. Bradbury, who had approached the card table.

"Did you say game?"

Arabella inwardly groaned. This was why she struggled with patience. You ran the risk of missing out on opportunities.

Mr. Bradbury surveyed the different stacks of cards between them. "You *are* playing a game without me." He pulled out an empty chair and took a seat. "What are we playing?"

"*We* were playing battle," Arabella replied, not hiding the frustration in her tone.

Mr. Bradbury eyed her skeptically. "You know, if you want to attract a husband next Season, you would do well to do a lot less of this"—he pulled a ridiculous looking face and flapped his fingers in the form of a mouth—"and a lot more of this." He smiled sweetly, pressed his hands together, and fluttered his eyes.

She swatted his shoulder—hard—and he reeled back in mock outrage.

"For someone who is so terrified of marriage," Arabella said, folding her arms, "you have a lot of advice on the subject."

"She has you there, Bradbury," Lord Northcott said.

"What's this?" Bradbury turned a surprised scowl on Lord Northcott. "I let you into the brotherhood and you turn your back on me?"

"I'm not turning my back," Lord Northcott replied. "But Miss Latham is smart enough to know her own mind. If a man cannot accept her for who she is"—he turned to look at her—"then he is not worth her time."

His words stole her breath as he continued to hold her eyes with his intense gaze. Was he offering to be that man?

"What are you two doing?" Mr. Bradbury asked with a heavy dose of suspicion, severing their connection. He looked back and forth between them, his scowl growing.

Lord Northcott cleared his throat and turned to look at his friend. "Did you want to play?"

Mr. Bradbury didn't immediately respond, though his scowl lessened. "Battle, you said?"

"Yes," Arabella replied. "Only the winner gets to ask the other player a question."

"That is boring." Mr. Bradbury reached over and drew a small stack of cards off each of theirs and set them in front of him. "Let's change it to coin."

"No," Arabella replied, not wanting Lord Northcott to withdraw from the game. "It's more fun this way."

Mr. Bradbury scoffed. "You and I have different definitions of fun."

Ignoring his grumbling, Arabella reached for her stack, then waited for the others to do the same before flipping over her top card.

Mr. Bradbury won with the king of diamonds.

"So what now?" he asked. "Do I ask a question to the both of you, or do I just pick one of you?"

"Just pick one," Arabella replied, anxious to get to the next hand. She wouldn't be able to ask Lord Northcott the more personal questions she'd been hoping to, but she could still learn more about him.

"That still makes it difficult. I do not find either one of you that interesting." Mr. Bradbury tapped his chin in thought. "Oh, I know." He turned toward Arabella. "Tell me about this cousin of yours, Sebastian Latham. Why have I never met him before?"

Arrabella's lips twitched, but she managed to hold back her laugh. She'd been wondering when the timing would be right to inform Mr. Bradbury he'd lost his wager, and he had unknowingly provided the perfect opportunity for her.

"Sebastian was not my cousin," she replied, glancing toward Lord Northcott to see if he wanted to be part of her reveal.

He sat stiff in his chair, but a subtle spark beneath his dark eyes told her he was enjoying this part of the game.

She met Mr. Bradbury's gaze with a wide, smug smile. "It was me."

Bradbury laughed. "Very funny." He looked to Lord Northcott. "Can you believe this?"

"It was her," he said.

Bradbury's eyes nearly bulged out of his head as he looked between her and Lord Northcott. "What? How did you—Why on earth would you—" He stopped short, realization washing over him as he stared open-mouthed at Arabella. "Emerson's study." He swallowed, cursing under his breath. "Why would you *ever* take my words seriously?"

"I shall remember that in the future," she said, finding an unholy delight in tormenting him.

He moaned and dropped his head into the palms of his hands. "Your brother is going to murder me."

"No, he is not," Arabella said. "We are not going to tell him—or my mother—about any of this." She paused and looked to Lord Northcott. "Anything that happened that day is now in the past, never to be revisited."

His eyes thanked her.

"Agreed," Mr. Bradbury said, letting out a breath as his body sagged into his chair with relief.

"But you still owe me for winning that bet," Arabella added, bobbing her brow. She'd be a fool not to try for something.

"Like what?" Bradbury asked with a hesitant tone as he sat up straighter.

"Take me to the Sadler's Wells Theatre," she said, risking a glance at Lord Northcott, whose lips twitched as he subtly shook his head.

"No," Mr. Bradbury said with the added emphasis of a pointed finger in her direction. "That place is questionable at best. Your brother *would* kill me if I took you without his permission."

Arabella shrugged; it had been a long shot. "Then I would like a driving lesson in Hyde Park." At least that would get her out of doors.

And with any luck, Mr. Bradbury would ask Lord Northcott to come along.

SEVENTEEN

Henry's butler was waiting for him the moment he walked through the front door, as always, playing sentinel for his aunt. Samson took his hat and then glanced with questioning eyes over Henry's shoulder.

Bradbury had followed him home.

"Good afternoon," Bradbury said, holding out his hat for the old butler.

One invitation to dinner and he was making himself at home. Henry was relieved. Grateful, even, but he could never tell Bradbury that.

The old butler looked to Henry and then to Bradbury's hat, his expression as stiff and lifeless as a gargoyle's.

"Or not, I suppose . . ." Bradbury said, his tone unsure as he looked at Henry with a quizzical brow. "Is he all right?"

"Come on," Henry said, taking Bradbury's hat and pushing it into Samson's hands before heading toward his study.

He didn't want to explain to his friend that he and his aunt were quarreling. Samson had likely been instructed to send Henry to his aunt the moment he returned home. Bradbury's presence was preventing him from doing that.

The situation between Henry and his aunt had gone from strained to tense. After his visit to Guy's Hospital, he and his solicitor had spent two days searching for any information regarding his mother and sister's admittance to the old Bedlam. They did everything they could think of, from sending an inquiry to the old family solicitor to asking Dr. Stafford for what information he had. The letter to Dr. Stafford had so far gone unanswered, and the old family solicitor told them nothing and had instead informed his aunt.

She'd stormed into Henry's study that morning with fire in her eyes, demanding he cease looking into the past before he risked exposing more of his family's failings and ruin what was left of the Northcott family reputation.

He made her no promises and left the house.

Instead, he'd collected Bradbury from Brooks's and gone straight to the Lathams' house, hoping his friend's presence would help disguise his reason for visiting. He doubted it worked after the way Mrs. Latham had discreetly watched him. She no doubt suspected something had shifted between her daughter and himself.

He bit back a groan. He was getting in far too deep, and he was proving hopeless in being able to stop himself.

Entering his study with Bradbury just behind him, Henry ignored the portraits of every previous baron that ran down the length of the room. He knew he was risking all they'd built, but he *wanted* a different future for himself and his sister

He stopped at the sideboard that he rarely used, and never for himself, and reached for a crystal decanter of brandy while turning toward his friend. "Would you like a dri—"

His words were cut short by the impact of Bradbury's fist as it struck him.

Henry's head snapped sideways, and pain radiated from his chin all the way through his teeth.

Bradbury let out a loud hiss. "Blast, that hurts as bad as I thought it would." He shook his hand, flexing his fingers.

"What the devil was that for?" Henry growled, rubbing at the throbbing muscle at his chin.

Bradbury shot him a stern glare and pointed an accusatory finger at him. "That is so when Emerson returns home and finds you making moonstruck eyes at his sister, I can look him in the face and say I defended his sister's honor. How long have you been secretly courting Miss Latham?"

He's caught you now. The voice inside his head laughed.

Henry's hand froze on his chin. He didn't know what to say.

They stared each other down for several long minutes, and then Bradbury let out a huff of frustration and dropped his hand.

"I knew this was going to happen. Once one fool gets married, the next fool follows."

Henry held up a hand and shook his head as panic settled in. He was far from being able to make a proposal of marriage. "It's not exactly what you think."

Bradbury's scowl deepened. "What do you mean it's not what I think?" His voice was sharp with impatience. "Because I can tell you that is exactly what Miss Latham is thinking. Are you leading on our friend's sister?"

"No," Henry said adamantly.

"Then what are you doing?" Bradbury asked, confusion warring with exasperation across his face.

Henry shoved a hand through his hair, trying to figure out what to say that would satisfy his friend but not divulge his family's secrets. "It's . . . complicated."

That will satisfy him, the voice said with sarcasm.

Bradbury threw his hands in the air and began to pace. "Of course it's complicated, you bacon-brained fool! This is Emerson's *sister.*"

Henry stood in stunned disbelief. Had that explanation truly worked?

Bradbury tapped his hand against the side of his leg as he continued to pace. "Now, we need to come up with a set of rules, ones that will keep Emerson from pummeling us—well, primarily me—you may very well have to take at least one facer for going behind his back." Bradbury abruptly stopped. "Although, he did go after his sister's friend behind *her* back, so maybe lead with that." He paused, then winced. "On second thought, do not do that."

Henry agreed. If he was so fortunate as to have that discussion with Emerson, he'd use no such excuse.

Bradbury resumed pacing. "Rules. We need rules."

Henry remained silent, knowing his friend was correct.

Bradbury held up a finger. "First, you must no longer call upon the Lathams without me in attendance."

Henry nodded. That was actually a good idea, which was shocking coming from Bradbury. Until Henry was able to sort out everything with himself and his sister, what had started between him and Arabella could go no further. He'd not distance himself from her entirely, but he wouldn't allow another situation like what happened in his study the night of the dinner party. His fingers still twitched at the thought of being able to touch her again, to hear her sudden intake of breath when he did. It was the honorable thing, until all could be resolved. And with Bradbury present, he would be able to keep his control.

"Second . . . second . . ." Bradbury turned quick on his heels to face Henry, throwing up his hands once again. "For pity's sake, I am no Lady Bixbee. I do not know what strategy to make. Heaven knows I am never courting anyone."

A knock sounded at the study door.

"Enter," Henry called, a knot of unease forming between his shoulders as he anticipated seeing his aunt enter.

What tactic would she try next? He'd never gone against her before, and she was not handling it well.

Instead of his aunt, however, Samson walked in along with a boy Henry recognized as a runner from his solicitor's office.

"The boy refuses to give the missive to anyone but you, my lord," the old butler said with a tight scowl.

The boy squeezed past an unmoving Samson and handed Henry a rectangular, brown-paper parcel.

"Good lad," Henry said, his heart picking up its pace. Had Mr. Tompkin finally found something related to his mother's history?

Henry had instructed his solicitor that all letters were to be delivered directly to his hand, and he would cover all costs. There would be no more letters easily read by his aunt.

"See the boy is paid," Henry directed Samson. "And have something brought up from the kitchen." The boy was cleaner than most runners, but Henry remembered being that age. He had been constantly hungry and growing out of his clothing.

Samson nodded, though Henry knew he wasn't happy about it. Turning his back to both the door and Bradbury, Henry untied the string holding the parcel together, praying it contained what he'd been searching for.

Peeling open one side of the stiff brown paper, he quickly read his solicitor's very short message that sat atop a folded letter.

This just arrived from Dr. Stafford.

Finally.

His heart pounded as he retrieved a second letter from the stack of papers with shaking hands.

He skimmed over the proper greetings and got to the heart of the matter.

I have been called away on a matter of the Crown and do not know when I will be allowed to return. But I agree, we must talk.

Henry cursed. Of course—why would anything come easy for him?

Until then, I will have a trusted member of my staff send you what I have on your sister, along with this letter. But I must warn you, there is not much. The old hospital was not the only thing to succumb to rot and decay.

On the matter of your mother, though, there is much to discuss, and it must be in person. I will call on you the moment I am free to do so.

Henry clenched his eyes shut and let out a frustrated breath. Again, he was left with more questions than answers. How could there be a thin stack of papers about his sister but much to discuss about his mother?

He doubted he would get many answers soon if the rumors about the current state of the king were to be believed. Dr. Stafford's absence could be for some time.

Bradbury cleared his throat. "Is everything all right?"

Henry looked at his friend and secured the parcel under his arm. "I do not know," he said, being fully honest with himself *and* Bradbury for the first time that day.

But he would have hope and read and wait.

"Is there anything I can do to help?" Bradbury asked, a hint of concern in his tone.

Henry shook his head as he heard hurried, feminine footsteps outside his open study door. His aunt had apparently grown inpatient. "Go to the club. I will meet you there later," he said.

Bradbury hesitated, his eyes glancing from the door to Henry. "Whatever is going on, I hope you know you can trust me . . . Goosey." Then he winked.

A soft chuckle found its way out of Henry's tight chest, and he shook his head at the familiar ridiculousness of his friend. Bradbury, it seemed, was circling Henry's nest, waiting to be allowed closer.

If only he could.

EIGHTEEN

Henry raked a hand through his hair and pulled the ends taut. After the second confrontation with his aunt yesterday, when she'd demanded to see the parcel the boy had delivered and Henry refused, she'd taken to playing the pianoforte—often—and loud enough that it seemed to reach him in any corner of the house. His head pounded, and he fought against a deep feeling of guilt. She only played the songs he knew to be his uncle's favorites, and he could feel her anger and disappointment by how purposefully she struck every note.

Sitting at his desk in the study, Henry stared at the thin stack of papers from Dr. Stafford. The papers were yellowed and stained, and the faded ink of the notes made by the doctors and nurses from the old Bedlam made the reports difficult to read. But he'd read them all, several times. He had hoped to find answers, but even the admittance form left him with more questions.

Patient name: Vivian Sarah Northcott

"Sarah," Henry repeated on a tortured whisper. His younger sister had been named Vivian after their mother, but everyone but their mother had called her Sarah.

Sex: Female

Age: 13

The number splayed him. She was too young, and after seeing the conditions at the old Bedlam, he doubted she'd had anyone there to protect her.

He should've protected her.

His aunt hit a loud, dissonant chord on the pianoforte, and it felt like a knife to his temple.

Scrubbing a hand across his forehead, he ignored his aunt and read on.

Admitted: 21 June 1805

Eight months after their mother was admitted. Henry's indifference toward the woman who'd given him life was not lost on him. But he was certain the guilt he felt toward Sarah would last his lifetime.

Rank or profession:
Sister to the Right Honorable Baron Northcott

Henry had been fifteen, and not ready to take on the burden of a title.

Family history:
Father deceased. Mother living—treated for insanity in 1804.

So the doctors knew that their mother had been treated for insanity, but there were no other details given. Is that what Dr. Stafford wanted to discuss with him?

Henry let out a heavy breath. Always more questions than answers.

Continuing, he read,

No history of insanity on father's side. Mother's side unknown.

Henry's mother had been an only child, the daughter of a poor French aristocratic family. From what Henry had been told, his parents had claimed their union to be a love match, but the Northcott family had disapproved of the connection. When Henry's grandfather discovered they'd secretly married, he had cut them off. Henry's father had supported and then bankrupted their family through gambling.

Facts indicating insanity observed at the time of examination: Patient is slight and girlish, and appearance and hair were in disarray upon arrival. Eyes are wild and vacant. Patient tried to attack the nurse upon admittance.

Henry ran a hand down his face. More violence.

Just like your mother, the voice inside his head whispered. Henry clenched his jaw and read on.

Facts communicated by others: Family reports the patient refuses to speak and is prone to hysteria and screaming during sleep.

Henry read the last line over again. He couldn't remember his sister's screams nor any hysterics. They slept in separate rooms, but surely he would've heard something or been called to comfort her.

He pinched the bridge of his nose hard, welcoming the pain. Why couldn't he remember? He could remember his mother's hysterics; they haunted him in his dreams.

He needed answers. He needed . . . hope.

His aunt missed another chord. The sound bit into the back of his ears, and his neck cringed against the sting of it.

Just once, he wanted to know a modicum of peace, when secrets didn't haunt him around every corner, trying to upend his existence.

An odd, light tapping reached his ears during a short-lived break in his aunt's playing.

It couldn't be rain; the sun had finally pushed through the clouds for the past few days.

Henry sat up straighter and listened intently.

Tap. Tap. Tap. There it was again.

Gathering up his papers, he put them in the bottom drawer of his desk and locked it. Then he followed the sound, which had grown more persistent.

He stopped at one of the two large windows and stared down at the top half of—

"What the blazes?" Henry muttered.

Bradbury's hand was pressed against the glass, shading his eyes as he scanned the room. He startled when his eyes met Henry's middle.

Bending down slightly, Henry undid the latch and pulled up on the window. "What the devil are you doing?"

Bradbury scowled up at him, his hands on his hips. His hat sat atop the large rose bush next to him, and the bottom of his boots were speckled with dirt from trampling through the back garden to get to the window.

"Paying a call," Bradbury said with an exasperated breath. "Now move over so I can climb in."

"Use the front door," Henry said.

Bradbury huffed. "I did, but your ogre of a butler said you were not receiving callers and shut the door." He shot Henry an annoyed glare. "Now move."

Without waiting for Henry to comply, Bradbury propped both hands on the windowsill and lifted himself upward until he could swing one leg over the opening.

Henry stepped back, then offered a hand to help his friend the rest of the way in.

Henry's frustration—no, anger—that had been building was beginning to crackle and burn. He'd never felt such a way toward his aunt, who was keeping him like a prisoner inside his own home.

Many doors. Many locks. The voice echoed Henry's thoughts from Guy's Hospital.

A chill scraped like stone on steel across his spine.

"You know," Bradbury said, leaning his top half back out the window to retrieve his hat from the rosebush, "when you said you were going to meet me at our club later, I did not understand that to mean an entire *day* later, nor that I would have to be the one to come in search of you." His eyes snapped with annoyance as he brushed the dirt and leaves from his clothing.

"I was . . . " Henry let his words trail off, not knowing what to say. He was growing tired of all the secrets.

His aunt's angry playing filled the silence.

"I think it's time you tell me what is going on," Bradbury said, all the frustration and annoyance gone from him. "The parcel yesterday? Your guard dog of a butler? The . . ." He nodded toward the study door, wincing as Henry's aunt hit a minor chord. "What has been brewing inside this house?"

Henry shook his head, struggling, and probably failing, to keep his frustration and near exhaustion from his expression. He truly was growing tired of keeping it all in.

But he must.

"I cannot say," he replied. There was more than his own reputation at stake.

The corners of Bradbury's mouth dipped into a frown, but he nodded.

His look of disappointment hit like a cudgel to Henry's gut. His secrets were going to cost him his friends one day.

"Well, then," Bradbury said, blowing out a breath as he looked around the room. "Should we use the door or the window?"

"We?" Henry asked, flummoxed.

Bradbury huffed and looked to the ceiling. "Always about the details with you." He stepped closer to Henry and patted him aggressively on the shoulder. "*We* made a promise to take Miss Latham for a driving lesson, and now that the sun has finally come out, it's a perfect day for a ride in the park."

"You made that promise," Henry replied, not entirely sure why he was fighting an opportunity to escape his house.

Not to mention, see Arabella, the voice whispered.

Henry's heart picked up its pace.

"Again," Bradbury said, throwing up his hands. "It's always about the details with you." He stared Henry down. "You are just as complicit in all this as I am. After all, you were the one leading her around inside the club." Bradbury paused. "As a matter of fact, when did you realize it was her?"

"From the start," Henry replied, making Bradbury scowl. "The only way to get her out was to show her that blasted betting book that *you* made that wager about."

"Would you just come?" Bradbury moaned. "Do you know what will happen if Lady Bixbee hears I was riding around alone with Miss Latham? That meddlesome matron is your problem; I do not want her to be mine."

That was yet another problem he would have to resolve along with Dr. Stafford and his sister. Everything was a muddled mess.

"Let's go," Henry said, letting out a frustrated breath and nodding toward the door.

"Good," Bradbury smiled, and they started for the door. "Also, I shall need to borrow your phaeton."

An unexpected chuckle found its way out of Henry's chest. It sounded odd yet felt restoring. "Perhaps your next winnings should go toward purchasing a more dependable conveyance." Henry always seemed to be giving Bradbury a ride to somewhere.

"And deprive you of my company?" Bradbury scoffed. "Admit it, Goosey. You like having me around."

Henry shook his head and chuckled as they left the study. His friend was right, but that didn't also mean that Bradbury was not a complete miser.

NINETEEN

Henry pulled back on the reins to his two matching grays as they came to a stop in front of the Lathams' home. He'd driven alone in the front of his phaeton coach while Bradbury had lounged across the back seat.

"Not too badly done. A little slow for my taste," Bradbury said, using one of the larger back wheels as a step to hop down. He looked up at Henry from the pavement, a smile playing at the corner of his mouth. "But I can see that I will have my work cut out for me if I am to teach both you and Miss Latham to handle the conveyance properly."

Henry didn't bother looking to the heavens for patience; they'd not answered any of his other prayers after all. "Would you just go and fetch Miss Latham?"

"You do not want to come in?" Bradbury asked, tilting his head with a perplexing glance.

"I should double-check the horses," Henry said, suddenly feeling nervous that he'd not be able to control his need to touch Arabella. He'd tried telling himself that just being in her company would be more than enough, but he could already feel himself slipping from that resolve. He needed a moment to clear his head and regain the tight control he held over himself.

"Very well," Bradbury said. "Though if we die today, I doubt it will be because of a poorly fastened buckle." He chuckled before dashing up to the front door.

Instead of regaining control, Henry felt a nervous energy humming through him, making the muscles in his arms feel tight while his hands slightly shook. And all because of one woman. A traitorous smile crested his lips.

Climbing down from the phaeton, he rechecked the straps and buckles on the horses.

They began to fidget, no doubt sensing Henry's unease. He placed a hand on each of their necks and stroked the silky short hairs in a bid to calm them.

The front door to the Lathams' home opened, and he turned his head to watch as a glorious figure in sky blue practically skipped down the front steps. Her lips looked kissed by the sun.

She is breathtaking, Henry inwardly groaned. Enduring an outing where one could look but not touch should've been one of Hercules's twelve labors.

Her eyes brightened the moment their eyes met, and her cheeks flushed to the color of a sun-ripened peach.

"*A horse, a horse, my kingdom for a horse,*" she called out with a smile he wanted only for himself.

She stopped next to him on the pavement and placed a hand close to his on the horse's neck. She had the most infectious smile, one that instantly pulled an answering smile to his own lips.

"*Richard the Third,*" Henry replied, his littlest finger turning on him and sliding across until it rested atop of her own. And just like that, a lifetime's resolve for control was obliterated.

Red colored her cheeks, and she stared up at him through her long, dark lashes.

"Come on, Goosey," Bradbury said, clamping both hands on Henry's shoulders, nearly making him jump out of his own skin, and hauling him back a few steps.

Henry gave a slight shake of his head. He'd been so enraptured by the bewitching creature before him he'd completely forgot his surroundings.

Still holding onto Henry's shoulders, Bradbury leaned close to his ear. "Could you at least wait to fawn all over your ladylove until we are out of sight of Mama Latham? We do not need her writing to Emerson."

Henry swallowed. That would be his luck.

Clapping Henry on the back, Bradbury jumped up into the

driver's seat and untied the reins from the brake lever. "Come on, you two, let us get this driving lesson over with. Death—I mean time—waits for no one." He winked and shot them both an amused grin.

"I shall make you eat your words once again, Mr. Bradbury," Arabella challenged with her usual spark of determination.

Bradbury barked out a laugh. "Touché, Miss Latham."

Henry shook his head and laughed to himself. It was most certainly going to be a ride to remember.

He held out a hand to Arabella and enjoyed the warm pressure of her touch in his palm as he helped her up into the conveyance. He climbed up after her, envious of Bradbury's position next to Arabella, while he took the seat behind them.

࿔࿎࿇

As soon as they entered Hyde Park, Bradbury directed the horses to turn from the thoroughfare and down one of the more private gravel lanes in between the Serpentine and a copse of trees. The sunbathed park was bustling with almost every member of the *ton* who remained in London, enjoying the warmth after what felt like months of rain.

"All right, Miss Latham," Bradbury said, pulling the horses to a stop and dropping the reins haphazardly into Arabella's hands. He leaned back in his seat, stretched out his legs as far as they could go, and crossed one ankle over the other. "Have at it."

Henry lunged forward, nearly clearing the back of their seat as he took hold of the reins before Arabella could do any such thing. "What in the devil is wrong with you?" he yelled at Bradbury, his voice sounding hoarse, whether from his barely suppressed anger or because he couldn't remember the last time he'd raised his voice at anyone, he couldn't say.

"What?" Bradbury asked innocently. "She said she wanted to make me eat my words, so here is her chance."

Henry sucked in a deep breath through his nose, trying to calm his anger, and the scent of primroses immediately filled his senses. In his haste to grab the reins, he had inadvertently wrapped his arms around Arabella from behind. Her back was firmly pressed against his chest, and he was quickly growing distracted by the feel of her in his arms.

He swallowed, his mouth suddenly dry. Was she as aware of him as he was of her?

You could lean in closer and find out, the voice inside his head whispered.

Henry cleared his throat and forced himself to focus on the twelve hundred pounds of powerful horseflesh before them.

He quickly untangled his arms from around Arabella and repositioned the reins between her and Bradbury. Because of the short length of the reins, he was forced to lean over the back of their bench, which still put him near Arabella, but at least he was no longer touching her.

She turned her head to smile at him. The apples of her cheeks were the most fetching shade of red, and he felt her awareness of him like a dart of pleasure and pain, tempting him to touch her again.

Bradbury. He needed to focus on the dim-witted Bradbury.

Tearing his eyes away, he glowered at his senseless friend. "You cannot just hand over the reins to animals that have enough force and weight to kill a man."

"I did no such thing," Bradbury argued over his shoulder at Henry. "I have had my hand on the brake lever this entire time." Bradbury lifted his hand from where the lever rested near his thigh and mockingly wiggled his fingers. Then he stood and faced Henry.

"Furthermore, my reflexes are just as quick as yours, and I would have jumped in at the first sign of trouble." He placed his boot on the back of the bench, forcing Henry to look up to meet his eyes. "But if you think you can do better, then, by all means, take over the lesson." In the blink of an eye, Bradbury had stepped over the back of the bench, crowding the space where Henry was standing.

"What is the matter with you?" Henry growled, glaring at Bradbury. He had to juggle moving himself into position on the front bench while also trying to hold the pair of horses steady.

"Nothing," Bradbury said with a confident smile as he leaned back on the bench and placed his hands behind his head. "Now, do not keep Miss Latham waiting." He winked. "Show the lady a *proper* driving lesson."

Henry stared at Bradbury in stunned disbelief. Had his friend just pulled off a brilliant matchmaking stratagem and secured Henry time with Arabella while Bradbury served as chaperone?

His jaw nearly dropped in astonishment. If that was Bradbury's intention, the man who had renounced love could prove to be a rival to Lady Bixbee.

"I would advise closing your mouth," Bradbury said, leaning forward to pat Henry on the shoulder. "Horses are known for their attraction to flies."

Henry clamped his mouth shut. Heaven help him, his friend had orchestrated the whole thing.

Arabella giggled.

Henry slowly turned his head toward her. "What are you laughing about?"

"Nothing," she said, smiling up at him with a look that was both adorable and provoking.

"Do you want to learn to drive the phaeton or not?" he grumbled even as a grin pulled at his lips.

"Yes, very much," she replied, a spark of nervous excitement in her eyes.

Henry nodded, reminding himself to focus on the task at hand and not solely on the beautiful woman next to him.

He held out the reins to her, trying—and failing—to not breathe in her sweet scent. Another whiff and he would demand his aunt plant primroses in all the gardens.

Arabella hesitated for a moment, her brow lifting as her front teeth caught her bottom lip. "I thought you said I was not supposed to just be handed the reins?"

"You are not," he said to reassure her. "Now take—"

Before he could finish, she snatched the reins out of his hands, teasing him with her eyes as the horses rocked back and forth from the sudden motion.

"*Who seeks and will not take when once 'tis offered shall never find it more.*" Her lips quirked in a mischievous smile.

"*Antony and Cleopatra,*" Henry replied with a smile. He loved her games.

"I am beginning to think I shall have to work harder to try to stump you, Lord Northcott."

In that moment, he wanted nothing more than to ask her to call him by his Christian name.

What was that about not letting it go any further? the voice whispered.

Taking a breath, he positioned her fingers into the correct grip. He was teaching her to drive a phaeton, nothing more. "The reins should start between your little finger and the next finger, and then up along the palm and out through your thumbs."

She nodded, her breaths coming out in shallow pants that tickled his cheek.

He swallowed past a growing lump in his throat as his fingers slowly guided the leather straps along the delicate shape of her palm. The world around them fell silent until all he could hear was his breath beginning to match her own.

"What do I do next?" she asked in a soft whisper, her eyes dipping to where his thigh pressed up against her own.

"You will want to—" He swallowed, trying not to focus on the heat radiating through him from that simple touch. "To hold the reins out in front of you with enough tension to give the horses leave but also keep them steady."

She nodded, her eyes holding his for a long, penetrating moment.

"Now," he said, the inexplicable dryness in his throat forcing him to clear it. "You will want to press the toes of one foot up against the footboard to help you hold fast against the initial pull of the horses while leaving the other foot flat against the floor."

She adjusted her seat, her leg rubbing even closer against his.

He held back a groan. He couldn't take much more of this.

"And now?" She sounded almost breathless as she stared up at him, as if anticipating something different from what she was asking for.

"And now, I have grown a beard." Bradbury startled them both by standing from his seat and jumping off the phaeton. "If ever you decide to do some actual driving, circle back around to collect me. I think I saw Lord Darby; he owes me money."

Henry stared at his friend's retreating form, unblinking. So much for sticking to his promise to never leave him alone with Arabella. Henry was in so much trouble.

"Does everyone owe him money?" Arabella asked.

Henry turned back to her. "Only those who are foolish enough to wager against him," he replied. Their legs were still pressed together on the tiny bench. Why were benches made so small?

Arabella laughed. "I wagered against him."

"You are a rare exception," Henry replied, believing those words to be true in more ways than one. There was no one like Arabella in the entire world, he was sure of it.

Her smile was broad—and perhaps a little smug.

Henry shook his head with an uncontrollable grin as he released the break. Task at hand. "Now, brace your feet and then gently flick the reins."

She adjusted her position on the seat, driving him once again to distraction with all the touching, and then flicked the reins.

The horses jumped, jerking the conveyance forward and nearly pulling a yelping Arabella with them.

Henry reached out, grabbing her hips and pulling her back into the seat.

"Flick with your wrists, not your arms," Henry instructed, keeping one arm firmly wrapped around her. He wanted to make certain she stayed in the seat—not because he was enjoying the feel of her next to him. With his other hand, he helped adjust the pressure of the reins in her hands until the horses fell into a smooth, steady gait down the gravel path.

"Well, that was certainly thrilling. I see why you wanted me to brace my feet." Arabella sheepishly laughed, her eyes dipping down to his arm that was still wrapped around her waist.

He should remove it. Luckily for him, they were coming upon a rounded turn.

"Pull—slightly—on one of the reins." He helped guide her hand until they safely turned the bend.

Another conveyance was coming toward them, forcing Henry to remove his arm.

Arabella smiled at him, the warmth in her eyes making him feel as if she regretted the removal of his touch as well. His heart should not be warmed by that fact.

They fell into a somewhat comfortable silence. He didn't feel awkward, but he kept trying to think of something to say. She was a quick learner, and the lane was easy to navigate, making it unnecessary for him to offer her any more instruction.

"This might seem completely forward of me," Arabella started, glancing toward him before returning her attention to the horses as they passed the other conveyance. "But I had hoped to ask you this the last time we were together, and if I do not ask it now, I am afraid we shall be interrupted again."

Henry nodded hesitantly, not knowing what to expect.

"Did you visit your sister?"

Henry's back stiffened, and he looked away on impulse.

The conveyance jerked to a stop. He felt the reassuring touch of Arabella's hand on his back, and his heart quickened in response.

"I do not ask to pry," she said in a gentle tone.

"I know," Henry said, distracting himself with securing the brake.

What could he say? He'd already told her more than he'd ever told anyone else. But if they were ever going to be given a chance to pursue an attachment, she'd have to know the truth.

He turned to face her, her hand slipping from his back. He wished he could pull it back. "I did go and see her," he said, meeting her gaze.

"And?" Arabella prompted, her soft tone washing away the last of his resistance.

"And she was like a shell of herself. She had been given a drug by a doctor. There had been an incident, though I am not entirely certain what to believe happened." He paused and gripped his hands together in front of him. "Whatever Dr. Stafford expected me to find, I am trying hard to believe that it could not have been that."

Arabella placed a hand on top of his. "I am certain it was not." Her voice was gentle and soothing, her eyes imploring him to continue to hope. "You must try again. For her sake as well as yours." Tears filled the corners of her eyes. "Family is all we have."

He slowly nodded. She was no doubt feeling the immense loss of her father. But he had grown up in a family much different from her own.

Turning one of his palms upward, he twined his fingers with hers. And in that moment, he felt as if he was holding on to everything he had.

TWENTY

"I don't know why I let you talk me into this," Hattie said, wincing into Arabella's bedchamber mirror for what had to be the hundredth time that morning.

"I am beginning to wonder the same thing," Arabella replied, struggling to shove one of her pearl hairpins into the horribly plaited chignon that sat lopsided on the back of Hattie's head.

Arabella had awoken before dawn, her mind and body restless after yesterday's ride in Hyde Park. Her chest infused with warmth at the memory of Lord Northcott's arms around her after he'd lunged for the reins.

How his chest had pressed hard against her back, allowing her to feel the pounding beat of his heart.

How his fingers had curled around hers while she held the reins, adjusting her fingers with a gentleness she was learning was very much him.

How he'd opened up to her about his sister, and how he'd comforted her when her thoughts went to her father.

"Ouch!" Hattie hissed, rubbing the back of her head.

A tiny pearl pin-turned-dagger was sticking slightly askew out of the back of Hattie's hair.

"I am so sorry. How have you never made my head into a pincushion?"

"Honestly, never thought it difficult before now," Hattie said, letting out another sharp hiss. Her hands shot up to her head, her fingers pressing around the area where Arabella had managed to finally shove the pin.

"Finished," Arabella said, taking a step back with a forced smile. It looked horrendous.

Hattie studied her hair in the mirror. "'Tis . . . lovely," she said after a moment. "What shape were you hopin' for?"

"A bird's nest," Arabella replied, saying the first thing that popped into her head. Though this one looked as if it'd fallen from a tree and blown through the countryside.

"Elegant," Hattie replied, forcing a smile.

They stared at one another in the mirror for an entire minute before their lips began to twitch.

"*Cuckoo, cuckoo, cuckoo,*" Arabella chirped, mocking herself using Shakespeare's words from *Love's Labours Lost.*

They burst into fits of laughter until Arabella had to wrap her arms around her sides while Hattie brushed away the tears beneath her eyes.

"I don't think ye should put this on your list of accomplishments," Hattie said.

"I could not agree with you more," Arabella replied, trying to catch her breath. "I should help you take it out."

"No!" Hattie jumped from the chair. "I'll do it. 'Tis fine. In fact, I should pin your hair up, then ye can go and break your fast."

"Do not worry about it," Arabella said. "I think I will leave it down for the morning." She ran her fingers through her long, dark locks, arranging it all to one side. "The sun is out. I think I will walk through the back garden."

Staying in London for so long while they waited for Emerson and Olivia to return was beginning to make her truly miss the openness of the countryside. There was nothing more freeing than the smell of earth, dew, and pine while the breeze whipped through your hair.

"Very well, miss," Hattie said as Arabella made her way out the door.

When she reached the bottom of the stairs, she paused.

Something heavy momentarily scraped across the floor, followed by several distinct grunts. Was her mother having the servants rearrange the furniture?

Following the sound, she passed the breakfast room, then turned down the side corridor at the back of the house. She found two men with their sleeves rolled up, hefting a large rectangular table turned on its side into the room next to her brother's study. Their grunts quickly changed into grumbles as they pivoted the table, trying to fit it through the doorway despite its curved, ornate legs that continually caught on the doorframe.

Studying the table, she noticed a hole had been cut out of each visible corner and net-like bags hung beneath them.

Billiards!

A rush of excitement filled her, and she followed the movers into the room. She needed to see for herself the green baize and padded wood rails before she'd truly believe it.

Emerson had often teased their mother that he'd someday purchase a billiards table for the house. Their mother had, in her motherly way, told him he'd be doing no such thing. Billiards tables were for gentlemen's clubs and not a home. Apparently, Emerson had finally followed through on his threat by having one delivered while he was conveniently more than a hundred miles away, and with enough time between the delivery and his return to give their mother's ire time to abate.

A familiar deep timbre sounded from somewhere inside the room, and Arabella stopped inside the doorway, her heart racing.

Her eyes scanned the space, looking for Lord Northcott; the billiards table could wait. She quickly counted three men in the room, one on either side of the billiards table, which they still carried on its side, while the third man was one of her footmen. He had his back to her as he bent down to grab the edge of the table closest to the floor.

As the men began flipping the large, rectangular table to stand on its feet, Arabella caught sight of two well-polished boots slowly being uncovered as the table was placed on its legs.

"That will do," Lord Northcott's deep tone once again filled the room, and, like the curtains in a play drawing open, the righting of the table revealed the man himself.

Her breath arrested in her lungs, her chest and throat suddenly tightening as she watched a rugged-looking Lord Northcott in a charcoal gray waistcoat and rolled-up white shirtsleeves help steady the substantial table and position it in the room.

The muscles exposed on his lower arms flexed and strained against the weight of the table, and his firm jaw clenched as his eyes remained solely focused on the task.

Romeo had said it best: *Did my heart love till now? Forswear it, sight! For I ne'er saw true beauty till this night.*

He was so strong. So handsome. And not above working alongside others, just like her father had been. That thought alone warmed her heart to near bursting.

The table securely placed, the other men began to hurry about, making final adjustments.

Lord Northcott took a step back and bent his neck from side to side before brushing his hands together. He released a deep exhale, looked forward, and froze.

Their eyes locked, and a rush of heat climbed up her neck and flooded her cheeks. His shoulders stiffened, and his eyes instantly looked anywhere else but at her.

Before she could say anything, he bolted to a chair at the back corner of the room.

With the skill of a valet, he whisked his discarded black jacket off the back of a chair and over his head, sliding one arm into the sleeve. But his rolled-up shirtsleeve caught in the tight fit of his jacket, and he began to flail his arm, trying to force it the rest of the way through.

Arabella's lips twitched, and she covered a giggle behind her fingers.

Struggling, he turned his back to her, his arm still flailing in his jacket-turned-flag. Taking pity on him, she went to him, passing the two men and her footman who were doing their best to look busy.

"Here," she said, coming around to face Lord Northcott and placing a staying hand on his shoulder.

He immediately stopped, and his eyes met hers with a scorching stare that heated the air around them. Slowly, his gaze moved to her hair that lay loose around her shoulders. He visibly swallowed, and his eyes snapped upward to meet hers again.

"May I?" she asked, her stomach giving an unexpected leap at the thought that he was fighting back the urge to touch her hair.

He nodded slowly, his eyes never leaving hers.

Sliding her hand from his shoulder to his forearm, she proceeded to pull his arm free from his jacket. His muscles twitched beneath her fingers, and his chest rose and fell with his quickened breaths.

When she freed his arm, she turned to place his jacket over the back of the chair. She took an extra moment to steady her own anxious breaths.

Turning around, she found him watching her as if he wasn't certain what to do next. She reached out with slightly shaky fingers and slid them beneath the warmed material of his shirt-sleeves, unrolling them until the cloth reached his wrist. They stood so close, she could smell the familiar, inviting scent of leather and warm spice upon his skin.

Finishing the first sleeve, she moved to do the other, but he finally moved and began unrolling the second sleeve himself. She collected his jacket and held it up for him to slip into.

He turned his back to her, though his eyes still watched her over his shoulder as he threaded his arms into his jacket. "Thank you," he said, his voice gruff.

She smiled, any and all words fleeing from her mind as he turned to face her.

"My apologies for—" he began but was cut off as one of the men approached.

"Will that be all, my lord?"

He quickly surveyed the room. "Yes, thank you."

The man nodded and pulled his cap from his back pocket, placing it to his chest. "Mr. Thurston thanks you and Mr. Latham for your business."

On those parting words, the two men exited the room, leaving only the footman, who appeared to be busying himself with something by the fireplace.

Lord Northcott cleared his throat. "My apologies for the earliness of the hour. I hope we did not disturb you." His eyes moved to her hair once again and jerked away.

"Not at all," Arabella replied, unable to stop another smile.

"Your brother asked me to see to the delivery." He was acting so stiff and so formal; she didn't like it.

"My brother takes advantage of you," she said.

He frowned in incomprehension.

"Because he is over a hundred miles away," she explained. "And because he knows my mother would disapprove of having a billiards table in her home."

His eyes briefly widened. "Forgive me, I was not aware."

"Do not worry," she teased. "She would never blame you. Any displeasure will be directed at Emerson, which could prove to be most entertaining—for us."

A smile ghosted his lips, and he shook his head. "I would prefer to be left out of all of it."

"I am afraid it is too late; *what's done is done.*"

"*Macbeth*," he replied, all stiffness melting away.

"The iron is ready, my lord," the footman called from the fireplace, flames flickering beside him.

"Excuse me." Lord Northcott moved to join the footman, and Arabella followed a few steps behind him.

The footman put on a large, thick black glove that Arabella imagined a blacksmith might use near his forge. He reached without hesitation into the flames and withdrew what appeared to be an iron brick, his gloved hand grasping a handle attached to the top.

"What is that?" Arabella asked, coming closer.

"It's an iron used to smooth the green wool baize of the table." Lord Northcott took a step back, giving plenty of room for the footman to walk to the billiards table.

Arabella watched as the footman carefully dragged the hot iron from one end of the green baize to the other. The noticeable bumps that had been near the center smoothed out until they were nonexistent. It was all so simple, and yet fascinating to watch. Who'd have thought one had to iron a billiards table?

"May I try?" Arabella asked, unable to resist.

"You wish to iron a billiards table?" Lord Northcott asked, amused.

"Why not?" she asked, shrugging. Her answer wasn't a good argument, but it was the truth. She didn't need to know how to iron a billiards table, but she wanted to try.

Another smile tugged at his lips. "If you wish."

TWENTY-ONE

"There is another glove on the mantel, my lord," the footman said.

Lord Northcott nodded and stepped away. But instead of bringing the single glove to Arabella, he slipped it over his own fingers and retrieved the iron from the footman. "If you would give your glove to Miss Latham," he directed the footman while holding the iron out in front of him.

The footman was quick to comply. "Will that be all, my lord?"

"Yes, and thank you for stepping in at the last minute to help."

The footman bowed and excused himself, leaving the door fully open behind him.

Putting on the oversized glove, Arabella found it difficult to bend her fingers against the material's stiffness. "What must I do?" she asked, feeling both excited and slightly nervous about holding something that'd been completely consumed by flames.

Holding the iron at a safe distance, Lord Northcott moved to stand behind her, pinning her between himself and the billiards table.

When he remained silent, Arabella looked at him over her shoulder. "Lord Northcott?"

His eyes were fixated on her hair that flowed down her back and over her shoulder. "You—" His voice caught, and he cleared his throat. "You should do something to pin up your hair." His eyes darted toward the hot iron in his hand. "It could . . ." His words trailed off, and he swallowed, tentatively meeting her eyes.

"I do not have any pins," she replied. "But here—" Arabella

removed the large glove and gathered her hair, draping it over the shoulder farthest from the iron. "Will this work?"

He nodded and took half a step closer, his eyes lingering on her hair. With his free hand, he moved a few strands she'd missed. The light brush of his fingertips left a trail of warmth across her neck.

Clearing his throat, Lord Northcott dropped his hand and moved the hot iron around to the front until it hovered over the table. She could feel the heat rising from it and leaned forward with him until it touched the green baize.

"The idea is to pull the iron across the baize with enough pressure to smooth out the creases but not burn the wool." He demonstrated the technique, his chest pressing up against her back the further he moved the iron toward the center.

Arabella's breath hitched at the feel of his warm breath and the sound of his voice so close to her ear. She was fully engulfed in his arms. If only he'd kiss her.

"Would you like to try?" he whispered, his voice husky and deep.

Arabella felt a flash of heat all along her body, her heart racing. Had she said that last part out loud?

"Try what?" she asked, breathless.

He took an almost imperceptible step back. "The—" His voice caught, and he cleared his throat. "The iron." He held it out to her.

Feeling a little foolish, she reached out and awkwardly attempted to slip her oversized glove beneath his to hold on to the end of the handle.

He put his free hand on the small of her back as if to steady her and helped her adjust the positions of their hands until she had a firm grip on the iron. It was heavier than she anticipated, and she was shocked she couldn't feel the heat of it rising through her glove.

He guided her hand, and together they made a few passes over the table. The feel of his arms once again around her and his hand pressed over her own was calming. She let out a contented sigh, and then froze.

Please. Please. Please. Do not let him have heard that.

He cleared his throat.

Zounds! He had.

"Here," he said, letting go of the iron while taking a step back. "You try."

Internally berating herself, Arabella tightened her grip on the handle and acted as if nothing humiliating had escaped her lips. The weight of the iron was much more noticeable without his added strength, straining the muscles of her arm and wrist. The fear of dropping the iron and scorching the table was a good distraction.

Taking a fortifying breath, she lowered the iron to the table. Her hand shook, whether from the strain of the weight or because she was holding something that could very well burn the baize of her brother's new billiards table she couldn't tell. Perhaps she hadn't thought this through . . .

She had to do it, though, so Lord Northcott wouldn't suspect that she'd only suggested he teach her so he'd have to put his arms around her. She gently pressed the iron to the green baize. Instantly, it began hissing, and she jerked the iron away from the table while clamping her eyes shut.

"Did I burn it?" she asked, too nervous to even look. Emerson would never let her live it down if she had.

"No," Lord Northcott replied from behind her. "It barely touched the table."

Cracking one eye open, she looked at him, her wrist aching from holding up the iron for so long. "Did you not hear it hissssss?" She dragged out the word to further emphasize her cause for concern.

He stared down at her with a soft smile, and a chuckle rumbled deep within his chest. "It is going to hiss. Just keep moving the iron. You will be fine."

"It did not hiss the first time," she said adamantly.

"Yes. It did," he replied with the utmost confidence.

Very well, perhaps it could have, though it was his fault for distracting her so she didn't notice. But she couldn't tell him that.

Knowing she had no argument, she returned her attention to the iron in her hand. Her wrist was about to snap under the strain, but she could complete at least one pass over the table; her stubborn spirit demanded it.

Lowering the iron, she prepared herself for the hiss. The muscles in her shoulders tensed while she squinted. She felt the iron meet the table, and she pressed against the green baize. There was no sound.

A surge of triumph filled her, and she swung around to face Lord Northcott, who lunged out of the way as she lifted the iron high. "Ha! See, no hiss!"

"That is likely because the iron has gone cold." He reached for the iron with his gloved hand, taking it from her.

The screaming muscles in her weakening arm thanked him, while the triumphant fire in her chest burnt out. "Oh."

His dark eyes flickered with humor, and she noticed how his mouth pressed into a thin line as if he were trying to hide a teasing smile from her. She liked seeing this side of him. He seemed lighter, happier, and it made her happier knowing she could bring that spark out in him.

"*You mock me, sir,*" Arabella said, placing her hands on her hips while holding back a smile.

"*Hamlet,*" he quickly replied. "And not at all." Turning away from her, he returned the iron to the fireplace.

Unsure of what would happen now, but knowing she wasn't ready to abandon this moment with him, Arabella moved to the sideboard, where an array of objects had been laid out.

"What are these?" she asked, abandoning her oversized glove and running her fingers along an ornate rectangular box. Carved on top of the box was a canopy of trees with three elephants standing beneath them.

Opening the small gold latch, she found three polished balls lying in blue velvet. Two were white and one was red.

Lord Northcott came to stand next to her and picked up one of the white balls. "These are referred to as cue balls, while the red is the object or target."

Arabella picked up the other white ball, slightly surprised by its balanced weight. "What are they made from?" She tossed it up into the air and caught it again. It was too light to be marble or stone.

"Ivory." He turned the ball around in his hand and examined it. "There should be a small spot on one of the cue balls to differentiate them during the game."

Arabella searched her own, finding a dark blue dot near her thumb. "How is the game played?"

"Have you never played before?" He sounded surprised, though she probably deserved his disbelief considering that he knew how curious she could be.

"I have been able to watch a few games. My uncle—the earl—has a table, but none of my cousins have been willing to take the time to teach me."

"Will your mother approve? Given her dislike of the game?" he asked.

Arabella shrugged. "No, she will probably not approve. But as the table is already in the house, we might as well use it to its full advantage."

He nodded and returned his ball to the ornate box.

She nearly laughed with excitement. She couldn't wait to best some of her cousins when next they visited her uncle.

Returning her ball to the box, Arabella picked up one of the long smooth sticks, which she knew were used to hit the balls around the table, and held it up like a sword.

"Is this for dueling when someone cheats?" She lunged forward, pretending to slice the air in front of him.

He caught the end of the stick easily, stopping her from landing any "fatal" blows. "The *cue* is not used as a weapon, though the mace sounds as if it should be." He reached with his other hand for another stick that leaned against the sideboard. Instead of looking like the one she grabbed, the mace had a wide triangle piece at its tip.

"And why are there different sticks?"

"I will show you," Lord Northcott replied. He released his hold on her cue stick and grabbed one of the white balls and the red ball from the box.

Placing the red ball on one side of the table and the white on the other, Lord Northcott motioned for her to join him. She pretended to sheath her sword at her hip and marched to stand next to him.

He shook his head fondly at her, his deep, soft chuckle heating her insides. She liked hearing him laugh so much.

"There are many different rules to play the game," he began. "So, before a game can start, the players must agree upon them. For your first game, we shall say that cannons—which are points—will count as one when your cue ball hits your opponent's cue ball and the red ball in succession. Hazard points—which are harder to get—will be two points for sinking the opponent's cue ball in a pocket, and three points for pocketing the red. A foul—which occurs when you sink your own cue ball into a pocket—will result in a loss of two points."

Arabella's head was swimming with numbers and the actions associated with them. No wonder she couldn't puzzle out the rules while watching. She might have to ask him to write them down for her to study later.

"Perhaps we should start with simply hitting the balls," he said with an apologetic smile, no doubt reading the confusion in her face.

She nodded several times. "That would be greatly appreciated."

"Switch me weapons." He held out the mace to her. "The mace is generally used by beginners and ladies as it has a greater surface to strike the ball with."

"Very well," she said, trading him her cue stick. "But do not be surprised when I prove to be a quick learner and ask for my sword back." She raised a challenging brow and quirked her lips, earning another chuckle from him.

Stepping up to the table, she tried to mimic on her own how her cousins had played. She gripped the thicker tail of the mace with her left hand, while her right hand slipped the skinnier tip with the flat triangular piece at the end between her pointer and middle finger. She leaned forward, resting her right hand on the baize, feeling awkward and strange.

"Almost," Lord Northcott said, coming up behind her.

Her nerves jumped with anticipation. It was the iron all over again.

He placed both hands at her waist, guiding her to straighten her posture. She thought she'd melt on the spot, his hands warm at her sides.

"What does my posture have to do with hitting the ball?" she asked, grateful there was only a slight tremor in her tone, her heart racing.

"Much," he replied. He released his hold on her waist and removed her hand from the cue's tip. Enveloping her hand in his much larger one, he brought it to rest on the oak rail of the table.

Taking her other hand, he moved it to palm the butt of the stick, and then he helped her hold it at an angle until the flat triangular piece rested flush against the baize. The distracting pressure on her fingers made it difficult to pay attention to anything else.

Her cheeks flushed as she realized how big of an error she'd made.

After a much longer pause than necessary, he released his grip on her hand and cleared his throat. He took a step back. "Now, all you have to do is line up the mace with your cue ball in order to hit the red ball."

That seemed simple enough.

Squaring her shoulders, she stepped to the right, leaned her neck forward for a better line of sight, and pushed with a good heave until the triangle piece connected with the ivory ball.

The cue ball shot forward, echoing a loud *swack* upon impact. It missed the red ball completely, but it hit the rail with such force that it bounced upward, going over the edge of the table and crashing to the floor.

With a terrified gasp, she dropped the mace, picked up her skirts, and ran for the fallen ball on the other side of the table. "Did I break it? Oh, please do not say I broke it!" Falling to her knees, she picked up the ivory ball and frantically searched for a chip or a crack.

Lord Northcott lowered himself beside her. "I am certain there is no harm done. Lord Digby sent a ball through a window once, and it landed in a garden without a scratch."

Arabella recollected the very drunk Lord Digby from her adventure inside Brooks's. "He could see straight enough to hit a ball?" she asked, already feeling better about her mishap.

"He did not hit it with a stick." He smiled. "He was drunk and pitched forward, sprawling across one of the billiards tables. He, miraculously, hit one of the balls with a flailing hand, and his momentum was enough to send the ball over the edge of the table and through the nearby window."

A laugh exploded from her lips, her delight in the comical image causing her shoulders to shake. "Oh, Lord Digby."

"Come on." He stood, offering her his hand. "Let's have you try it a second time—just maybe not with so much force."

Arabella slipped her hand in his, and he held on longer than was necessary after she regained her feet.

She took her cue ball and placed it directly behind the red ball, thus eliminating the risk of hitting the ball too hard and having it shoot off the table again. Lining up the mace, she made a second attempt.

The cue ball bounced backward, and the red ball stopped near one of the side pockets.

"Nicely done," Lord Northcott said, a gentle smile on his lips. "How about trying to knock the red ball into the pocket?"

"All right," Arabella said, feeling more confident this time. She lined up the mace with the cue ball and tried again.

The cue ball nicked the side of the red ball—nowhere near the spot where she'd been aiming—and ricocheted off the rail near the pocket and rolled toward the back end of the table.

"Close," Lord Northcott said, coming up behind her and showing once more how to correct her posture.

"Will you take a turn?" she asked after another attempt.

He hesitated, then nodded, moving to retrieve the second cue stick. Lining up behind the white cue ball, he leaned forward. He held the cue how he'd taught her, though he looked much better doing it. The shoulders of his jacket bunched, and the seams of his sleeves strained against his muscles. She wondered why he didn't remove the garment. She wouldn't mind seeing him in his shirtsleeves once again.

Rocking the cue stick forward, he struck the ball with the tip. The white ball shot even faster than her first attempt had, but his appeared much more controlled as it hit the red ball at the edge, shooting it into the nearest corner pocket while the white ball spun in the exact place where it had collided with the red.

"You could easily beat my cousins," she said with a devilish grin. "Where did you learn to play?"

He straightened from the table, the light gone from his eyes. "My father."

She knew his father was dead, and she wondered if he still mourned him. She knew she would never be able to fully get over the loss of her own father.

"My apologies for bringing it up," she said. "Were you close?"

"Not at all," he said, shocking her with how cold and detached his tone sounded. "Forgive me; you did not need to hear that."

"No, it's all right," she said, moving to him and grabbing his arm so he wouldn't pull away from her. "I wish to know more about you. I—I care for you," she said, imploring him with her eyes not to push her away. "Please, Lord Northcott," she said after another long moment of silence.

There was so much to unearth about his family and their past. It had to be a heavy burden for him to bear alone.

His eyes studied her carefully. "Henry," he said quietly.

"What?" she asked, not understanding.

"You may call me Henry." He looked so nervous, waiting to hear what she'd do after he'd asked something so intimate of her.

"Henry," she repeated, his name rolling naturally off her tongue as if it had always belonged there. Feeling emboldened by this sudden gift of trust, she asked, "If I let you call me Arabella, will you tell me about your father, Henry?"

His eyes lit with emotion, but there was no warmth to it. There was pain, there was heartbreak, and there was fear. His whole expression tightened, and for a moment she thought he wouldn't agree.

"My father was a reckless gambler," he began, and the indifference in his tone cut her. She couldn't imagine feeling that way about her own father, and her heart broke for Henry.

Stepping away from her, Henry moved to the pocket where he'd sunk the red ball and pulled it out of the net, placing it back onto the table. He didn't look at her as he started to play, his dark eyes solely fixed on the game as the balls collided and the red ball sank into another pocket. "His game of choice was billiards, and, unfortunately, he forced me to play as well."

Regret instantly gripped her heart for asking him to teach her. "Forgive me; if I had known, I—"

He held up a hand and stopped her before she could finish. "Whatever you feel you need to apologize for, do not. He does not deserve another thought. His greed cost my mother, my sister, and me our home more times than I care to count. After the last time, all he could think to do was kill himself and leave us to fend for ourselves."

Arabella's heart shattered, and she rushed to his side. "Oh,

Henry." Tears burned her eyes as she watched him try to maintain an unaffected expression. Taking both of his hands in hers, she closed her eyes and pressed his fingers to her cheeks. "What can I do?"

She wanted to comfort him. Comfort the innocent child he'd obviously never had the chance to be.

"Kiss me."

His words were so soft, she'd thought she misheard.

"Kiss me," he whispered again, "so that I might know bliss."

She opened her eyes to find the deepest, darkest eyes watching her as if Henry were a drowning man and she was his only rescue.

She wanted to be that rescue. Dropping her hands from his, she nodded, and her breath hitched.

His hands gently cradled her face, slowly tilting her lips toward his. Her heart pounded in her ears, and her breath froze in her lungs at his reverent touch. She thought she might die if he waited much longer.

His head lowered toward hers, and he touched his forehead against her own. She could hear their ragged breaths mingling. Then he bent his head the rest of the way down and captured her mouth in a slow and devastatingly thorough kiss.

His lips were warm and soft as they slanted over hers. Using his thumbs, he nudged her chin upward, deepening the angle of the kiss. She pressed her hands to his chest, needing to maintain her balance. Her every nerve burned with the overwhelming sensation of bliss. His hands slipped into her hair, and her knees went weak as he began to run his fingers through the long strands.

She sighed or he moaned, and the kiss deepened once again. She didn't know if it was because of something she did or him. All she knew was that she didn't want it to end.

"Arabella?" Her mother's voice called out, and Henry pulled back mere moments before she stepped into the room. "What on earth is this?" she asked, her eyes fixed on the billiards table.

Henry turned to face the table, his back to Arabella's mother, while Arabella, still in a kiss-induced haze, struggled to think of anything to say.

"Arabella?" her mother asked with concern as she looked at her more closely.

Arabella placed a hand over her mouth, knowing her lips had to be red or swollen from her passionate kiss with Henry. "Emerson ordered a billiards table," she managed to say after another moment.

Her mother's brow raised, but, mercifully, she said nothing.

Lord Northcott finally turned to face them, his posture rigid. "Forgive me, Mrs. Latham. I arrived earlier. Emerson wrote, asking me to oversee the table's delivery."

"I see that," she replied, watching them carefully.

"Yes, well—if you will excuse me," Henry said and, without waiting for a response, left.

"Heavens," her mother said, watching his retreat. "I see you and I will have much to talk about at breakfast this morning." Her eyes darted to Arabella's lips and her wild, unbound hair.

Arabella's cheeks burned, and she found it difficult to look her mother in the eye. She wouldn't wish back what she and Henry had shared, but how to explain what had happened to her mother? And what would happen now between her and Henry?

TWENTY-TWO

Henry's head pounded, but not because of an overindulgence in drink. Unfortunately for him, he wasn't that sort of man. Though he'd be lying if he said he hadn't been tempted to start. He'd completely ignored his resolve to not take things further with Arabella and instead kissed her until he'd lost all sense. Then, like a coward, he'd left her to face her mother with the evidence of what they'd done written all over Arabella's swollen lips.

How easy it would've been for even a night to forget he'd run from the Lathams' home, but forgetting was only ever temporary. Eventually the truth had a way of clawing itself free.

And the truth of Henry's reality arrived in a letter sent to him by Mrs. Latham late that same evening. She'd put to him a very particular request. One that, if he refused, would've proven he had no conscience.

A request, which, at the moment, was eating him alive.

Scrubbing a hand down his face, Henry let out a groan as the carriage dipped and swayed beneath him.

"Are you going to vomit?" Bradbury asked from across the carriage, watching him with a worried look.

"No, I am not," Henry said. He needed to do better at controlling his emotions. He'd already made such a mess of things, and he couldn't afford for the situation to get any worse.

Says the man who's already given up two of his family's greatest secrets, the voice inside his head whispered.

Henry groaned again. Arabella was proving to be his undoing.

"Are you certain you're all right?" Bradbury asked, subtly sliding away until he was no longer seated directly across from Henry.

"Yes," Henry replied, pressing his lips together and turning to stare out the window.

Control. He needed to regain control.

They rode in silence for nearly a minute—which was longer than Henry had anticipated—before Bradbury spoke again.

"Remind me again why we are escorting Mama Latham and Miss Latham to Sadler's Wells Theatre?"

"Because Mrs. Latham has asked it of us," Henry stiffly replied, still in shock that her letter hadn't called him out for his actions toward her daughter but instead requested him to escort her and Arabella to the infamous aquatic theater. His refusal would've proven he was even more of a cad. She'd played him quite well, and he feared coming face-to-face with her.

"No," Bradbury said, shaking his head. "Mama Latham asked it of *you*. I never got a letter." He was watching Henry suspiciously.

Henry couldn't afford for him to discover the true reason.

"If you did not want to come, then why did you get into my carriage?" Henry asked, trying to ignore the fact that the throbbing inside his head was worsening.

"Because," Bradbury said with a grunt as they went over a rather jarring dip, "if one of us is going to do something utterly foolish—and to be quite frank, I am shocked that it is not me for once—then the other one of us has to come along to present some semblance of sense."

Henry shot him a brooding glare. But as always, Bradbury didn't look the least bit affected. They both knew Emerson wouldn't be happy to hear that Henry had taken his mother and sister into such a precarious situation, but he had no other choice. He needed to try to recover what was left of the situation.

"I will say it again," Bradbury said, staring at Henry more pointedly. "It is rather *unbelievable* that I have become the sensible one. But I guess that is what love does to a man. It robs him of all common sense. Let us hope Emerson will believe you when you tell him the *full* story."

Henry was not a praying man, but if he was, he'd pray it would never come to that. "I shall inform Emerson that you advised against the outing."

"Splendid." Bradbury smiled. His posture immediately relaxed into his seat.

Leaning his head back against his own seat, Henry closed his eyes. He was in a tortured mess. He'd taken advantage of Arabella by asking for that kiss, yet he couldn't regret the taste of her on his lips.

Why not blame your father? the voice whispered. *It was your story about him that prompted Miss Latham to allow you that kiss.*

Henry shook his head. He'd already spent too many years of his life blaming his father, and little good had ever come of it.

No, Henry would own up to his errors in judgment—something his father never did.

Nathaniel Henry Northcott had been nothing more than a discontented second son of a baron, who, instead of doing something of purpose with his life, preferred to gamble and drink.

The last memory Henry had of his father was the very one he'd let slip to Arabella. He'd been a boy of thirteen, walking toward the stables just before dawn. His father had—once again—not returned home after an evening of gambling, leaving Henry no choice but to go out in search of him before his mother awoke to find her husband missing.

His mother had always been prone to hysterics. Whenever anything upset her, she'd dissolve into shrieking fits, which affected the entire household. Henry would hide Sarah in one of the farthest rooms until their father or the doctor with his many tinctures managed to calm their mother down.

On that particular morning, Henry had been surprised to find his father's horse standing in the center of the stable, its saddle still on its back. Their groomsmen had left the previous month after not being paid for several weeks.

At first, Henry had thought perhaps he'd missed his father

somewhere inside the house, but as he guided the horse to its stall, he caught sight of a familiar pair of boots.

He found his father lying on his side in a pile of musty straw, unmoving. His eyes were open, staring blankly up at the roof slats that were in desperate need of repair. A shattered bottle lay beside him, the red upon the jagged edges of the glass matching the red staining his father's side, arm, and wrist.

His father was dead, leaving behind a widow and two children with nothing—not even the roof over their heads once his losses at the billiards and card tables had been called in.

The carriage rolled to a stop in front of the Lathams', pulling Henry from his dark memories. It was time to meet whatever fate awaited him.

"Daft weather," Bradbury said, squinting up into the sky, half-filled with clouds. "The rain cannot decide whether to go or stay."

"Let us hope it stays away," Henry replied. Driving to Clerkenwell just outside of London was precarious enough even without the rain.

Stepping up to the front door alongside Bradbury, Henry could feel his palms begin to sweat beneath his clenched fists. He didn't know what kind of reception to expect behind that door.

Smith, the butler, was swift in welcoming them with his usual greeting. "Good day, Lord Northcott, Mr. Bradbury."

"Good day, Smith," Bradbury said, his eyes scanning the empty entry hall. "Have the ladies changed their minds about our outing?" A hopeful smile spread across his face.

All Henry could do was swallow past a dry throat.

"No," Smith replied, and Bradbury's smile vanished. "They were just coming down when flowers for Miss Latham were delivered."

"Flowers?" Henry repeated before he could stop himself, a sharp pang of possessiveness shooting through him.

"Yes, pink roses," Smith replied. "Miss Latham wanted to

arrange them herself. I suspect the ladies will only be a moment longer."

Henry fought the urge to discover who'd sent Arabella the roses. He couldn't allow himself to lose control.

Arabella's laughter soon filled the corridor, followed by a smile so sweet and brilliant it warmed him from the inside out, and she wasn't even looking at him. She was talking to her mother and hadn't realized he and Bradbury were standing at the other end of the entry hall.

She was breathtaking in Pomona green—she could be the goddess of the apple orchard herself, whom the color was named after. The vibrant shade only enriched her dark hair, and his fingers itched to run through her tresses once again.

"Good day to you, ladies," Bradbury called out, catching them by surprise.

Arabella and her mother's conversation ceased, their eyes snapping toward him and Bradbury. Henry's heart missed a beat as Arabella's eyes met his. She looked—dare he believe it?—*happy* to see him. Shouldn't she angry with him for running away? Or could her smile be because of their intended destination?

"I did not know you were joining us on our outing, Mr. Bradbury," Mrs. Latham said, offering them a welcoming smile as she and Arabella came to stand before them.

Henry waited for her look of censure, an expression he'd seen in many forms from his aunt, but Mrs. Latham merely looked at him mildly. He didn't understand what was happening.

"I did not know anyone was coming," Arabella said, her eyes alight with curiosity. "Where are we going?"

Her question rendered Henry speechless. Indeed, he couldn't feel more off-balance if she'd cracked him over the head with a billiards mace.

She didn't know about the outing? His heart skipped a beat. Was she truly happy just to see him, then?

"I planned a little surprise outing for us this afternoon," Mrs. Latham replied. "And Lord Northcott is—"

Mr. Bradbury coughed.

"Excuse me, Lord Northcott *and* Mr. Bradbury are being gracious enough to escort us."

Arabella opened her mouth to speak, her entire being alight with excitement, but Mr. Bradbury cut her off with a raised finger.

"Actually, might I argue against such an outing? Emerson wouldn't approve of us going without his permission."

"Well, you see, Mr. Bradbury," Mrs. Latham said in a tone that brooked no argument, "when my son decided to have a billiards table installed inside *our* home without seeking *my* permission, I felt I, too, could make this decision without him."

"Billiards table?" Bradbury jerked his head toward Henry. "Emerson finally got a table?"

Henry swallowed, and he felt heat crawl up his neck as he nodded.

"Is someone going to tell me where we are going, or must I continue to wait *with bated breath*?" Arabella asked, staring right at Henry. She was practically bouncing on the balls of her feet in anticipation.

Bradbury groaned. "Was that Shakespeare?"

"*The Merchant of Venice*," Henry replied, a smile tugging at his lips as he watched Arabella's cheeks turn the most fetching shade of pink.

"Lord Northcott," Mrs. Latham said, delicately clearing her throat.

Fearful he was about to be reprimanded for his rakish behavior, he was stunned to find Mrs. Latham holding back a smile.

"Would you do the honors?" she said.

Arabella's unbridled enthusiasm was as bright as the sun. The spirit in which she chose to live her life, even after heartache and loss, called to him, making him want, for even just a moment, to forget everything and get lost in her light.

"We are going to Sadler's Wells Theatre," he said, one side of his mouth ticking upward.

Arabella squealed and jumped toward him, throwing her arms around him.

Henry wrapped his arms around her, just to steady them both.

Liar, the voice whispered.

Henry braved a glance at Mrs. Latham. Her eyes held a spark of genuine happiness as he—the man who had kissed her daughter and then fled—held Arabella in his arms. There was no judgment or accusation for his past transgression, only grace. He didn't know how to feel, but with the warm pressure building in his chest, and the lump forming in his throat on top of the burning sensation behind his eyes, he was beginning to see what happiness in life could be like.

TWENTY-THREE

Arabella could do very little to contain her excitement. Jumping into Henry's arms had perhaps stepped beyond propriety's bounds, but that had been the last thing on her mind. It was also the last thing on her mind as she dragged her mother down the front steps and into the carriage before anyone could say anything.

Seeing a performance at Sadler's Wells Theatre had been a dream of hers ever since her father had described a naval battle there with replicas of ships armed with cannons and fired by children dressed up as naval shipmen. Arabella had been captivated by his retelling and determined to one day witness the show beside her father.

"When you are older," he'd said over and over. Now she was older, but she would have to see it without him.

Against her will, a heavy lump formed in her throat. Her eager footsteps slowed. She didn't want to feel this way every time she thought about her father. It seemed cruel to his memory to always feel the loss instead of remembering the good.

Everyone can master a grief but he that has it. Shakespeare. *Much Ado About Nothing.* The words were becoming more poignant to her as time without her father continued to pass.

Unbidden, her eyes moved to Henry, who sat opposite her, apparently staring out the window. But after a few moments, she found him stealing a glance at her. She softly smiled, catching his gaze.

His eyes smiled back though the rest of him sat rigid, portraying his usual stoic countenance. But Arabella didn't see it that way anymore. Not after that searing kiss. Now, she knew he wore his control like a mask. A role he'd created over time and circumstance to protect himself from his past.

Only with that kiss, he'd let her in. And she had no intention of turning back.

"We have arrived," her mother whispered to her, startling Arabella from her thoughts.

Henry and Mr. Bradbury climbed out of the carriage. She was next to follow, but her feet remained unmoving on the carriage floor.

"Arabella?" her mother said, confused.

With her eyes fixed on the open door, Arabella spoke, "I cannot decide if it feels wrong to go in without him."

Her mother's arms wrapped around her shoulders, pulling her into an embrace. "Many things feel wrong without him," she whispered into Arabella's temple as she slowly rubbed her hand up and down Arabella's arm. "But he *wanted* you to experience this, and he would be overjoyed to know you did so with . . ." Her words trailed off, but her meaning was clear.

Somewhere outside the carriage door stood Henry. The man she was falling in love with.

"Lady Bixbee is not going to be happy you are matchmaking behind her back," Arabella said, grateful her mother had been so understanding after Arabella confessed about kissing Henry.

Her mother patted her leg. "You leave Lady Bixbee to me."

"Gladly."

"Now, shall we go in?"

Arabella nodded, her excitement returning.

"Good," her mother said with a slow smile. "Because I, for one, am looking forward to your brother's reaction when he discovers where we have been."

A burst of laughter escaped Arabella's lips.

She always assumed she'd received her spirit from her father, but now she was beginning to believe it could've come from her mother.

"Is everything all right in there?" Mr. Bradbury called out before sticking his head into the carriage. "Oh, good, you are both smiling," he said with relief. "Might I suggest you continue your little tête-à-tête inside the theater? The crowd is growing disorderly, and if you do not want Northcott to take them on single-handedly, then we had best get to our box where we shall be safe. Relatively speaking."

"I do not think that will be necessary, Mr. Bradbury," her mother said with slight exasperation.

"Tell that to him," Bradbury scoffed, pointing a thumb toward Henry, whose attention was fixed on the bustling crowd. "The man is about one scuffle away from going all Mother Goose and charging at anyone who gets close."

"Mother Goose?" Arabella asked as she gathered her skirts and reached for Mr. Bradbury's hand to assist her. "I thought you always teased him with 'Beasty'?"

"I did, but it no longer fits. Trust me; he's a goose." Bradbury winked.

Arabella shook her head and laughed. "I have no idea what that means."

"One day you will," he replied while helping her to step down. "Now, can you manage to stay out of trouble while I help your mother?"

Arabella shot him an annoyed glare before moving toward Henry.

"Quite a crush of people," she said, stopping at his side and placing a hand on his arm.

He startled, the muscles under her fingers drawing taut as his eyes snapped to hers.

Goodness, Mr. Bradbury hadn't been exaggerating. Henry was on edge.

Sadler's Wells Theatre was known for its more uncouth crowd due to its rural location and the fact that it only ran during the summer months when London's more fashionable occupants left for the country. But they'd come more prepared than most with two additional groomsmen, which was more than the single escort the theater provided for its higher-paying patrons.

"*The path is smooth that leadeth on to danger,*" she said to try to reassure him.

"*Venus and Adonis,*" Lord Northcott replied. "And that does not make me feel any easier."

Arabella recognized a few people she'd met during the Season, but they were far outnumbered in the shoulder-to-shoulder crowd of working-class people who bumped and pushed at each other as they moved toward the theater.

Henry placed his hand over hers. The pressure conveyed that he'd no intention of letting her out of his sight, but when she met his eyes, she thought she saw a flash of enjoyment.

"Shall we go in?" she asked, placing her other hand on his. She was enjoying the feel of his touch too.

He nodded and glanced over her shoulder just as her mother and Mr. Bradbury came to stand beside them.

The two groomsmen led the way, making space in the slow-moving crowd.

Her eyes, however, couldn't move fast enough as she took it all in. The river, which ran somewhat parallel to the theater, was her most pressing interest. She stretched up on the tips of her toes, leaning heavily on Henry's arm as she craned her neck to try to follow the river until it disappeared behind the theater.

"What are you doing?" Henry asked, his tone neither annoyed nor teasing. He kept up their steady pace, his eyes darting between her and navigating the crowd.

"I was trying to see the river," she replied, giving one last effort to stretch up on her toes before they reached the covered walkway that would take them through to the entrance.

"The river?" he asked, bemused.

Arabella laughed. "Well, not *only* the river. I was hoping to see a glimpse of the Archimedes screw. They say it takes twelve men working half a day but that it can pull water directly from the river and into the theater's stage. I was hoping to see how such a feat could be accomplished."

He smiled and shook his head. "You and your inquisitive mind." He was teasing her.

"You should not smile while you say that, or I shall begin to believe that is one of the many things you like about me."

He did not answer, but his heated gaze dipped toward her mouth, turning her cheeks into flames.

The moment, however, was cut short by another shoving match that erupted next to them.

Henry moved faster than she could blink, shielding her in his arms while also maneuvering them away.

There was much yelling, and she could feel the pressure of the crowd as it pushed into him. Arabella's heart picked up its pace, and she looked for her mother, who was being similarly protected by Mr. Bradbury. The two groomsmen worked even harder to clear enough room around them as they neared the front doors.

As soon as they stepped through the theater doors, Arabella was overwhelmed by the dampness in the air and a musty smell that was decidedly river water—a far better smell than the Thames—but still heavy enough upon her senses that she found it easier to breathe in short puffs through her mouth.

"Your lungs will soon become accustomed to the dampness," Henry leaned down to whisper.

Her heart warmed at how attuned he was to her.

"Thank you," she said, picking up her skirts as they followed a thinning crowd up a large staircase, while the majority of the patrons broke off to sit in the pit.

They, along with the wealthier patrons, stopped halfway up, and took their seats in the private boxes. The poorest souls continued upward toward the highest gallery seats. They would have to strain their eyes to see the stage.

Entering their box, Henry escorted Arabella to the row of chairs placed at the front. Her mother and Mr. Bradbury were close behind, while the two groomsmen remained as sentinels at the curtain-covered doorway.

Henry directed her and her mother to take the two middle seats while he took his seat to Arabella's right and Mr. Bradbury took the seat next to her mother.

Leaning forward to the edge of her seat, Arabella looked to the stage. She couldn't believe the size of the water tank; it covered almost the entire length and width of the stage. A wooden walkway ran along both sides and the front of the tank. It reminded her of a giant brewing vat, which sounded silly, considering people would eventually get inside it.

"What do you think?" her mother asked, gently guiding her back into her seat.

"I cannot quite believe it," Arabella said, unable to hold back her smile. "It is almost exactly as father had said. Look!" She pointed toward the very back of the stage. "There truly is a waterfall, just as he said. How can it be possible?"

"Many inquisitive minds," her mother replied with a smile and a wink before turning to talk to Mr. Bradbury.

Arabella felt Henry's eyes on her long before she turned to look at him. He did nothing more than stare, as if memorizing her and this moment for a cherished memory.

Soft music filled the circular theater, and Arabella's nerves jumped with anticipation as the crowd hushed and the music built into an attention-grabbing crescendo.

The play was introduced as a forbidden lovers' tale, and Arabella was completely transfixed. From the music that made her want to move with the performers to the acting that made her gasp and openly laugh, she couldn't look away.

When she finally glanced at Henry, guilt-ridden for ignoring him, she found him once again watching her as if he were content to do so for the final two acts.

"You are missing the performance," she whispered, leaning closer to tease him.

"I assure you, I am not," he whispered with a soft smile that had her entire body overheating with the force of her blush.

Checking that her mother was occupied with the perfor-mance, Arabella stealthily slid closer to Henry and playfully knocked his boot with her own.

He didn't react. She kicked him again. This time, he adjusted in his seat to lean closer to her and tapped her foot in response. His attention moved to the play, though she swore a corner of his lip twitched.

Arabella intended to retaliate but was stopped by the lovers running out onto the boards. Hand in hand, they were smiling and laughing as they approached a small rowboat tied at a small dock.

They got into the boat and pushed off. The hero broke out in song, naming the many wonderful things about loving a beautiful woman. The scene was so cheery, so tranquil, Arabella doubted it would last for long. Tragedy would strike soon.

As she predicted, a man sat up in the back of the boat. His face was painted white, and his lips and cheeks painted a bright red. He smiled with a sinister grin, bobbed his eyes to the crowd, and raised a quiet finger to his lips as the lovers stared into one another's eyes.

"That is 'the clown,'" Henry whispered.

"Joseph Grimaldi?" Arabella asked with a hushed reverence. The man was well-known for his comedic high jinks and perfor-mances at Covent Garden and Drury Lane.

Henry smiled and nodded, and they turned back to see what his mischievous character would do next.

A dark figure appeared from out of the shadows on the left side of the stage. Arabella recognized him as the suitor whom the hero had previously dumped into the water. He followed the lovers along the shoreline, ducking behind tree after tree. When he got close enough, he signaled to the clown, who nodded in return. Inch by inch, Grimaldi made his way toward the center of the boat where the hero rowed with his back to him.

"'E's behind you!" a man with a heavy Cockney accent yelled from somewhere in the pit. The rest of the crowd burst into laughter as the clown scowled at the interruption.

The hero and the heroine remained unaffected by the crowd's interaction, and soon the clown began his quest again.

Kneeling behind the hero, the clown waited until the heroine reached a high point in the song. Then he reached out, tucked his hands beneath the hero's arms, and flipped him out of the boat. There was a large splash, and the theater roared with laughter.

The heroine uttered an ear-splitting scream, horror written all over her face.

"I'll save ye!" another Cockney man yelled from the pit. He stood from his seat, threw off his worn brown jacket, and ran to the stage. He climbed onto the boards and dove into the tank.

The crowd erupted into a mixture of applause and laughter as the spectator-turned-actor popped out of the water in a soggy, sputtering fit. "As cold as pompous Prinny!" he yelled out, before he swam away from the woman and dragged himself over the rim of the stage.

Arabella's sides ached and tears fell from the corners of her eyes as she laughed. One would never witness such a sight at Covent Garden or Drury Lane. She could think of many overly proper ladies from the *ton* who would swoon at the mere idea.

"Here," Henry whispered, handing her his handkerchief. His breath was warm on her skin, and chills of anticipation pricked her cheeks at the sudden memory of his warm lips.

She dabbed her eyes with the cloth, but instead of handing it back, held it hostage in her hand.

He raised a brow to her.

"A token," she said with a mischievous smile. "To remember possibly the most memorable day yet."

"And my token?" he whispered, a teasing smile on his lips.

Arabella's heart stuttered, and she knew immediately what she would like to give him.

TWENTY-FOUR

Henry navigated his horse through the busy streets of Southwark just south of the Thames. The ride hadn't been overly long, but it was warm, with a heavy dampness in the air that added to the perspiration dripping down the back of his neck.

A letter from Dr. Stafford had arrived that morning, asking him to come to the new Bedlam, where Sarah had been transferred earlier in the week. At long last, the time had come to determine his and his sister's fate.

The moment the new hospital came into view, Henry waited for that impending feeling of dread. The fear had nearly choked him the last time he went to Guy's Hospital, but this time something was different. His heart still knocked an unsettling rhythm, but now he wasn't a man driven by just hope; he was also a man driven by love.

He loved Arabella.

He'd experienced glimpses of what a life with her would be like, and he wanted that life. He wanted the same happiness for his sister.

Directing his horse down the gravel drive toward the front iron gate of Bedlam, Henry slowed his pace. The same two haunting statues from the old Bedlam, one of a man writhing in chains and the other man lying in a relaxed state, had been placed on square pillars on either side of the gate.

Despite his resolve for hope, a chill skittered down his spine. Of all the wretched things to have survived that place . . .

Behind the iron gate and surrounding wall, the grand Portland stone building stood three stories high with windows running along the entire length. It was a far cry nicer, and much larger, than its predecessor, with roofs and walls that didn't look as if they might topple over in the next gale. He only hoped it was more than a pretense for how it looked on the inside.

Dismounting, Henry tossed a coin to the stableboy who'd run up to collect his horse. The lad snatched it out of the air and beamed when he saw it was more than a simple farthing.

Henry reached out and tousled the boy's unruly hair, freeing several bits of straw from the dark strands. "See that he gets fresh water." He nodded to his horse. "And there will be another coin in it for you when I return."

The boy's smile widened as he vigorously nodded. Taking the reins from Henry, he turned to leave with the horse but stopped short and stared at something behind Henry.

Looking over his shoulder, Henry followed the boy's gaze. A man on a horse had stopped in the center of the busy gravel drive, forcing others to go around him. He was staring at Henry and the boy, and then he briefly glanced at the building before he kicked his horse and rode away.

"Does that happen often?" Henry asked. Something about the way the man watched them unsettled him.

"Aye, seen it a few times. Some folks do love a gawk. But nobody ever sees nothin'. The only times I ever do is when they're walkin' in the front gardens." The boy pointed a bony finger over the solid wall Henry still needed to cross to get to the hospital.

"Gardens?" Henry asked, deciding to disregard the incident. He'd more pressing concerns than a random rider who was looking for something to see.

"Aye, airing grounds I thinks they calls 'em. Big, open lawn with lots of trees."

Henry was relieved to hear the new hospital governors and doctors were seeing to the patients' privacy and care. It was a far cry from the governors at old Bedlam, who sold tickets so spectators could tour the patients like animals in cages.

Thanking the boy, Henry climbed the few stone steps to the

iron gate and crossed into the courtyard that led to the front
doors of the new Bedlam.

Once inside, he was greeted by a nurse and, once again, admitted simply by giving his name. This time, however, there were
no doors or locks, but a single corridor that led to a private study
at the front of the hospital. The nurse asked him to wait there
while she went in search of the doctor.

Taking in the room, Henry determined rather quickly that
Dr. Stafford was nothing like his grandmother. The old matron
seemed to take enjoyment in overwhelming her guests with dec-
oration, while Dr. Stafford would underwhelm them. There was
only one painting on the wall, and a single shelf of books stood
on the opposite wall near a window. A desk and chair sat near the
center of the room, with two more chairs facing it. The window
brought in the majority of the light, and a single candle, almost
burned down to the nub, sat atop a stack of papers and old ledgers with cracked and stained leather bindings.

Knowing he wouldn't be able to sit in a chair and wait, Henry
moved to the window. He stared out into an expansive lawn en-
closed by a wall and rows of trees. It had to be one of the airing
grounds the boy had mentioned, though it was currently empty
of any patients. He wished he could've found Sarah out walking;
it would've helped free him of the memory of her being nothing
but a shell of herself.

He didn't know how long he stood there, but eventually he
heard the doorknob turn, and Dr. Stafford walked in.

"Forgive me; I was held up with a patient," Dr. Stafford said,
shutting the door behind him. "Shall we sit?"

"I would rather stand," Henry replied. He moved to the
chairs in front of the desk and gripped the back of one to try to
stop his hands from shaking.

Heaven for once help him, this visit needed to go better than
the last. He'd had a taste of what a future with Arabella would
be like, and he didn't want to lose it. He doubted he'd ever get
enough.

"As you wish," Dr. Stafford said, his eyes looking toward Henry's hand.

Henry silently cursed; the man was far too observant.

Or your control is slipping, the voice inside his head whispered.

Henry moved his hands behind his back. No matter what happened, he needed to remain in control.

Dr. Stafford moved to stand behind his desk and pulled out two old ledgers from beneath the stack of papers. "I imagine you want to get straight to the point?"

"How is my sister?" Henry asked.

"She is settling in," he replied. "The airing grounds have been good for her."

Henry nodded. "They are a good addition."

"Thank you," Dr. Stafford replied. "They are one of many things I am hoping to see changed."

"Many things?" Henry asked, curious.

Dr. Stafford didn't immediately reply. Instead, he studied Henry, as if contemplating whether to trust him with something.

"What I am about to tell you," he began, sliding the ledgers across the desk toward Henry, "can go no further than this room."

Henry nodded, not wanting to hold on to another secret, while also knowing he had no choice.

"When I told you I had been called away by the Crown, what do you think it was for?" he asked.

"To help treat the king," Henry replied.

Dr. Stafford slowly shook his head, his eyes watching Henry carefully. "I was not. I was reporting to the Home Office."

"The Home Office?" Henry repeated. As a member of Parliament, he'd had some briefings with the group whose purpose it was to keep law and order by investigating conspiracies or rebellions. But he'd never heard about any investigations involving Bedlam.

Dr. Stafford nodded.

"What are you investigating?" Henry asked.

"Corruption."

Henry shook his head, not understanding. The corruption had been stopped when Parliament removed the old governors and negotiated the building of the new Bedlam.

"You should see this," Dr. Stafford said, opening one of the two ledgers and pointing to a spot on one of the pages. "It's a record of patients admitted and discharged."

Henry walked closer to the desk and leaned over the stained and ink-spattered page. He saw his sister's name written in one of the rows, next to the date she was admitted. It matched the day his aunt told him his sister had been taken away. He hadn't even been given the chance to say goodbye.

Instead of a discharge date was the word "Incurable."

He swallowed against the lump in his throat, and he tried to remember Arabella's voice, telling him to have hope.

"I already know all this," Henry said.

"That is not what I am trying to show you." He slid the ledger closer to Henry. "Do you see this small symbol here?" He pointed to a spot after the word "Incurable" that Henry had mistaken as a splatter of ink.

Looking closer, Henry recognized the distinct outline of a spade, like the one found on a gaming card.

"What does it mean? Is it found anywhere else?" Henry asked, scanning the rest of the names for the symbol. There were none on that page, but after flipping through a few pages, he found two more. One of the surnames he recognized as a prominent family from the aristocracy, though the other he didn't.

"For some time now, I have suspected that members of British nobility have been paying corrupt governors and doctors to lock away their unwanted relatives." Dr. Stafford crossed his arms over his chest. "Regardless of whether they truly have an incurable condition."

Henry's gut clenched, and he shook his head while bile rose in his throat. The spade on a gaming card represented nobility. He grabbed the ledger and checked the two patients' discharge dates. Both read "Incurable."

If this was true, that would mean that his aunt—

He couldn't finish the thought.

No, she couldn't be capable of something so vile. She lived her entire life for her family.

Not your *family*, the voice whispered.

Henry was going to be sick.

"Do you have the ledger with my mother's information?" Henry asked, needing to see everything that had been kept from him for so long.

Dr. Stafford retrieved a much older and much more haggard ledger, opening to a premarked page. "This is the day you were told she was admitted?"

Henry checked the date and nodded. He was haunted by that date just as much as he was haunted by the day of his father's death and the day his uncle was murdered.

Scanning the surnames, he ran his finger all the way to the bottom of the page, but "Northcott" wasn't on the list. He looked to Dr. Stafford, his stomach twisting into another unsettling knot. What was going on?

There was no mistaking his mother was mad. He'd been inside the house the night she'd murdered his uncle. He'd heard his mother's sickening laughter and his aunt's screams. His mother had to be inside that book.

"Your mother was French?" Dr. Stafford asked.

Henry nodded.

"Do you know her parents' surname?"

It took Henry a moment to remember; he hadn't heard it since he was a boy. "Dubois," he finally answered. He checked the surnames again and found it low on the page.

"V. Dubois," Henry whispered aloud. *Vivian Dubois.*

His aunt must've stripped the Northcott name from his mother. He checked the date of her death, and it matched what his aunt had told him. He'd been sixteen and had struggled with the shame that he shouldn't—and didn't—cry for his dead mother.

"How would my sister come to have the spade?" Henry asked. If his aunt had the ability to make arrangements for his mother, she must've been able to arrange Sarah's diagnosis. Though why his aunt would want to be rid of Sarah, he didn't know.

"I suspect your aunt met the right people in order to both avoid a public trial and have your mother committed."

Henry wished he could deny his aunt's involvement in such a scheme, but recent events had opened his eyes to her manipulative ways. But why would she lock Sarah away?

"Was my sister truly mad when she was admitted?" Henry asked.

"I cannot answer that. I did not come to know her until years later," Dr. Stafford replied. "But what I can say is that I believe your sister was not left unaffected from what happened during her childhood."

"What do you mean?" Henry asked, his shoulders tense. He needed to understand for his sister and himself. Could this be the answer he was looking for? Could he be cured of the voice inside his head?

"I mean that, much like our soldiers who are coming home affected by the war, your sister—and even yourself—did not leave childhood unscathed."

"My childhood was nothing like a war," Henry replied, not understanding. His father's gambling and his mother's hysterics couldn't be compared to the atrocities of war.

"No, not exactly. But you both experienced sudden and sometimes violent changes to your lives, as well as a lot of deaths, one of them quite horrific. I have treated patients afflicted from less traumatic situations."

Henry took a shaky breath, and the tension in his shoulders clawed its way up his neck. He should tell Dr. Stafford about the voice. The very thought twisted into a sickening knot inside his stomach. If the doctor believed there was hope for Sarah, there had to be hope for him. But could he trust him?

"I need to see my sister," Henry said. If he could actually see the hope Dr. Stafford had in Sarah, then Henry could trust him.

"Of course," Dr. Stafford said, but he didn't move to the door. "There is one more thing I must tell you about your mother."

"What is it?" Henry asked, his head beginning to hurt.

"There is no other proof of her ever having been inside the old Bedlam. I never found a doctor's note or a nurse's log. Nothing. All I have is the record of the day she was committed and the day of her death."

"Could the records have been lost due to the dilapidated condition of the old hospital?" The knot in Henry's stomach grew.

"It is possible," Dr. Stafford replied. "But I find that highly suspicious. Your sister was only admitted six months later, and I was able to find information on her." He paused and took a deep breath. "If you want my opinion, it is as if someone wanted your mother completely scrubbed from existence."

Henry's mind flashed to his family's portrait that had been taken down and then to how his aunt had been fighting for him to leave the past alone.

She was trying to hide all of this. But there had to be more.

"I will send for your sister," Dr. Stafford said, snapping Henry from his thoughts.

Henry nodded, his temples pounding from the mess of it all.

Dr. Stafford stepped from the room, though Henry could hear him speaking about Sarah to a nurse just outside the door. Henry finally took a seat, propping his elbows on his knees and leaning forward until his head rested in his hands. What he wouldn't give to hear Arabella's soothing voice, to feel her comforting touch.

He heard the door open, and Dr. Stafford stepped back into the room. Henry slowly sat up, his legs unsteady.

"I know this is jarring," the doctor said with a gentle tone that Henry found almost grating. The last thing he wanted was pity. "But—"

His words were cut off by the shrieking voice that had been

torturing Henry inside his home for the past week. His aunt had somehow found him.

One might think she had someone following you, the voice whispered.

The rider from earlier. Of course. He cursed himself for continuing to underestimate his aunt.

"Is he in here? Henry?" his aunt's voice demanded, her footsteps hurried and clacking against the polished marble floor.

The door to Dr. Stafford's study burst open, and his aunt stormed inside. "I demand you stop this at once," she said, pointing a finger at Henry. Her entire body shook with her rage, and her eyes burned like the devil's flame.

"Or what?" Henry snapped. His nerves hummed to the point that his hands were visibly shaking, and he had to work for every heaving breath. He was losing control.

"Lady Northcott, if you would give us a moment," Dr. Stafford said, holding his hands up and slowly moving between them. His tone was calm, but there was alarm in the doctor's eyes.

Henry clenched his fists, his short nails stabbing into his palms as he tried to regain control.

"No," his aunt snapped. "I will not leave. Not until—"

Her words were cut off as Sarah rushed through the door, her eyes quickly taking in the occupants of the room.

"What is going on?" Nurse Maggie asked in alarm as she followed after Sarah.

"You!" his aunt screeched with hatred.

Sarah let out a vicious scream of her own, and they lunged for one another, landing in a heap of flailing skirts and arms, yelling and scratching.

Henry moved to separate them, but Dr. Stafford and Nurse Maggie were faster and pulled Sarah off his aunt.

Henry knelt by his aunt. She lay on her back on the floor, her hair almost completely ripped free of its pins. Three distinct red marks ran down one of her cheeks.

She clutched his arm, terrified. "Do you see what I tried to protect this family from?" she ground out through gritted teeth. "Now do you see?"

Henry was completely numb. His sister had just attacked his aunt. That wasn't the hope he'd been looking for. None of this was.

"Take me home," his aunt demanded, her eyes glaring.

Henry glanced over his shoulder and found Dr. Stafford with his arms wrapped protectively around Sarah, who was shaking and crying. Nurse Maggie was at her side, running her hands through her hair, whispering something into her ear.

"Take your aunt home," Dr. Stafford said, though Henry wanted to go to his sister.

But the doctor was right. He needed to deal with his aunt first, and then he'd decide what was to be done about his and Sarah's futures.

TWENTY-FIVE

Riding his horse alongside his aunt's carriage, Henry used the journey home to try to sort out all that had happened. A thousand questions about his sister, his mother, and his aunt twisted and knotted together until he no longer knew where one conscious thought ended and another began.

And what about Arabella? the voice inside his head whispered.

Henry's gut clenched, and he felt an unmistakable ache inside his chest.

In that moment, he wanted nothing more than to steer his horse away and not stop until he was in front of her home. He'd pull Arabella into his arms and hold her against his chest until the ache dissipated. Until all that mattered was how he felt about her and how she felt about him.

But that was never how his fate worked. And even though he'd allowed himself to hope, his hope was beginning to wane.

When they arrived home, his aunt stepped from her carriage just as he dismounted his horse. She stared at him with wounded eyes, her lace handkerchief pressed against the scratches on her cheek.

"We need to talk," he said, but she turned away and walked toward the front door.

She paused at the top of the steps and glared down at him as if he had been the one to maim her, then entered the house.

He felt the sting of her disappointment, but it no longer gutted him as it once had. He'd been a dutiful nephew to her, acquiescing to practically every wish. He hadn't forced her to move out of his house and into the home his uncle left for her. She still slept in the same set of rooms she had when his uncle was alive while

Henry remained in the same room from his boyhood. He'd never asked for anything, and he was done with the guilt.

Giving his aunt time to right her appearance in her rooms, Henry paced inside the entrance hall. But when she didn't come down after ten minutes, he took the stairs two at a time, his nerves on edge.

As he drew outside his aunt's sitting room door, which was connected to her bedchamber, Henry could make out her voice directing her maid to hurry.

"It does not matter," she barked. "Throw them in."

Not bothering to knock, he opened the door, not trusting the agitation in her tone.

His aunt sat in a high wingback chair in front of the fireplace, her hair still a tangled mess, her maid frantically trying to stoke a fire.

The hairs on the back of Henry's neck stood on end. It was too hot outside for a fire. "What are you doing?"

His aunt's eyes snapped to him in shock, while her maid startled and dropped the hot poker before scrambling for something on the floor and tossing it into the fire.

The maid lunged again at what Henry now recognized as a stack of letters tied together with a black ribbon.

"Stop!" he ordered, charging across the room before she could also toss them into the flames.

The maid's complexion drained of all color, and she dropped the letters onto the floor.

Henry snatched them up, gripping them tight in his hand.

"Give those back," his aunt ordered, pushing herself out of her chair and reaching for them.

Henry stepped out of her reach. "What are these?" He waved the stack of letters, his anger rising.

"My personal correspondence," his aunt snapped, her nose high in the air.

He believed her, but he didn't trust her enough to return them to her.

Turning his back to her, he walked to the other side of the room and ripped open one of the letters.

"I demand you stop!" his aunt yelled.

He could hear her swift footsteps as she moved toward him, but he didn't care.

The letter was yellowed and faded, the paper smudged with soot. He turned it over in his hands, noting that nothing was written on the outside nor was there any sign of a wax seal. He unfolded the paper, and it opened without any stiffness. The letter had been read often.

His aunt pulled hard on his arm, and he nearly dropped the letter. Her physical assault was nothing compared to the distrust coursing through him.

She doesn't want you to see something, the voice whispered, echoing Henry's thoughts.

The letter was indeed addressed to his aunt. His eyes jumped down to the bottom, and what he saw there knocked the air from his lungs.

The letter was from his mother. His eyes jerked back to the top to see if there was a date, but there was none. Nothing was conventional about the letter. The large stroke of his mother's pen and the many inkblots splattered and smeared spoke of her rage as she wrote.

> *You will pay for this! My son is the baron now, and he will get me out. When he does, I shall see you—*

Henry stopped reading, not wanting to know what she said next. It was clear to him that his mother wasn't in her right mind.

But why does Auntie have the letter? the voice whispered.

His aunt's fists beat against his back, her demands to see her letters returned to her more adamant.

Holding her away with one arm, he reached again for the stack and opened the next letter which was just as yellowed and worn as the letter from his mother had been.

There was a date to this letter, and the writing was as pristine as what Henry would expect from any gentle-born lady. His mother's name stared up at him from the top of the page, while his aunt's signature glared up at him from the bottom.

There was only one, small sentence written on the entire page.

I have won.

"What is all this?" Henry whirled around, startling his aunt, who stumbled a few steps back. "What did you win?"

She met his questions with a long, chilling silence followed by the most bitter and cold laugh. "You want to know what this is?" She smiled like a wolf. "This is twenty-three years of watching your trollop of a mother get—and take—*everything* she ever wanted."

"I do not understand," Henry said. His childhood had been barely a step above poverty because of his father's gambling. And that was before his parents' marriage had gone from utter infatuation to all-out hatred. What about his mother's life had his aunt—the wife of a baron—coveted?

"Of course you do not understand," she scoffed. "Because you have never been told."

"Told what?" he gritted out, growing tired of being kept in the dark.

"Your parents were never a love match," she began. "Your parents *had* to marry because she was already with child. With *you.*" She pointed an accusatory finger at him.

Henry's stomach dropped. Her words contradicted everything he'd ever been told.

"Your mother," his aunt continued, her eyes flashing with pure hatred, "managed to seduce your dim-witted father into marrying her instead of doing what his family said and sending her away." She shook her head, disgusted. "She became like a weevil to the stock of this family. Finding her way in, corrupting everything, until there was nothing left untouched.

"Every time your father's gambling left them destitute, she would find a way inside my home, preying upon my husband's weaknesses until she gave him the one thing I never could." Her eyes darkened, and they flashed with such malice it turned the blood in Henry's veins to ice water. "A child."

"Where is this child?" Henry demanded. The only children ever inside this home had been him and his sister.

And then the answer hit him, knocking the air from his lungs.

Sarah wasn't his sister but his half sister.

"There was nothing ever wrong with Sarah. You had her committed to spite my mother," Henry seethed.

"Oh, there was much wrong with her. You saw it today. She was always violent toward me. No doubt from your mother's influence."

Bile rose in his throat. He wanted to refute his aunt's accusations, but after what happened today . . .

His head pounded, and he pressed his hands to his temples, wanting it all to stop.

He needed time to think—alone.

"You will leave this house," he said, dropping his hands from his head.

"I will not," she said in outrage. "This is my home. My husband—"

"Your husband," Henry snapped, his anger raging, "arranged for you to have a home after his death, and it is time you used it."

"You cannot banish me," she shrieked, her face turning a dark red. "I took you in. I made you who you are. You will be nothing but fodder for the gossipmongers without me and my husband's reputation to raise you up from the failings of your parents."

"Better that than to go on living an absolute lie with you," he said. "You will leave and never set foot inside this home again."

Not caring what she had to say, he left the room.

He'd thought his family's madness to be their most damning trait, but he could see now that it went much deeper than that.

His mother and aunt had poisoned everything with their jealousy and hate, leaving a path of destruction and pain in their wake.

The last flickering flame of hope he had for a brighter future with Arabella went out. He and Sarah would carry these scars for the rest of their lives. That had to be what drove Sarah into madness—to violence just like their mother before her end. He wouldn't risk the day when the same madness finally overtook him and he hurt Arabella.

TWENTY-SIX

Had Arabella seen Henry in the past five days since their enchanting outing to Sadler's Wells Theatre, she might've been content to simply watch the twenty or so goldfish swim about in Mrs. Twickum's fountain. The fish were a new addition and the reason for the current garden party, which, as fate would have it, was being held inside the protective glass walls of an orangery while the rain descended once again over London.

Admiral Twickum had built the haven as a gift to his wife in an attempt to make up for their time apart while he was at sea, and Arabella and her family had been invited there many times. Each visit was as pleasing as the last with the delightful smell of citrus in the air and the eye-catching array of flowers and ornately trimmed shrubberies. But for the first time, Arabella couldn't enjoy any of it.

She'd hoped to see Henry escorting his aunt amongst the other guests, but so far, they'd yet to arrive.

"I wonder what could be constantly pulling your attention away, Miss Latham?" Lady Bixbee asked, a warning of annoyance in her tone.

Arabella snapped her attention back to her small party, which consisted of her mother and Lady Bixbee. They stood near the rectangular fountain, though the water's calming ripples and the bright colors of the goldfish did nothing to ease Arabella's growing feeling that something wasn't right.

Her mother offered her a sympathetic smile. She knew of Arabella's concerns and was certain Henry would have a good reason for his absence. His aunt had also not attended the last charity meeting at Lady Bixbee's, which only unsettled Arabella further.

His aunt was clearly against Henry marrying, and Arabella feared she was meddling again.

"I was admiring the goldfish," Arabella replied, forcing a smile.

Lady Bixbee scoffed. "And I will be the next emperor of France," she said, eyeing Arabella through her quizzing glass. "What do you think?" she asked, though the question was not posed to Arabella.

Looking to her left, Arabella startled to find Dr. Stafford standing beside her. He looked tired. There were dark circles beneath his eyes, and the smile he usually wore was weak. Her mind immediately went to Henry. She knew the two men had been trying to meet to discuss Henry's sister. Had something happened?

"France would not deserve you, Grandmother," Dr. Stafford replied.

Lady Bixbee heartily chuckled. "There, you see?" she said to Arabella, pointing a finger at Dr. Stafford. "Unabashed flattery. Now that is a quality you want in a husband."

Arabella held back a groan. She didn't have time for Lady Bixbee's machinations. She needed to find a way to talk privately with Dr. Stafford.

"Dr. Stafford, have you been inside the Twickum's orangery before?" Arabella asked, a plan to extract them both already forming.

"This is my first time," he replied.

"Then you are in luck." She smiled, grabbing him by the forearm and tugging. "I have been here many times. I will show you around." He was kind enough to go along without any protest.

Lady Bixbee's laugh followed them. "The girl is just like me."

Arabella was no longer certain that was a good thing.

Directing them to a pair of lemon trees tucked farther away from the fountain but still visible to her mother for propriety's sake, Arabella released Dr. Stafford's arm and faced him. "Can you smell the citrus? I just love the smell of lemon," she said loud enough for a nearby couple to hear. The smell was so strong she could taste it on her tongue.

Dr. Stafford raised a brow.

"Forgive me," she said the moment the couple were out of earshot. "I know that was a silly question, but I did not want to draw any lingering ears."

Dr. Stafford nodded, and a soft, genuine, smile crested his lips. "I prefer lime, actually."

Arabella's lips twitched, relieved he was teasing her. "I hope you will forgive my forwardness once again, but I must ask. Is everything all right? You look tired." She flinched at her bluntness.

He shook his head and chuckled. "You continue to surprise me, Miss Latham." He met her eyes, and she knew he meant that as a compliment. Letting out a breath, he rubbed a hand across the back of his neck. "To be honest, I *am* tired. What I have been trying to bring about for months has quite possibly fallen from my reach."

"Are you speaking of Lord Northcott and his sister?" she asked, the pit in her stomach growing.

"You know about his sister?" Dr. Stafford asked, surprised.

Arabella nodded. "Lord Northcott has told me about his conversations with you and about his family." Again Dr. Stafford looked shocked. "Please, if you know something, tell me. I have not seen him in five days, and I am worried."

He briefly closed his eyes and let out a breath. "I have been trying to contact him as well, with no response."

"Why? What happened?" she asked, resisting the urge to cling to his arm. But she couldn't make a scene. She needed to know what happened.

"Miss Latham, I must ask—" His words were cut short by the sudden whispers that spread across the orangery.

Turning her head, Arabella's eyes crashed like waves upon the dark rocky shore that was Henry as he descended the steps. Gone was the man who'd teased and smiled with her at the theater;

instead, he was replaced by the ever-stoic visage of the Brooding Baron.

Her heart threatened to shatter, and without thinking or caring what others might say, she moved to be with him.

"Miss Latham." Dr. Stafford's hand stopped her. "Please, before you go, we have an opportunity here to help two people we care for."

"How?" Her eyes darted desperately toward Henry and back.

"My honor as a physician prevents me from telling you the specifics, but what I can say is that I have nothing but the hope to repair a family that has been broken."

Arabella's chest grew tight, and she fought back tears. If she had the chance to repair her family and bring her father back, she would do anything.

"What must I do?" she asked, taking a fortifying breath.

"Can you arrange for Lord Northcott and me to meet privately, here, before he can leave?"

She nodded. "I could bring him to you behind there," Arabella said, pointing through the row of orange trees, ferns, and palms to a wall of vines at the back of the room.

She knew the wall hid a door wherein the gardener could enter from the outside garden. The space was just big enough for a workbench, a stool, and some tools to be kept. It would be close quarters—especially with someone as broad as Henry—but in a room made of glass walls, it would have to do.

Dr. Stafford nodded.

Arabella took a shaky breath and quoted from *Henry VI, Part Two* to herself: *God shall be my hope, my stay, my guide, and lantern to my feet.*

TWENTY-SEVEN

If Henry hadn't been in such a miserable and dark mood, he would've been impressed by how effortlessly Arabella managed to break him away from Admiral Twickum, who'd cornered Henry upon his arrival. Henry had no interest in attending this party, nor did he care about the price of goldfish; he'd only come to speak with Arabella. To tell her in a public setting, where she wouldn't be able to argue with him, that nothing more could happen between them. If she fought his decision, he feared he would be powerless to resist. But he was doing this for her, and if she hated him for it, all the better. It would make it easier for her to forget him.

She'd told Admiral Twickum she was bringing him to her mother, which he was glad about. He wanted her to have the support of her mother when he left. But then she suddenly turned, weaving them through a grouping of citrus trees.

"Where are we going?" he asked, not wanting to be completely alone with her.

She glanced over her shoulder and offered him a nervous smile.

He didn't like the fact that Arabella Latham of all people was remaining silent, so he pulled against her grip.

"Please," she said, slipping her palm from the crook of his arm and taking his hand

Powerless at her touch, he allowed her to pull them deeper into the jungle of trees and ferns.

The farther they went, the more he wanted to thread his fingers with her own. But he couldn't. To do so would give her the impression that such intimacies could continue.

Or you could be selfish, the voice whispered.

Henry gritted his teeth. He wouldn't bring the darkness of his family down upon her.

Breaking out of the trees, she pulled him toward a wall of vines near the back of the orangery. An abrupt right at the wall of vines brought them to a smaller, hidden room. They would be completely and inappropriately alone. He *should* stop her before—

Dr. Stafford stepped forward.

Henry's body stiffened, and his shock turned to fury.

He'd purposely been avoiding the doctor. He was done with the man's false promises of hope. There was no hope. Sarah would stay at Bedlam, where Dr. Stafford would continue to give her the care and protection Henry couldn't provide once the madness finally overtook him.

"What is this?" Henry demanded in a harsh whisper, ripping his hand free of Arabella's and taking a step back.

"Henry, please. Let me explain," she said, stepping toward him with her hands held out. Her eyes were wide, making her look almost frightened.

His gut twisted at the thought of her being afraid of him, and he glared at Dr. Stafford. "You could not get to me, so you used her?" He clenched his jaw. "What did you tell her?"

"I told her nothing," Dr. Stafford replied, his calm but cautious demeanor made Henry feel more out of control. "I only wish to talk."

Henry scoffed. "Do you truly expect me to believe that?"

"He is telling the truth," Arabella said, moving to stand between them like a warrior standing before a beast. Jealousy that she was defending the doctor reared its ugly head. "He has told me nothing, even after I continued to ask. He only wants to speak to you. To help you."

"Help me?" Henry mocked with a disgusted shake of his head. He was already too far gone. "And what do you believe I need help with?" He glared down at Arabella, daring her to give him an answer.

"I do not know," she said. "I wish I did, so that *I* could help you. But I know enough about you to know something is not right. You look . . . Your eyes, they . . ." She trailed off, as if she were hesitant to speak her mind.

Arabella was never hesitant to say anything.

Make her say it, the voice whispered.

"I look like what?" he asked, letting the voice win.

She hesitated again, her eyes looking deeply into his. "Haunted," she finally said, proving to him why he needed to end this. He would not risk having his family or himself tarnish the beautiful light that was her spirit.

"Haunted is only touching the surface," Henry said, taking another step away from her before looking to the doctor. "Are you happy now?"

"None of us will be happy if you persist in acting like this," Dr. Stafford said, taking a few cautious steps closer to Arabella. His demeanor remained calm, but his actions proved that he thought Henry volatile enough to lash out, and Arabella was closest.

Here is your chance, the voice whispered. *To end all hope for the both of you.*

"Acting like what?" Henry said in a biting tone, ignoring both the sadness in Arabella's eyes and the feeling of his heart being ripped from his chest. It was time to finish what he'd come to do.

Dr. Stafford's jaw remained determinedly set, and he gave no answer. Instead, the doctor stepped protectively beside Arabella.

"Tell her," Henry ground out, his anger at everything that had ever happened to him in his life igniting like a keg of gunpowder that'd been carelessly left by an open flame. "Tell her what my sister did. Tell her how she attacked my aunt—"

"Your aunt attacked *her*," Dr. Stafford cut him off, his jaw clenched. "You do not know the history betwe—"

Henry bitterly laughed. "Oh, I know. I know exactly what

my aunt *and* my mother have done. It is a plague upon my and
my sister's lives, and there is no cure for such darkness and hatred.
My sister is better where she is. I failed her then, and I will only
fail her now."

"Henry, do not say that," Arabella cut in, tears glistening her
eyes.

The pity he saw there was all he needed to say the one thing
he'd never told anyone. He wanted no one's pity; this was what
he was.

"Before you or the doctor try to convince me otherwise, there
is one more thing you should know." Henry swallowed, and it
felt as if fire burned through his throat. "I hear a voice inside my
head."

But his admission didn't give Henry the response he wanted
from Dr. Stafford. Instead of being shocked, the man remained
watchful and calm. "I've seen this before from those who have
suffered trauma, as you have. I can help you," he said, his words
slow and careful.

Henry scoffed. "I am beyond help."

Dr. Stafford studied him, and Henry stared him down. The
doctor could disagree all he wanted, but that fact would never
change.

A gentle pressure touched Henry's chest, and his eyes jerked
down. Arabella stood directly in front of him, her eyes cautiously
watching his, her hand covering his pounding heart.

"Please." Her voice caught, but her eyes never wavered from
his. "Let him help you."

Henry shook his head. The woman had more fight in her
than a hundred men, but Henry knew when it was time to sur-
render.

He removed her hand from his chest and returned it to her
side. "What was happening between us can *never* be."

"Why not?" She reached for him again, and he took a step
back. But instead of looking hurt by his forced distance, she only
looked more determined.

"Do you not understand what my family is capable of?" he said, clenching his jaw. "My father killed himself. My mother *murdered* my uncle. And I have heard about and witnessed my sister's violent outbursts. *We* are not safe, and I will *not* risk anything happening to you," he ground out.

"And what about what I want?" Fire burned in her magnificent eyes, and she stubbornly raised her chin. "How I feel?"

He shook his head. "It does not matter."

"It does matter," she demanded. "I am in love with you."

Whatever remained of Henry's heart shattered into thousands of irreparable pieces. He cursed the heavens for putting him through this. She loved him, and he'd never get to have that bliss.

He hated himself even more for what he was about to say.

"You of all people should know, Miss Latham, that *love is blind.*"

Her eyes widened in shock at his cruel use of her beloved Shakespeare. For a moment, he thought he'd finally got through to her. She needed to go with Dr. Stafford, who still stood behind her.

"*The Merchant of Venice,*" she replied, straightening her shoulders. It was clear she was going to play her game to win. "And you should know that *the course of true love never did run smooth.*"

He glared and took a step closer to her. "*Loving goes by haps; some Cupid kills with arrows, some with traps.*"

"*A heart to love, and in that heart, courage to make's love known,*" she retorted, lifting her chin and taking two steps toward him.

He scowled down at her. They were close enough that either one of them could reach out and touch the other. "*Love is a familiar; love is a devil. There is no evil angel but love.*"

"*My bounty is as boundless as the sea. My love as deep. The more I give to thee, the more I have, for both are infinite,*" she shot back.

"*Love is a smoke made with the fume of sighs; being purged, a fire sparkling in lovers' eyes; being vexed, a sea nourished with lovers' tears. What is it else? A madness—*" He choked on the word, then closed the last distance between them, forcing her take a step back into the protective reach of Dr. Stafford if she wanted to meet his eyes.

His heart turned cold. The pain was so intense. It was time to end this.

"A madness most discreet, a choking gall, and a preserving sweet." He took a painful breath. "I want nothing to do with love."

His parting words cut like a knife in his chest, but he forced himself to turn and walk away. He was a beast. But at least she would be safe.

TWENTY-EIGHT

Wrapping her arms tightly around her middle, Arabella stared up into the portrait of her parents that hung above the fireplace inside her brother's study. The early morning was slightly chilled from yesterday's constant rain, and a small fire flickered in the hearth, but she could feel none of it. The way Henry had ended things between them the day before had cut her most deep. It was almost cruel how one could feel numb and yet ache unbearably all at the same time.

"I do not know what to do," she whispered to her father's image. Her chest grew tight, and tears threatened to fall as she struggled with the thought that she wouldn't be able to keep her last promise to him and marry for love.

What could be done? Henry had said and done everything in his power to push her away, and yet her heart wouldn't let him go. What he'd said—and how he'd said it—frightened her. She knew little about madness beyond what Dr. Stafford had told her. The rest was speculation and rumor, and that part of it frightened her.

The church claimed it was God's judgment upon the wicked. But now, faced with the king's own madness, could that be true when he was chosen by God to rule?

Henry was a good and honorable man who hadn't harmed a soul. She couldn't believe God would have cause to strike judgment upon him. It didn't make sense.

Her mother's voice outside the study door drew her attention.

"Will you have a tray of drinking chocolate brought up?" her mother said.

"Yes, ma'am," a footman replied.

Arabella took a steadying breath. She'd finally come out of

her room with the intent to speak with her mother. It was time to tell her what had happened. She needed her mother's wisdom. Her comfort. Her guidance. Anything to make the bleakness of the situation not feel so desolate.

After Henry walked away at the Twickums' party, her heart had buckled and threatened to take her to her knees. Dr. Stafford had graciously helped her to a nearby gardener's stool, then left to find her mother.

The gentle but worried look on her mother's face when she'd appeared told Arabella that she knew what sort of state she would find her daughter in. What Dr. Stafford told her mother Arabella didn't know, and her mother had yet to ask her anything.

The door to the study opened, and she heard her mother's graceful footsteps.

"Feeling any better?" her mother asked with a soothing tone. She stopped beside Arabella, her eyes glancing toward the portrait and then away.

"A little," Arabella lied, her voice faltering.

She wanted to be strong. She *needed* to be strong, or else she might as well give up.

"Will you tell me what happened?" her mother asked, guiding her toward the nearby wingback chairs.

Arabella took a deep breath and nodded, knowing where she must start. "I told Henry that I loved him." The pain from his rejection threatened to resurface, but she forced it back down.

Her mother's head snapped to fully look at Arabella. Her eyes wide, she pressed a hand to her chest. "In front of Dr. Stafford?"

Arabella internally groaned, only now realizing that she'd indeed confessed her love for one man while in front of another whose grandmother was quite determined to see them wed.

"I did."

"Merciful heavens," her mother said, taking a seat, her voice barely louder than a whisper.

"Indeed," Arabella said, dropping into her chair.

She'd need to apologize to Dr. Stafford—if she ever saw

him again. Though they'd agreed from the beginning not to feel rushed by Lady Bixbee's persistent machinations and hadn't discussed their feelings toward one another since, Arabella felt it was the right thing to do. She only prayed she hadn't hurt him. He was a good man, and he deserved happiness.

A maid entered the study, carrying a silver tray with a tall, silver pot and two white cups.

Arabella's mother instructed her to leave it on the small table between their chairs, and they were left alone once again.

Her mother poured both of them a cup and then took a sip, licking the chocolate from her lips. "What happened after you told Lord Northcott that you loved him?"

Arabella took a sip of her chocolate, determined to tell all without crumbling.

A level head, a level course, as her father would say.

Starting with her conversation with Dr. Stafford and his request, she explained how she'd, in way, deceived Henry by omission by bringing him to the waiting doctor.

Her mother looked at her with disappointment.

Arabella then recounted the painful details about how badly Henry had reacted and what he'd said about his family. She left out the part about the voice inside his head. That secret was Henry's and Henry's alone.

"So you see," Arabella managed through a tight throat, "I told Henry that I loved him, and he pushed me away." Her voice faltered as she fought the burning sensation behind her eyes. It was like feeling her heart break all over again. "He is hurting, and I know he thinks he is doing this to protect me, but I do not feel protected. I feel broken." She took a shaky breath. "What can I do?"

Her mother didn't have an immediate response. In fact, she'd barely looked surprised through most of what Arabella had said. Which led Arabella to suspect . . .

"Did you already know about Henry's family?" she asked.

Her mother returned her cup to the table and folded her hands in her lap before meeting Arabella's eyes. "I have always been aware of the rumors surrounding his uncle's death. But at the dinner party, his aunt informed me about the truths surrounding his parents' deaths."

"Why would she tell you this?" Arabella asked.

"I believe she saw the possibility of an attachment forming between you and her nephew. She said she wanted to . . ." Her mother's words trailed off, uncertainty lingering in her tone. "She wanted to warn me about what you would face should the *ton* ever discover the full truth about his family."

A surge of betrayal on Henry's behalf coursed through her. Why would his aunt warn away someone who cared for him? The night of the dinner party, she'd preached about duty to one's family, yet, clearly, she didn't care about *family* at all. She only cared about herself.

"And now, knowing more of Henry's family's past, do you wish for me to avoid such a connection?" Arabella asked. Her heart pounded in her chest. She feared not having her mother's support.

Her mother took hold of Arabella's hand. "I said this to your brother when he returned with Olivia all battered and bruised by her father, and I shall say it to you. I cannot fault you for whom your heart loves." She rubbed her thumb gently over Arabella's knuckles. "Do his family's past and present worry me? Of course they do. But I also feel that I have come to know Lord Northcott, and nothing he has ever done has given me a moment's hesitation about his goodness." She squeezed Arabella's hand. "But my sweet, spirited, stubborn girl, if he wants to spare you from his past, you cannot force him to change."

Arabella made to argue. Deep down, she knew he loved her. She didn't need to *change* his mind. She needed him to trust her. To trust that their love would see them through anything.

Her mother held up her hand. "I do not say this because I doubt his feelings for you. I am saying this because, for once in your life, you are going to have to use patience."

Her mother's advice was sound, but that didn't mean Arabella wanted to follow it.

"I know you want to jump in and fix this," her mother continued. "But what he needs from you is time. *He* needs to find his way through what life has dealt him, and when he does, he will find you there waiting for him."

"But he is alone," she argued, her chest growing tight with worry.

"He is not alone," her mother said, placing her hands on Arabella's cheeks, her eyes staring hard into hers. "He will have Mr. Bradbury, and when your brother returns in a few days, he shall have Emerson as well." She dropped her hands. "Give him time."

Arabella reluctantly nodded. Time was too fickle for her. What was endless to some was ripped short from others. But her mother was wise, and, besides, what other choice did she have?

Though patience be a tired mare, yet she will plod.

"I beg your pardon, ma'am," Smith said from the doorway. "Dr. Stafford is asking to see you and Miss Latham."

"What? He is here?" Arabella asked, jumping to her feet. "Yes, of course I will see him." She moved to collect him herself, but her mother caught her by the arm and stopped her.

"Bring him to the parlor, Smith," her mother said. Then to Arabella she said in a low, teasing tone, "What did we just discuss about patience?"

Arabella offered her mother an apologetic smile before following her to the parlor.

Dr. Stafford walked in and stiffly bowed, hesitating before meeting her eyes. "Forgive the early intrusion; I—I thought to see how Miss Latham was faring."

"I am a little better," Arabella said. She offered him a friendly smile, but he still looked uncomfortable. She worried her confession to Henry had hurt him. "I am relieved you called."

His wide eyes snapped to hers in shock. "You are?"

"I am," she replied.

"You are," Dr. Stafford repeated, glancing to her mother as if he expected her to protest his visit.

Arabella couldn't help but awkwardly laugh. He was acting so nervous it was making her nervous. "Yes, I am."

"You are," Dr. Stafford said slowly, as if he were finally coming around to believe it.

"I wonder, Dr. Stafford," her mother cut in, which was good, as they were getting nowhere, "if *I* might ask something of *you*?" Her choice of words hinted toward what he'd asked of Arabella the previous evening. The way she tilted her head and raised one rebuking brow told the rest.

Dr. Stafford was getting a mother's warning.

He nodded, a penitent look upon his somber face.

"I promised Arabella a walk in the back garden, but I just remembered something I need to write to Mr. Bradbury. Would you be so kind as to go in my stead? I always find the air so . . . restorative after it rains."

Arabella could have kissed her mother on the cheek. With one simple request, she'd orchestrated a means by which Arabella might find some relief from two of her greatest worries. Arabella would apologize to Dr. Stafford during their walk in the garden, while her mother would write to Mr. Bradbury to make certain Henry wasn't left alone.

"I would be happy to," Dr. Stafford said, looking to Arabella. "If Miss Latham would not be opposed to my company?"

"Of course not," Arabella replied.

Leaving her mother at a writing table near the window overlooking the back garden, Arabella led the way onto the terrace and down the steps to the same gravel path she and Dr. Stafford had taken before.

Waiting to speak until they reached the bench beneath the plum tree, Arabella took a seat, and gestured for Dr. Stafford to join her. But he hesitated.

"I must admit," he said, looking down at her, one hand on his hip while the other rubbed at the back of his neck, "I thought, after what happened yesterday, you would not want to see me ever again."

"Why would you think that?" she asked, patting the bench next to her, inviting him to sit down. "Truly, you did nothing as terrible as what I did."

He sat but looked at her as if she'd grown a second head. "You? No, I—"

She held up her hand. "Please, allow me to explain." His argument halted, though his confusion remained. She took a fortifying breath. "I wanted to apologize if—that is, if what I said to Henry about how I—" Heat ran up her neck and into her cheeks, and for a moment she had to look away. It was quite uncomfortable talking to a man about your feelings for another man. She wished she could say it in a way that didn't fully embarrass the both of them. "I need to apologize to you if what I said to Henry about my feelings for him . . . hurt you, in any way . . ."

They sat in silence for two solid heartbeats before realization flashed in his eyes. He shifted uncomfortably in his seat and cleared his throat. She struggled not to do the same.

"Yes, uh . . . allow me to assure you, Miss Latham, that no offense has been taken. Though I know my grandmother has been in earnest for a union between us, I have come to look upon you as a cherished friend."

Relief flooded through her, and before she could think better of it, she grabbed both his hands with hers. "Oh, thank goodness."

He chuckled. "Had it been any other time, my pride might not have survived seeing such relief on a woman's face when being freed from my affections."

Her entire body burned with the force of her embarrassment, and her hands flew to cover her cheeks. "I am so sorry—that did not come out right."

Dr. Stafford laughed and reached up to pull her hands down. "It is all right. In a way, I understand how you feel."

"What?" she gasped, an excited smile bursting across her lips. "Are you saying you are in love with someone else?"

He looked down into his lap and shook his head. "I would not call it love. It is . . . complicated."

"Because of Lady Bixbee?"

He let out a breath and leaned forward until his elbows rested upon his knees. "Unfortunately, my grandmother's displeasure is the least of my problems."

Arabella studied him, the look of forlorn hope evident in the dip of his head and shoulders. She hated feeling that way herself. "Is there anything I can do?" she asked, placing a supportive hand on his shoulder.

He turned to look up at her. "You have helped more than you know. I just seem doomed to failure."

She blinked, certain she must've misheard him. "I beg your pardon. I have helped you? How?"

He looked away and rubbed his forehead. "I guess I owe you an explanation, considering everything that has happened."

Arabella stared at him, even more confused.

Sitting up straighter, he turned until they could look one another in the eye. "Have you never wondered why I practically begged you to orchestrate my talk with Lord Northcott?"

"Because you treat his sister," Arabella replied, and then it hit her. "His sister! You care for his sister!"

He hesitated. "I care for her well-being . . . I can admit nothing more than that," he replied, looking almost ashamed of his feelings. "She should not be a patient at the hospital, but no matter how many ways I have tried, I cannot get her out."

"How many ways?" Arabella asked.

"I have tried everything from relentlessly contacting Lord Northcott to the Home Office."

"The Home Office?"

He nodded. "I should not tell you this, but I believe Lord Northcott's sister was part of a group of old Bedlam patients who were admitted under false pretenses."

An icy chill settled over Arabella's skin. "False pretenses?"

"Bribes."

Arabella felt as if she might be ill. "Does Lord Northcott know this?"

"He knows, and I hoped he would do something. But after what happened with his aunt, I cannot get him to face the situation."

But I could, the thought instantly flew through her mind. This was more than just about Henry; this was about saving what was left of his family.

But would Henry see her? He'd made it very clear that he wanted nothing more to do with her. She needed a way to make him come to her. To face this and not hide himself away. But how?

"Will you and your mother be attending my grandmother's card party this evening?" Dr. Stafford asked, no doubt trying to lighten their conversation.

"I–I am not certain," she said. "Though I know my mother has accepted the invitation."

"I hope that you do. A distraction would be good for the both of us." He offered her a half-hearted smile.

A distraction . . .

Instantly, a reckless plan began to formulate in her mind. One that was worthy of a Shakespearean play.

If Bedlam was what haunted Henry's family, then that is where she needed to go. She would show him that *she* wasn't afraid of his past and that she would risk everything for him and his sister to have a future.

All she needed was for her mother to be occupied at Lady Bixbee's party—and a bribe.

TWENTY-NINE

"We shouldn't be doin' this, miss," Hattie said from inside the darkened carriage outside the new Bedlam. Her voice was uneasy, her grip on Arabella's hands tense.

"Yes, well, many people throughout history have done things they probably should not have," Arabella managed to say with some degree of normalcy, though her heart pounded in her chest.

The sound of approaching voices outside silenced them. Arabella recognized Hattie's brother, Jim, the groomsman who'd taken her to Brooks's. He was talking to someone, though they were too far away to make out any words.

Hattie's hand remained firmly clenched in hers as they waited, and Arabella thanked the heavens for such a friend.

"You remember what to do with the letters?" Arabella whispered, needing to fill the silence.

"Yes, miss. My brother will get yer letter to Lord Northcott, and I'll give the second to yer mother."

"Good," she said. The guilt for the worry she was about to inflict on her mother—and on Hattie—sat like a boulder atop her chest. "And after, you are not, under any circumstance, allowed to let my mother dismiss you. I have explained my actions in the letter and how you and your brother are in no way responsible."

"Yes, miss." Hattie didn't sound confident in the plan, but Arabella chose to believe her mother would forgive Hattie and Jim for their part in it.

The male voices ceased, and a few moments later, the carriage door opened. Arabella and Hattie jumped.

"They'll take ye, miss," Jim whispered. "But he says the doc won't do it for less than fifty pounds."

Arabella swallowed. She'd foolishly hoped it wouldn't come to that amount. Fifty pounds was all she'd found inside Emerson's desk; she would have to thank Mr. Bradbury later for showing her where her brother kept the additional monies.

She handed the banknotes to Jim while Hattie started to needlessly fidget with Arabella's disguise. Arabella had thought it best to arrive in a dressing gown to give the impression that her family had suddenly decided to be rid of her and would pay to do so.

Hattie had used white powder to give Arabella's complexion a more ghostly finish and had rubbed soot around her eyes to make them look tired and sunken. Next was her brown traveling cloak; the hood would keep her face hidden until she got inside.

She just had to get inside and then find her way to where the patients were kept and then locate Henry's sister—whom she'd never met.

She quoted Shakespeare's *Merry Wives of Windsor* to herself—*Good luck lies in odd numbers*—and then took a deep breath. She'd take it one step at a time. It was the only option, other than panic.

"Be careful, miss," Hattie said, sniffling.

Arabella fought back her own tears and patted Hattie's hand, balled tightly in her lap. "I shall be back before you know it," she said, praying her words would be true.

What she was about to do was beyond reckless. If she were found out, more than just her reputation would be ruined. But she had to do this. Love was worth every risk.

Scooting to the carriage door, she took a deep breath and yelled out into the night, "No! No, I will not go!"

Hattie and Jim moved into action, pretending to struggle in removing her from the carriage.

"Come now, miss. 'Tis our stop," Hattie said in a coddling but forceful tone that was worthy of any stage.

Arabella continued to thrash about, grunting against their fake protestations. The plan was to make her wild nature convincing for any observer, but before she could step down from the carriage, the man from Bedlam shoved Jim out of the way, clamped two burly hands around Arabella's waist, and tore her free from the carriage.

She screamed against the rush of pain to her ribs, then again as her feet hit the ground. Fear clutched at her insides, and she briefly closed her eyes to block out what was happening.

"We'll take it from here," another man said, walking up to them. He grabbed her by the arm, and she cried out from his hard grip.

Out of instinct to survive, Arabella fought to be free herself, but their hold only intensified.

"Let go of her," Jim protested, moving toward them.

But Arabella couldn't allow him to take her back. She needed to get inside.

With all the strength she could muster, she threw her head back and her legs up into the air. "Let me go! Let me go!" she yelled, shaking her head, hoping to deter Jim from trying to rescue her. Her response caught one of the two men off guard, and he stumbled to collect his footing.

His reaction was harsh and quick. Grabbing the hood of her cloak, he twisted the material around his fist and shook her viciously. She heard the crack of her teeth as her mouth clattered open and shut.

"That's what we do with animals," he hissed in her ear.

Terror turned Arabella's insides to ice, and her heart threatened to burst out of her chest. If Hattie and Jim hadn't been watching, she would've crumpled to the ground. But she'd talked them into this. She had to leave them with the belief that they hadn't made a terrible mistake.

Tears stained Hattie's cheeks, and Jim looked as if he was a hair's breadth away from ignoring her orders and taking her home.

Arabella wanted to go home; this was turning out to be much more frightening than she imagined. But she had to do this for Henry and his sister.

She knew Henry loved her. He *would* come for her.

THIRTY

Walking into his study, Henry slammed the door behind him, and he didn't stop until he reached the sideboard. He pressed both hands on top of the wood until his fingertips turned white. An array of amber-colored liquids in intricate crystal decanters stared back at him, offering the seductive power of oblivion.

I'd pick the brandy, the voice whispered. *It matches the color of Arabella's eyes.*

With a wordless roar, Henry swept his arms across the sideboard and sent everything in his path crashing to the floor.

He sucked in heavy, deep breaths and dug his fingers into his hips to distract himself from the pain of wanting her. Needing her.

It had only been one day.

Stepping over the broken glass, Henry moved to the wall of portraits where every Baron Northcott hung. One by one, he pulled them down and dropped them to the floor, not caring if their frames broke or cracked. With his aunt and the last of her things—watchdog butler included—removed to the house his uncle had left her, Henry no longer had to live with their judgmental stares.

A rapid tapping filled the room.

Turning toward the window, he scowled at Bradbury, who was standing in the bushes outside his study.

Henry marched over and pulled the window open. "Go away." He slammed the window shut, but not before he heard Bradbury curse.

Bradbury pounded on the glass, but Henry ignored him and moved to his desk, which was out of sight of any windows. He didn't want to talk to anyone.

Miserable, Henry sat with his head in his hands.

The pounding soon stopped, replaced by the sound of shattering glass.

Henry's head jerked up. A large stone from the garden lay on the floor. Bradbury's arm came through the window next, wrapped in his jacket, knocking away the jagged shards of glass from the window frame.

"What the devil are you doing?" Henry yelled, storming to the window.

Bradbury stuck his head through the opening and glared up at him. "Breaking and entering." Unwrapping his jacket from his arm, he tossed it through the window, followed by his hat.

"Burglary is a hanging offense," Henry said, gritting his teeth.

"Lucky for me, I plan on taking nothing," Bradbury grunted as he climbed through the window.

Henry did nothing to help him.

Straightening, Bradbury brushed the dirt from his breeches and then scanned the room. "What the deuce happened here?"

"I'm redecorating," Henry said in a wry tone. "Now leave."

Bradbury frowned. "Not until you tell me why no one is even answering your door." Stepping over the shattered crystal decanters and pools of liquor, Bradbury marched to the study's door, opened it, and stuck his head into the corridor. "It's like a graveyard in here."

He wasn't far from the truth. Henry had sent every servant from his home to work at his aunt's, while the servants previously working there were coming to work for him. The only servants left were two groomsmen seeing to the horses.

Bradbury walked back toward Henry. "You know, when Mama Latham's note asked me to come and check on you, I thought perhaps you and your lady love had quarreled, but . . . looking around . . ." His eyes paused on the pile of frames and broken decanters. "*What* is going on, Goosey?"

Why couldn't he be left to his misery?

"Stop calling me that," Henry snapped, sharp and harsh because he could be nothing else. "Look around you; I am no mother goose—I am a beast!" His voice practically shook the house, and his shoulders heaved up and down with every ragged breath.

Instead of cowering, Bradbury studied him with a look far too searching for comfort.

Needing to shield himself, to create the same distance that'd seen him through his childhood and beyond, Henry folded his arms across his chest and rid his face of any expression.

"Did you ever wonder why I called you Beasty?" Bradbury asked.

Henry scoffed. "Because I am the Brooding Baron, the beast the *ton* cannot stop whispering about."

"No," Bradbury answered, shaking his head. "Because you were *acting* like what those gossips made you out to be."

His words hit Henry hard in the gut, and he wanted to deny them.

"I called you Beasty," Bradbury continued, "because I thought as your friend, you would feel comfortable enough to tell me to shut my mouth." A faint, teasing smile lifted one corner of his mouth. "And that you would believe you were not what they were making you out to be, but the *good* and loyal Mother Goose whom Emerson and I have come to know."

All the anger inside Henry melted away, leaving him almost spent. His arms hung limp at his sides, the fight gone out of him, as he stared at his friend. It was hard to believe Bradbury was capable of something so . . . thoughtful.

A lump quickly formed in Henry's throat, and he tried to clear it. "Bradbury, I—"

Bradbury held up a hand. "I am going to stop you right there, Goosey. Whatever you were about to say, I did not say what I did so you could get all—" He waved his hand about uncomfortably. "I said it because it needed to be said. That is all."

Henry stared at his friend, taken aback by this hidden side of him.

They fell into an uncomfortable silence.

"You broke my window," Henry eventually blurted.

"You shut the window in my face," Bradbury countered with a challenging brow.

Another uncomfortable silence followed.

"Are you going to tell me why you shut the window in my face?" Bradbury asked.

Henry opened his mouth, but his instinctive refusal died upon his lips. He was tired of holding it all in.

"Yes," he said, his voice hoarse.

Bradbury nodded, looking almost relieved. "Good. But let's go to another room. I am not a fan of your redecorating."

An unbidden chuckle rumbled deep in Henry's chest, and Bradbury did a poor job of suppressing his own laugh.

They moved to a sitting room near the front of the house, and Henry told Bradbury everything—about his parents, his uncle's death, his mother's admittance to Bedlam. About his sister's existence and how she was currently a patient in the new Bedlam. About what he'd recently discovered about his aunt, and about his painful conversation with Arabella and Dr. Stafford.

Saying it all out loud for the first time made everything more real, and his stomach twisted into a painful knot as he waited for Bradbury's reaction.

Bradbury blinked a few times. "Heaven help me, Goosey." He ran a hand through his hair, making the red strands look like a rooster's comb. "What does one even say to that?"

Henry shrugged, having no answer himself. He was only relieved Bradbury hadn't gone running from the room.

"Actually, I know one thing I want to say." Bradbury met Henry's eyes. "Do not let that old harpy win."

"Harpy?"

"Your aunt. You pushing Miss Latham away only gives your aunt what she wants—you miserable and alone."

"It's more complicated than that," Henry argued.

"Hang complicated. You only get one life. Why let the actions of others determine how you live it? Trust me, once you start living for yourself, you will be much happier. And who is to say that is not exactly what you need?"

Arabella was what he needed. He just wished he knew he could keep her safe.

A heavy knock sounded at the front door.

"Do you want to answer that?" Bradbury asked.

Henry shook his head, not wanting to deal with any visitors. Dr. Stafford, in particular, had been adamant that they talk, but Henry was still too angry about how he'd used Arabella to get to him.

The knocking soon changed to pounding.

"That sounds urgent. I think I had better go check," Bradbury said, jumping up and going for the door.

"You are getting far too comfortable in my house," Henry called out.

"You like having me here, Goosey," Bradbury yelled over his shoulder before disappearing into the corridor.

One day Henry probably should tell his friends that he did.

Bradbury soon returned, his footsteps swift. "A coachman from the Lathams," he said, holding out a letter to Henry. "He said you needed to read this."

Henry grabbed the letter from Bradbury, immediately recognizing Arabella's feminine handwriting.

His heart pounded.

Tearing open the seal, he read the letter, trying to ignore the growing pit in his stomach.

> *I know you said you would not risk me getting hurt, but I can make no such promise. I am willing to risk all, because I know you and your sister are worth saving. I have gone to Bedlam with the hope that you will choose to face this. Please do not bar yourself away. Choose to save me, your sister, and, most importantly, yourself.*

I kiss thee with a most constant heart.

The reality of what Arabella had done slammed against Henry's chest to the point he could barely breathe.

"Northcott, what is it?" Bradbury asked. "You are white as a ghost."

Henry shoved the letter into Bradbury's hands, an invisible vise tight around his throat.

Bradbury scanned the letter and let out a curse, handing it back to Henry. "What do we do?"

"I have to go after her," Henry replied, heading for the door.

"I'm coming," Bradbury said, following him.

Henry stopped and turned toward his friend. "No, the fewer people there, the less suspicion. We do not want to risk ruining her reputation if she is found out. You go to Mrs. Latham, tell her what has happened, and stay with her until I have returned with Arabella."

Bradbury hesitated for only a moment. "Right. Be careful."

Henry nodded and ran for his stables. If he was going to get Arabella out unseen, he was going to need his carriage and, more importantly, the help of Dr. Stafford.

THIRTY-ONE

Even before Henry's carriage stopped in front of Lady Bixbee's London residence, he was out the door and sprinting up the front steps. He prayed the doctor would be in attendance. If not, Henry wasn't above begging the old matron for his whereabouts.

As he pounded on the door, absolute fear and remorse twisted and burned inside his chest. He knew he'd find no relief until Arabella was safely in his arms. Where she belonged.

He had been a fool to believe she'd accept his decision. Her stubbornness was proving to be more of a detriment to herself than his fears of his family ever were.

The moment the door opened, Henry barged past the unsuspecting butler and demanded to see Dr. Stafford. It took the butler a moment to collect himself, but then he led Henry to a nearby room.

"Wait here," the butler said sternly.

Struggling to keep an appearance of calm, Henry paced as the clock on the mantel ticked away more of his precious time. He'd no idea how long Arabella had been inside Bedlam, but a single moment was too long.

Your sister has been in there for much longer, the voice inside his head whispered.

Henry pressed his eyes shut against a heavy rush of guilt.

The door to the sitting room opened, and Henry moved to the doctor before he even had a chance to fully enter the room.

"We need to go," Henry said, grabbing Dr. Stafford by the arm and attempting to pull him back into the corridor and out to his waiting carriage.

With swift movements, Dr. Stafford twisted out of Henry's

grasp, reversing their hold until Henry's hands were pinned be-hind his back and the side of his head was pressed to the door-frame.

"Forgive me if I do not seem eager to be forcibly removed from my grandmother's home," Dr. Stafford said in a matter-of-fact tone.

"Do you use that move on your patients?" Henry ground out through his teeth, his temper rising. They were wasting time.

Dr. Stafford immediately released his hold, and Henry pushed himself off the doorframe, his cheek throbbing.

Dr. Stafford walked fully into the sitting room, removed his evening jacket, and threw it over the back of a chair. "I have never in my life intentionally hurt a patient." He began rolling up his shirtsleeves. "But I have no qualms about fighting a man who so easily breaks the heart of a woman as remarkable as Miss Latham."

The last hold Henry had snapped, and he charged for the doctor.

"Do you think that was easy for me?" Henry growled, swing-ing one fist for the doctor's face, anticipating the block. When his fist met the doctor's raised forearm, Henry swung low with his other arm and connected with Dr. Stafford's abdomen. "I was gutted."

Dr. Stafford doubled over, one arm wrapping around his stomach. Slowly, he straightened, shooting daggers at Henry. "You are a coward." Then he charged.

His shoulder rammed into Henry's chest, robbing him of breath and driving them both to the floor. Dr. Stafford remained on top, evading any attempt Henry made to knock him off.

"You could have accepted my help," Dr. Stafford grunted, taking a swing for Henry's face.

Henry raised a hand in time to partially deflect the blow, but it still hit the side of his head and left a ringing in his ear. With all his weight, he kicked upward and rolled to the left, unbalancing Dr. Stafford.

Moving quickly on his hands and knees, Henry dove for the

doctor. They tumbled, crashing into a small table and knocking it to the ground. More furniture crashed to the floor as they both fought and failed to remain the victor. After another round, they lay side by side on their backs, completely out of breath.

"I *need* your help," Henry said, his voice ragged.

Dr. Stafford tilted his head to look at him, blood dripping from one corner of his mouth. "I know," he said in a dry tone.

Henry pushed himself up on one elbow, his earlier panic ripping through him again. "Not that. Arabella has gone inside Bedlam."

Dr. Stafford sat straight up. "What? Are you certain?"

Henry nodded. She'd managed to get herself inside Brooks's; he dared not doubt she'd found a way to get herself into Bedlam.

She was there because of him, and he needed to get her out, body and reputation whole.

Dr. Stafford cursed, shooting to his feet. He offered a hand to Henry. "Why did you not say so? How long?" he asked, retrieving his jacket.

Henry moved quickly toward the door. The pain in his side made it difficult to draw a full breath, and his jaw ached with every movement.

"I do not know," he replied, entering the corridor where the butler waited by the front door, hats in hand, one brow inconspicuously raised.

"Thank you, Wilkinson," Dr. Stafford said, taking his hat.

Henry took his hat, finding it odd that the butler would be waiting for them.

Wilkinson nodded. "Of course, sir." He moved to the door, then stopped, blocking their exit.

"What is it?" Dr. Stafford demanded. "We are in a hurry."

Wilkinson cleared his throat. "Your grandmother asks that the next time you decide to fight a man over a woman, you take it to the Park at dawn like every other respectable gentleman and not her sitting room."

Henry stood in stunned disbelief while Dr. Stafford grumbled something about "his meddlesome grandmother."

"She also told me," Wilkinson continued, "that I was not to let you leave without securing payment for her damaged furnishings."

"Send him the bill," Dr. Stafford said in a droll tone as he pointed to Henry. "He is the one getting the girl."

"I will inform your grandmother," Wilkinson said, moving to open the door.

Henry followed Dr. Stafford to the carriage and was stepping inside when a boy came running up to him.

"Letter for the doc."

Dr. Stafford poked his head out of the carriage and took the note from the boy.

Standing in the light of the carriage lantern, Henry recognized the boy as the one who'd seen to his horse that day at the new Bedlam. He was hunched over, his hands on his knees as he struggled to catch his breath.

Henry cursed; that was a long way for a boy to run.

"Hip flask," he called up to his coachman, whom he knew always carried one full of water during the hot summer months.

His man tossed it down, and Henry handed it to the lad. The boy tipped it back for several seconds.

"Thank ye, sir," he said, wiping a dirty sleeve across his mouth.

"We need to go," Dr. Stafford said with some urgency, ducking back into the carriage.

"Hop up with my coachman," Henry said to the boy, who looked relieved. "We will take you back."

The boy jumped up onto the bench, and they were on their way.

"What was in the letter?" Henry asked, restless and fearful that it held something about Arabella.

"It was from my mother."

"Your mother?" Henry asked, not at all understanding her connection with their situation.

"You have met her before," Dr. Stafford replied as the carriage jerked and swayed. "Twice, actually. She was the nurse who walked you out the day you visited Sarah at Guy's Hospital. And she was the one who brought Sarah in when you came to the new Bedlam."

Henry nodded, remembering the woman who'd referred to his sister as "my Sarah."

"Why is your mother at the hospital?" Henry asked.

"She is a nurse. I brought her in to be my eyes and ears when I could not be there," Dr. Stafford replied.

Henry blew out a breath and shook his head, amazed at how resourceful the doctor was proving to be.

"A new patient was just admitted," Dr. Stafford said. "But our requirements state that new admissions occur only during the daylight hours and with at least two doctors' approval. If this new patient is indeed Miss Latham, she may have just given us our chance to catch whoever is taking the bribes."

"Who is the doctor on staff?" Henry asked.

"I believe it is Gladstone," Dr. Stafford replied. "And he is the worst of the bunch."

Henry's blood ran cold as he recognized the name of the pompous doctor he'd met at Guy's Hospital. The one who'd drugged his sister until she was nothing but a shell of herself.

Henry prayed they'd get there in time before Gladstone could do the same to Arabella.

THIRTY-TWO

Arabella stood shaking, her damp hair dripping down the back of the hospital's gray nightgown. She'd nearly been drowned and scrubbed raw in an ice-cold water bath.

"Did she give you any trouble?" Dr. Gladstone asked the older nurse who'd done the scrubbing. He was well-dressed, but his voice was as cold and hard as the grip he had on Arabella's jaw.

"She has some fight in her," Nurse Robins said, annoyed.

Dr. Gladstone tilted Arabella's head back and squeezed her cheeks even harder until she opened her mouth. The strain on her neck felt like a thousand pinpricks.

"We will soon cure her of that."

Nausea roiled in her stomach at his words. There would be more of this. Terror and panic mixed, forming a rancid taste she fought to choke down.

Henry, please hurry!

Dr. Gladstone released his grip, and Arabella thanked the heavens to be free of his ruthless touch. Pulling out a gold timepiece, he spoke. "It is nearly eight. Take her to the dayroom. The other females should be just about done with their suppers, and then have them locked in their rooms by nine." He stuffed the timepiece back into the pocket of his dark-green jacket. "Tuck her in a room somewhere, and I will arrange the paperwork to be delayed until morning."

He handed the nurse a banknote and left the room.

"Emma," Nurse Robins barked at the young nurse mopping up the floor, causing both her and Arabella to jump. "You heard the doctor. Take her to the dayroom and then get started on the beds."

Emma hurried to Arabella like a frightened rabbit dashing about to avoid a hungry fox.

She took her gently by the arm, but Arabella still flinched against the sudden, searing pain. Her previous handlers had left large bruises on her upper arms that stung at the slightest touch.

Emma led her through two sets of locked doors and into a corridor lined with doors on one side and arched windows along the other.

"I'm sorry," Emma whispered the moment they were far away from Nurse Robins. "I'll bring you an ointment to put on the bruises before you sleep."

Arabella swallowed against a rush of emotions. For the first time since she walked inside the hospital, she felt human. "Thank you," she whispered in a shaky voice.

"There are a few of us who aren't so bad," she said with a sad smile. "In time, you'll learn which doctors and nurses to avoid."

They were three-quarters of the way down the corridor when Emma opened a door on the side with all the windows. "This is the dayroom. You'll spend the majority of your free time here or on the airing grounds."

Emma directed her toward one of the many sofas nearest a low-lit fire. Arabella nearly wept when the first billow of heat brushed her frozen skin.

"Thank you," Arabella whispered, meeting Emma's eyes for the first time.

Emma nodded, offering a compassionate smile.

"Emma?" a woman's voice called from the doorway.

Arabella's heart began to race, and she prayed that whoever it was would be more like Emma than like Nurse Robins.

"That's Nurse Maggie," Emma whispered, nodding at the woman who looked even older than Nurse Robins. "She's a good one."

Arabella let out a sigh of relief for the first time that evening.

Nurse Maggie came to stand in front of Arabella. "I will sit with the new patient until the others arrive. You go and see to your tasks so you can get home to your little one," she said with a knowing smile.

"Thank you, ma'am," Emma replied most eagerly, before offering Arabella a reassuring smile and leaving the room.

"What's your name, child?" Nurse Maggie asked gently.

Arabella wanted to fall into the older woman's arms and cry. Her tone, the way she looked at her—it was how a mother would look upon her child.

"Viola," Arabella replied, keeping to her chosen *Twelfth Night* character—Sebastian's twin sister.

"Well, Viola, let's see if we can get your hair a little dryer and plaited."

Tears freely rolled down Arabella's cheeks as Nurse Maggie directed her to stand closer to the fire. The heat on her skin and the soothing feeling of a brush gently running through her hair melted away the final threads of fear and tension. For a moment, she felt safe.

"I will introduce you to my Sarah," Nurse Maggie said as she plaited Arabella's hair.

Arabella sucked in a breath, and her heart stilled.

Please be the Sarah I'm looking for.

"She will help you find your way in here," Nurse Maggie finished just before other female voices sounded in the corridor.

Arabella's eyes snapped toward the door, fear gripping her insides.

Twenty or so women, dressed in gray nightgowns like hers, filtered into the room. Some of them went straight to the single bookshelf, while others moved to different table games tucked in the quiet corners of the room. A smaller number were accompanied individually by nurses; those patients moved their lips but no words emerged.

No one looked wild or threatening.

Then Nurse Robins walked in, and the atmosphere of the room changed with her presence.

Arabella's breathing quickened, and every muscle tensed as she waited to see what the old battle-ax would do.

"Nurse Maggie," Nurse Robins barked in a curt and conde-
scending tone. "Come with me."

"Stay here, child," Nurse Maggie whispered, gently patting
Arabella's arm. "I will return as soon as I can."

Arabella nodded, more than willing to remain near the fire—
and away from Nurse Robins—while she tried to find Sarah.

There were several girls with hair as black as Henry's, though
hair color might not play a part. Arabella had dark-brown hair
while her brother's was more of a golden brown.

She exhaled. This was going to be difficult.

"You are new," a young girl said, coming up from behind
Arabella and causing her to jump.

The girl, who couldn't be more than twelve, had light-brown
hair that fell over her shoulders and the biggest brown eyes that
watched Arabella with pure fascination.

"I'm Hannah," she said.

Arabella hesitated, uncertain what to do about her visitor.
She didn't want to draw unwanted attention, but it was growing
harder to ignore Hannah's large, endearing eyes.

"It's nice to meet you, Hannah," Arabella replied with a
friendly smile. "My name is Viola."

Hannah tilted her head and stared at Arabella. "She doesn't
look like a Viola, does she, Anna?"

Arabella sat in stunned silence. There was no one else around
them.

"Anna is my twin sister," Hannah said, turning a bright smile
to her left. "Mother tells us apart by our hair color." She looked
back to Arabella. "Hers is much more golden than mine, don't
you think?"

"Uh, yes. Yes, it is," Arabella replied, not having the heart to
tell the girl her sister wasn't there.

"See, I told you, Anna," Hannah said, bouncing proudly on
her toes.

She stopped, then turned her head toward the empty space
next to her and giggled.

"Well?" Hannah said, turning back to Arabella.

"Pardon?" Arabella asked, not understanding.

"Aren't you going to answer my sister's question?" Hannah scowled.

Arabella panicked. "My apologies; I—I did not understand her question." She glanced toward the door, hoping to see Nurse Maggie returning.

"You're being rude," Hannah snapped, her eyes darkening as she glared at Arabella. "Everyone here is *always* mean to Anna." Her voice grew louder with every word, drawing eyes from around the room.

"No, no, you misunderstand," Arabella said, holding up her hands to try to calm her before Nurse Robins came over. "Please, I did not—"

"Can you make me a flower, Hannah?" a girl said, coming to stand next to her. She looked slightly younger than Arabella.

She placed a book in Hannah's arms, and Hannah giggled with excitement as she sat on the floor and opened the book. She began to round a single page, tucking the edge into the inside spine; the finished shape looked much like a flower petal.

"Hannah and Anna like flowers," the dark-haired girl said, taking a seat on the sofa next to Arabella.

"We've a pretty flower garden at home," Hannah said, her eyes focused on her task.

The dark-haired girl leaned toward Arabella and whispered, "Hannah's twin died a few months back."

Arabella nodded in understanding, tears quickly forming as her heart broke for the little girl who'd obviously loved her sister so much she couldn't let her go, even in death.

"Thank you for telling me," Arabella whispered back. "I'm Viola," she said.

"Sarah," the dark-haired girl replied with a soft smile.

Arabella sucked in a sudden breath, and her heart stuttered in her chest. Had she found Henry's sister?

THIRTY-THREE

Arabella, near exhaustion in mind and body, sat with Hannah and Sarah on one of the sofas, listening to them giggle as Sarah pretended her finger was a bee trying to land on one of the two book flowers Hannah had made.

"No! No!" Hannah laughed, swatting at Sarah's finger as it buzzed and tickled her cheek. "Tell her to stop, Anna," she called out, twisting to try to get away, and Arabella's heart broke all over again for the young girl's loss.

The book slipped from Hannah's lap, landing with a thud on the floor. Arabella bent down to retrieve it, finding several pages had slipped from their petal shape.

"I think this flower needs rearranging," she said, handing the book back to the girl.

"We can fix it. Right, Anna?" Hannah said with an eager smile, recreating the petals in her lap.

Arabella glanced at Sarah over the top of Hannah's head. She found dark eyes under dark brows watching her, reminding her of Henry. Her heart clenched, and she had to look away because of the pain.

Only to be met with an image far worse as Nurse Robins stepped back into the room—without Nurse Maggie.

Arabella swallowed down the feeling of dread.

Behind Nurse Robins was another young nurse, a tray in her hands. "Time for your biscuits, girls," she called out.

Only a few girls stopped what they were doing and went to the nurse with the tray.

"Go on, Hannah," Sarah whispered.

Hannah frowned from her spot on the sofa. "I don't like the biscuits."

"I know, but you must go."

Reluctantly, Hannah got to her feet, a frown marring her lips.

Sarah reached out and squeezed her hand. "Do the trick I taught you."

Hannah sighed. "Come on, Anna."

"What's going on?" Arabella asked as soon as Hannah was far enough away.

"They put something in the biscuits that make you sleep like the dead, and then you wake up feeling even more tired, and sometimes dizzy."

Unease tickled the back of Arabella's neck. "Will they make me take one?" She didn't want to fall asleep inside this place.

Please, Henry, hurry!

"Not unless—" Sarah's words were cut off by Nurse Robins.

"Viola," the old battle-ax barked. "Come and take your biscuit. Doctor's orders."

Arabella remained in her seat, her heart pounding. The fear of never waking up—never seeing Henry, her mother, her brother and Olivia again—held her in place.

"Viola!" Nurse Robins voice slashed through the air like a whip, her glare growing more intense the longer Arabella delayed.

"What do I do?" Arabella pleaded.

"Put it under your tongue," Sarah whispered, her lips barely moving as she looked elsewhere. "Then, after, spit it into your hand."

Arabella swallowed. She could do that. Slowly, she rose from her seat, her chest growing tighter with every step.

Reaching the nurse holding the tray, Arabella picked up one of the brown biscuits. It was small and easily fit in the palm of her hand.

"Put it in your mouth," Nurse Robins ordered, her tone perilously close to a growl.

Arabella's hand shook as she slipped the biscuit into her

mouth. She immediately tasted sugar, followed by a strong, bitter taste before she rolled it under her tongue.

Wanting it out of her mouth as soon as possible, she turned to walk away but was stopped by Nurse Robins, who moved to block her escape.

"I need to see you swallow," she ordered.

Arabella froze, knowing if she saved herself now and swallowed, it would only come back to harm her in the end.

"Open your mouth," Nurse Robins ordered, her watchful eyes boring into her.

Arabella slowly opened her mouth, praying the biscuit would stay under her tongue.

Nurse Robins grabbed her by the cheeks and pinched. The biscuit toppled out along with Arabella's startled cry.

"I knew it," Nurse Robins snarled, her grip tightening on Arabella's cheeks.

Arabella fought to break free.

Nurse Robins growled, shaking Arabella back and forth by her jaw. "Eat it!"

Arabella watched in sheer agony as Nurse Robins reached for not one biscuit, but two. She brought the biscuits up and pressed them to Arabella's mouth. The hard edges of the biscuit bit into her lips, making Arabella scream out in pain.

As soon as Arabella opened her mouth, Nurse Robins shoved both biscuits inside, and then she clamped a hand over Arabella's nose and mouth with a viselike grip.

Arabella couldn't breathe, her lungs and throat burning. She scratched and pulled, trying to break herself free from the nurse's clutches.

"Swallow!" Nurse Robins yelled into her ear.

Black spots began to form at the edge of her vision, and real, clawing panic overtook her as she feared she might die from lack of air.

A scream, angry and determined, rang out from somewhere in the room, and Arabella was knocked to the ground, finally free.

She clutched at her chest and gasped for breath. The blackness subsided, revealing Sarah and Nurse Robins fighting on the ground.

Two nurses ran over, one of them pulling Sarah off Nurse Robins. There was bloodlust in the old battle-ax's eyes as she regained her feet. She lifted a hand to strike Sarah, who was being held tight between the nurses.

Without a second thought about herself, Arabella jumped in the way of Nurse Robins opened hand and took a direct blow to the side of her face. A loud ringing filled her ears, and she fell to the floor once again.

Before she could even try to get up, Arabella was grabbed by the collar of her gown and hauled to her feet.

Nurse Robins looked wild as she pulled Arabella's face close to her own. "You are going to regre—"

"Let her go!" a deep, almost feral, voice called out.

Henry.

He had come.

THIRTY-FOUR

When Henry entered the hospital corridor and heard the screams, he knew he was moments away from being too late. He'd never run so hard in his life, terror mixed with rage pushing him beyond his mortal limits.

He outpaced Dr. Stafford and barreled through the doorway and into a room filled with screams and shouting, his heart threatening to beat out of his chest. His eyes locked onto the sight of Arabella being nearly lifted off the ground by the collar of her dress.

"Let her go!" The words ripped through him like thunder after an earth-shattering flash. Fury pumped through him, making his muscles shake from the ferocity.

The woman dropped her hold on Arabella, and the color leached from her skin, her eyes flashing wide with absolute fright.

She looks as if she believes you'll eat her, Beasty, the voice inside his head laughed.

Henry couldn't have cared less.

Arabella crumbled toward the floor, and Henry lunged, wrapping his arms around her and pulling her to him. He felt her heart racing against his chest, even as her body shook uncontrollably.

He ran frantic hands over her, looking for every injury. "Where are you hurt?" he asked, his voice hoarse and thick.

There were so many bruises.

"S-Sarah," Arabella struggled to get out, her teeth chattering though the room wasn't cold. She gripped at his clothing, but her shaking hands couldn't keep their hold. "Help . . . Sarah."

Henry jerked his head up, a hot iron of fear twisting inside his stomach. What had happened to Sarah? Was she in the room?

He found her flanked by two nurses as if she were about to be dragged to the gallows. Her wide eyes watched him through the wild, dark strands of her hair hanging over her face.

Dr. Stafford bolted past Henry in a blur of movement. He didn't stop until he'd ripped Sarah from the hold of the two nurses and pulled her to him in a protective embrace.

"What is going on here?" he demanded as the room descended into chaos.

An argument broke out between Dr. Stafford and Nurse Robins just as Nurse Maggie came hastily into the room. She took in the situation and immediately ordered the other nurses to remove all patients and staff not involved.

Arabella's grip on his jacket loosened, and his hold around her waist tightened. He wasn't ready to let her go. He doubted he ever would be after this.

"Henry?" She said his name in an entreating and gentle tone, and he knew she wanted him to look at her. But he couldn't. If he did, he would see the bruises across her face and arms. They were there because she'd done this for him.

Anguish and regret caught in his throat, and he swallowed hard.

She moved in his arms again, only this time she pressed the palms of her hands against his chest and slowly slid them up his shoulders and locked them behind his head. She pressed her face into the curve of his neck, and he could feel her hot tears against his skin.

No one had ever held him in such a way, giving comfort but also finding it.

"I love you," he whispered into her hair as he kissed the side of her head.

"I love you too," she whispered into his neck, her close breath igniting his senses.

"Lord Northcott?" Dr. Stafford's voice broke through the moment, reminding Henry there was much that still needed to be done.

Relaxing his hold, he met Dr. Stafford's watchful gaze.

"Is she all right?" Dr. Stafford asked, nodding toward Arabella.

Henry opened his mouth to reply but was cut off by the woman herself.

"She will be," she said in a muffled voice, her head buried in Henry's chest. There was a slight humorous lilt to her tone, as if she were trying to make light of how poorly she felt.

A smile tugged at the corner of Henry's lips, and he shook his head. What woman could go through what she had and still find a way to laugh?

A woman mad enough to love a man like you, the voice whispered.

Love is merely madness, Henry thought, quoting Shakespeare's *As You Like It* and kissing the top of his Arabella's head again.

"How is my sister?" Henry asked, nodding to the side of the room where Sarah was being tended to by Nurse Maggie.

"She will be all right," Dr. Stafford said, glancing at Sarah and then back to him. "She is stronger than you think."

Henry nodded, feeling like more of a stranger to his sister than the doctor was.

"What do we do now?" He'd never thought past getting Arabella back in his arms.

"Take her home," Dr. Stafford said, nodding to Arabella. "I will remain here and deal with Nurse Robins and Dr. Gladstone."

Henry had almost forgotten about the pompous doctor, who'd so far not even bothered to show his face. His blood boiled. It was men like him who gave hospitals their inhumane reputation, and Henry swore that he would see Gladstone—and any other doctors like him—removed from Bedlam by the next Parliamentary session.

"We cannot leave Sarah," Arabella said, looking up at Henry with pleading eyes.

Henry nodded in agreement. It was time Sarah came home. But would she even feel comfortable or safe with him after all this time?

Sarah's expression was unreadable, but he saw the way she leaned into Nurse Maggie's comforting arms. *That* was what Sarah truly needed.

"Can you spare your mother for a time?" he asked Dr. Stafford, nodding his head toward the two women.

"What about your aunt?" Dr. Stafford asked with caution and some confusion.

"No longer in my household," Henry replied with a finality that didn't make him feel a moment of remorse.

Dr. Stafford nodded. "Then I will make the arrangements."

"Thank you," Henry said, the sudden rush of emotions making his voice sound strained. "For everything."

Henry knew he hadn't made it easy on the doctor, but he was grateful the man cared so much about his patients to fight for them as he had.

"You are welcome," Dr. Stafford replied. "Take a left in the corridor; it will lead you to a side door. There should be a man stationed there who can let you out."

Henry nodded, then slipped out of his jacket and wrapped it around Arabella's shoulders. He lifted her into his arms, and she settled against him, sliding her arms around his neck.

"Are we going home?" she asked, her voice sounding tired.

"I am taking *you* home," he said, stepping out of the room and turning left.

"Henry?" Arabella let out a yawn, and her grip around his neck loosened. "I am going to fall asleep."

"Sleep if you need to, my love," he whispered. She'd been through much; he was sure she was exhausted.

She went quiet for a few moments, but then she murmured, "I tried not to take the biscuits."

"What biscuits?"

"Sarah said they use them to—" She took in a deep breath and let out a long exhale, as if it required considerable effort. "To put them to sleep."

Henry stopped, a cold sense of foreboding icing through him.

Something wasn't right. He and Dr. Stafford had missed something.

"I do not want to be Juliet," Arabella's words sounded distant, and she was growing heavier and heavier in his arms.

He turned around and picked up his pace. "Why would you be Juliet?" he asked, wanting to keep her talking.

"The potion made her go to sleep, and Romeo thought she died. And then she woke to find him dead."

"I will not take a poison, my love," he said, kissing her forehead and using his chin to keep her drooping head from falling forward.

His heart was pounding hard in chest, and his lungs were about to burst from the almost lifeless weight she was becoming in his arms.

Reentering the room, he yelled for Stafford, who took one look at them and came running.

"Henry?" Arabella mumbled.

He knelt on the floor before he lost his grip and dropped her. "Yes?" he asked, his throat constricting with panic. He needed to keep her talking; he couldn't lose her.

Dr. Stafford grabbed her wrist, checking her pulse.

"Will you be there when I wake?" Arabella mumbled before she went completely still in his arms.

"What is happening to her?" Henry shouted at the doctor.

Dr. Stafford grabbed her out of Henry's arms and laid her on the floor.

Henry took her hand, which thankfully still felt warm in his tight grip, but she didn't move. Their story would *not* end like *Romeo and Juliet*, not when he'd finally chosen to fight for it.

The doctor put his ear to her lips and, after a moment, sat back up. "Her breaths are shallow, but she is breathing."

Henry pressed her limp hand to his lips and let out a shaky breath of momentary relief. "What is wrong with her?"

Using his thumb and forefinger, Dr. Stafford peeled one of Arabella's eyelids open. She didn't stir.

The doctor checked her other eye and her pulse at her wrist once again before looking to Henry. "They must have given her a heavy dose of laudanum."

"What can be done?" Henry asked, fear clutching at his insides as he pulled her back into his arms.

"Take her home and watch her breathing. She will need time to sleep off the effects."

THIRTY-FIVE

Arabella awoke to the warming presence of sunlight. Her head felt groggy and her limbs heavy. She detested the feeling, like being held captive inside her body when all she wanted to do was open her eyes and move.

Forcing one eye open, Arabella recognized her bedroom and let out a sigh of relief.

She was home.

With stiff and strained movements, she pushed the coverlet, which felt more like a boulder than soft wool, off her.

Her arms free, she gritted her teeth and tried to push herself to a seated position. A wave of dizziness hit her, forcing her to clamp her eyes shut. She muttered a curse.

"Do I want to know where you learned that word?" her mother's voice said from nearby.

"Would it make you feel better," Arabella began, keeping her eyes shut as she waited for her head to stop spinning, "if I said I heard it from more than one person?"

"No, it would not." Her mother's hands pressed against her shoulders. "You should lie back down."

"No," Arabella ground out, fighting to stay upright. "I need to get out of this bed."

"You and your stubbornness," her mother said in exasperation. She moved her hands beneath Arabella's arms, and together they worked until she was fully sitting up in bed.

When the dizziness finally subsided, she cracked open her eyes and found her mother in a chair beside the bed. There were dark circles beneath her red, puffy eyes, and wisps of hair had come free, framing her worry-lined face.

Arabella felt the weight of that worry and fear she had put her mother through. "My stubbornness is sorry."

"Yes, well." Her mother moved to sit beside her on the bed, disappointment written across her face. "Your stubbornness has more than just myself to apologize to." Her eyes moved to the far corner of the room where Hattie slept hunched over in a chair.

Relief at finding Hattie still employed in their home washed over Arabella, followed by another wave of guilt. "Please do not be angry with her," she said, turning pleading eyes on her mother. "I gave her no choice. I would have found a way to do it without her."

Her mother let out a heavy breath. "I know. And while I will say that I am *not* happy, I take comfort knowing there is an entire army of people helping me try to keep you and your wild stubbornness alive."

"Army of people?" Arabella asked. She wouldn't consider a lady's maid and a groomsman an army.

"Yes," her mother said. "I understand it took a doctor, a nurse, a reckless gambler, and a baron to bring you back to me last night. Two of them spent the night in our home."

Henry.

Arabella's heart skipped a beat, and she found within herself a sudden burst of vitality. "I want to see him," she said, throwing off the coverlet and trying to swing her legs over the edge.

Her mother jumped from the bed. "Dr. Stafford said you should not be rushing this."

"Can you help me get dressed?" Arabella asked, pushing through another bout of dizziness.

"Yes, but you need to slow down."

Arabella managed to get her feet on the floor before the flash of strength faded and the weight of weariness returned. "You may be right."

"You say that as if it were not a common occurrence," her mother chided, her hands on her hips.

"*The quality of mercy is not strained; it droppeth as the gentle*

*rain from heaven upon the place beneath. It is twice blessed; it bless-
eth him that gives and him that takes,*" Arabella quoted from the
Merchant of Venice, with big, pitiful eyes.

Her mother looked to the heavens and then back at her. "You
and your Shakespeare. I told your father it would be trouble."

Arabella's heart warmed at the thought of her father. He'd
known then what she knew now: Shakespeare was *always* the answer.

With her mother's much-needed assistance, Arabella managed to change from her nightgown into a long-sleeved, yellow
morning dress that brought the gold out in her eyes. Hattie woke
in time to save Arabella and her mother from making a disaster
with her hair. She also provided an ointment and powder that
helped the bruises on her face fade.

After offering Hattie her most sincere apology and thanks,
Arabella was set to go down.

She held on to her mother's arm, her nerves on edge, as they
descended the stairs into the entry hall. Her mind felt clearer, her
strength almost restored.

"Good to see you up and about, miss," Smith said from his
position at the base of the stairs.

He held out his hand, and Arabella took it as she moved off
the last step. "It is wonderful to *be* up and about," she replied
with an exaggerated tone she knew would amuse him.

He gave a soft chuckle. "I am beginning to doubt there is
anything that can keep you down, miss."

"Do not encourage her," her mother added with a fond smile.
"Where are our guests this afternoon, Smith? Have they left the
rooms we prepared for them last night?"

"*Still* in the family parlor, ma'am."

Her mother's eyes widened. "They stayed there all night?"

"They did," Smith replied with a firm nod.

"Whyever would they do that?" her mother asked.

"I did not feel it my place to ask," Smith replied. "But, if

I might add, Lord Northcott did appear much distressed, and I believe Mr. Bradbury was trying to settle him."

That was all Arabella needed to hear before rushing to the family parlor.

Stepping inside, she was met by a warm afternoon sun and . . . snoring?

Following the sound, she found Mr. Bradbury asleep on one of the sofas, his jacket draped over him like a blanket.

There was no sign of Henry, until she saw something moving out the back window. He was in the garden, pacing.

She made it as far as the gravel path before he noticed her approach.

His bloodshot eyes flashed wide. "You are awake." He said the words as if he didn't know if he could believe them, and then he walked directly to her, cutting across the garden's circular path despite the plants and small bushes in his way.

"I am awake," she replied, falling in love with him all over again.

His hair looked as if he'd run his hands through it a thousand times, and he'd removed his jacket, waistcoat, and cravat. Her breathing grew uneven the more she took in his broad, muscular form.

They stood no more than a hair's breadth away, but he did nothing more than stare, as if he were drinking her in with his eyes.

Her heart's rhythm increased, and suddenly a hair's breadth felt too far away. Reaching up a tentative hand, she ran her fingers through his wild hair, unable to resist. "You look as if you have not slept."

Color tinged his cheeks, and he attempted to smooth his hair back down. "I found it somewhat . . . difficult."

"Because of me?" she asked, guilt hitting her again.

Henry hesitated to meet her eyes and slowly nodded. "And my sister," he added.

Seeing his pain and worry, and knowing his fears, she closed the last bit of distance between them and put her hands into his. They completely surrounded her own, and his grip was strong but gentle.

"I think I know a way to help you with both your problems."

Henry stared into her eyes and swallowed.

Why was he hesitating?

"Do you not want to marry?" she asked, her heart seizing.

"It's not that easy," he said after a moment.

"Why?"

He took in a shaky breath. "Because—" He couldn't finish his sentence.

"Because it is not worth the risk?" she repeated his previous words on a tortured whisper. Her heart wouldn't survive if he rejected her again.

"No," he said quite adamantly, bringing her knuckles to his lips for a kiss. "No, you are worth more than *anything* to me. But what can I be for you?" His lips thinned into a hard line, and he dropped her hands. "All I can bring you is uncertainty because of—" He briefly looked away, then pointed to his head as if ashamed of his confession. "We cannot just go on planning a life and act as if nothing is wrong."

She immediately grabbed his hand and pressed it to her heart. "I agree, which is why I am *willing* to take this at a pace that is comfortable to you."

He raised a questioning brow, which she knew was justified. Her mother had just yesterday lectured her on her lack of patience—which she'd ignored. But she couldn't lose him. At least, with this plan, she would keep his love.

It was time for her to learn patience.

She let out a small breath. "What if I promise to let you choose the timing in which we wed?"

He stared at her, unconvinced.

She pressed on, her tone firm. "I want you to take the time you need for you and your sister to heal. All I require is a promise that I will always have your love."

His eyes darkened into a deep and piercing gaze that sent heat through her. He reached out and slowly pulled her closer until she was pressed up against him.

"You have *always* had my love," he said, his voice hoarse. "From the first day I met you at your family's country estate and you quoted that first Shakespeare line—*Prepare for mirth, for mirth becomes a feast*—" He paused, shaking his head, a tear-filled, amused look on his face. "My heart knew then that I needed you in my life."

Tears clouded her vision, and she bit at her bottom lip. She was so overwhelmed with hope, happiness, and love she didn't know if she could hold it all in.

Using the pad of his thumb, he wiped the tears from her cheeks, his eyes watching her with such tenderness.

"Kiss me," she whispered, almost out of breath. "Please."

Without hesitation, he dropped his hands from her face and splayed them across her back, pressing her to him as his lips slanted against hers.

His kiss was both hard and sweeping, as if part need and part frustration.

She leaned into him, wrapping her arms around his neck, savoring the sensation of his hand moving from her back up to her neck as if he feared she might pull away from the intensity of his kiss.

This was heaven. This was bliss. This was—

"What the devil!"

—over.

Breaking apart, Arabella followed Henry's alarmed gaze to discover her older brother storming down the terrace steps with Olivia and Mr. Bradbury hard on his heels.

Fire blazed in Emerson's eyes as he ignored his wife's and friend's calls for calm. Her overly protective brother had finally returned home.

Arabella turned around to face him, shielding Henry with her body.

A large hand gently pressed on her shoulder, followed by Henry's breath on her neck. "While I admire your protectiveness," he whispered, a chuckle in his tone, "I believe I should take care of this on my own." His lips gently brushed against her ear, sending shivers up her spine.

Her body naturally leaned back into him, seeking more of his touch. Henry was right; she was jumping in before thinking—again.

Would she ever truly learn patience?

She stepped aside but remained close to Henry. She was giving him his way, but that did not mean she could not also offer him assistance. She knew how to handle her brother better than anyone.

Emerson stopped, leaving only a few paces between them, his nostrils flaring as he glared at Henry. "I trusted you to look after my sister, not take advantage of her."

"I told you this was going to happen, Goosey," Bradbury called out from behind Emerson's shoulder.

Emerson shot Bradbury a dark look. "I will deal with you next."

"Wonderful," Bradbury grumbled, throwing his hands up. "Exactly as I predicted."

Her brother turned back to Henry. "You *will* marry her," he demanded, pointing an accusatory finger at Henry as if he thought himself some saint riding in to save her.

Agitated, Arabella took a step toward him to remind him that *he* had secretly courted *her* closest friend behind her back, but Henry touched her arm.

"Allow me," he whispered with a wink that nearly stole her breath.

She loved when he came out from behind his walls and teased her.

Henry leveled a look at Emerson, with as much dignity as a man who had just been caught kissing another man's sister—and in his shirtsleeves no less—could muster. "If you had waited another two minutes, I would have asked her that question my-self."

A gasp exploded from Arabella's lips, and she jumped into his arms. "Do you mean it?"

He nodded, his arms holding her tight. "I agree to your terms."

"I told you," Olivia said to Emerson, coming up to stand be-side him. She rubbed a hand along his chest, slowly bringing him out of his stupor. "I told you your friend was falling in love with your sister."

Arabella snorted. Olivia was the best thing to happen to her brother.

Emerson blinked and shook his head. He narrowed his eyes at Henry. "Are you in love with my sister?"

Henry nodded. "I am in love with your sister."

Emerson turned to Arabella. "And you are in love with him?"

"Beyond any doubt," she replied, her heart near to bursting.

All the tension in Emerson's posture melted, and he extended a hand to Henry with a grin. "Welcome to the family."

Henry took it, forcing Arabella to step aside as they pulled one another into a sideways hug, pounding each other aggres-sively on the back.

"Oh, come on," Mr. Bradbury groaned. "This is not fair. Now you will all be related, and then there is me."

"We do have a few female cousins," Emerson suggested.

Mr. Bradbury blanched, and his eyes darted to Arabella be-fore he shook his head. "No. No more cousins."

Emerson looked to Henry with a raised brow. "What is he talking about?" Then he turned to Mr. Bradbury. "Are you saying you are considering marriage?"

Arabella cupped a hand over her mouth to hold in a snort of laughter. Bringing up her adventure in Brooks's would assuredly ruin the moment. Luckily Mr. Bradbury's aversion to marriage was taking precedence.

Mr. Bradbury scoffed. "I can easily say that you will *never* see me walk down the aisle to join that institution."

"*The fool doth think he is wise,*" Arabella quoted. "*But the wise man knows himself to be a fool.*"

"*As You Like It,*" Henry answered, smiling down at her as he pulled her back into his arms.

"I do not even know what that means," Mr. Bradbury replied, throwing his hands in the air.

"That might be the point," Henry replied with a teasing smile.

Mr. Bradbury scowled.

"I do not know about the rest of you," Olivia interjected, "but I have not seen my friend in almost five months and would very much like to spend some much-needed time with her." She looked at Arabella with the warmest smile.

Arabella nodded in agreement. She also wanted to hear about what had happened with Olivia's father. The large bruise under Emerson's chin was worrisome.

"Shall we all go back inside?" Olivia suggested. "I believe your mother said something about scones."

"You had me at scones," Mr. Bradbury said, hurrying toward the steps. Emerson and Olivia followed closely behind.

"Shall we?" Arabella asked, looking up at Henry when he didn't release her from his arms.

"Are you certain about waiting to get married?" he asked, as if he were still uneasy about their decision. "Once I tell your brother our plan, he will have questions."

Arabella reached up and cupped his cheek. He leaned into her touch. "Then we will answer them together."

Henry bent down and gently kissed her lips. "Thank you," he whispered so softly that she knew the words were meant as a prayer between him and the heavens.

Her heart was bursting, and her eyes blurred with tears. In a world filled with so much uncertainty, she knew she was beyond blessed to have found her spark.

EPILOGUE

Six months later

Henry sat next to Arabella in his newly decorated study inside *their* home.

It had taken him and Dr. Stafford five months working with the Home Office to see that Dr. Gladstone and the others connected to him would never hold positions of power over others ever again.

When that was settled, he could wait no longer, and he and Arabella married by special license, changing his life for the better—and all because of her.

She'd insisted they delay their bridal tour until she'd brightened and changed every square inch of their home. She worked so hard that many nights she'd fall asleep in his arms after dinner while he read to her on the sofa. He tried convincing her to slow down, that there was no hurry, but she, of course, would not listen.

Sarah had been discharged from Bedlam but had asked to stay with Dr. Stafford's mother in her home. She was not ready to return to a place where so many haunting memories of her childhood resided. Henry didn't argue with her and only asked that he be allowed to visit her so they could try to rebuild what they had lost.

Arabella was his saving grace in that as well. She accompanied him on every visit, bringing samples of wallpaper or fabric and asking his sister what she thought or what she would like so that Sarah could feel a part of their household.

He was beyond grateful. Arabella was his greatest blessing in life, and he only hoped he was proving to be half as much in hers.

"Shall we begin?" Dr. Stafford asked, sitting in a chair across from him and Arabella.

"What do we do?" Henry asked, shifting uncomfortably on the sofa. Despite all the wonderful changes that had been happening, there was one thing that remained. The voice. It had quieted some, but it was still there, inside his head.

Arabella slipped her hand into his and squeezed, as if she knew where his mind was wandering. He looked at her, and she smiled with unabashed love in her eyes.

"We talk," Dr. Stafford said. "And you hold on to what matters most in life."

Henry took a deep breath.

"*Men at some time are masters of their fates,*" he quoted inside his head.

Julius Caesar, the voice whispered, and he chuckled.

Scooping Arabella into his arms, she squealed in surprise as he dropped her into his lap and wrapped his arms around her tight. "Well, then, I think I can do that."

ACKNOWLEDGMENTS

If there was ever a book where I was in over my head before I even started writing it, it would be this one. But I can honestly say that this story—and myself—were saved because of the following people:

First, and foremost, thank you to my husband. This book would not have been possible without the many hours you gave when you stepped in and took care of the kids and the house. Thank you for the many conversations I forced upon you because I was stumped or frustrated and you playfully argued with me until I got back to work so I could prove you wrong. You know me too well.

Thank you to Camille Smithson, my friend and critique partner who has been with me unwaveringly since the beginning. I'm almost embarrassed at how many drafts of this story you had to read.

To Heather Warren, who swept in when I needed you most and helped bring this story over the finish line. To Shallee McArthur for being able and willing when I needed your thoughts. To Jenny, for helping me diagnose two of my characters—I bet you never thought you'd be treating fictional patients. To Megan Walker for answering my plea for help even when you were in the middle of moving—you truly have a heart of gold. And to Arlem Hawks for helping me with the most random French question—you saved me from hours of research!

And last but *far* from least: thank you to Lisa Mangum and Heidi Gordon at Shadow Mountain for taking this Shakespearean adventure and pushing me to give it the spark it was missing! The time you spent with me on Zoom and through emails was probably more than expected. I'm forever grateful.

ABOUT THE AUTHOR

JENTRY FLINT is a bookworm-turned-writer with the propensity to try just about anything. She has a true love of history and believes a good quote can fix most things. She lives in sunny southern Utah with her husband and three kids.

Her favorite things in life are flavored popcorn, her grandmother's purple blanket, and curling up on the couch to watch a movie with her husband.